MINERVA'S NET

MINERVA'S NET

Don Otey

Library of Congress Number: 2004093079
ISBN : Hardcover 1-4134-5627-8
Softcover 1-4134-5626-X

This book was printed in the United States of America.

To order additional copies of this book, contact:
Xlibris Corporation
1-888-795-4274
www.Xlibris.com
Orders@Xlibris.com

23553

CHAPTER 1

The moon sat high over the bay on a cool February night. Traffic was light. The Skyway Bridge was nearly deserted. An intermittent wind played against the concrete and steel arch while it gently swayed with the rhythm of the gusts. Viewed from above the bridge looked like a giant hill stretching more than four miles with ant-like vehicles laboring to its top then skittering down the other side. Two hundred feet below the bridge's crest lay the choppy waters of Tampa Bay.

A car sped southward through St. Petersburg, Florida with an eighteen-wheeler close behind. They rounded the last bend in the road and lurched forward toward the upward sweep of the Skyway. Midnight was fast approaching as they neared the highest point of the structure. Suddenly the car's driver slowed and brought his car to a halt in mid lane. The truck driver behind him braked hard and sounded a loud air horn.

"Hey, dipstick. What do you think this is—a parking lot? Move it, lame brain."

The grating sound of the truck's horn pierced the night air but there was no response from the car's driver. Moments passed then the small, thin man opened his door, left it ajar and calmly stepped out into the path of oncoming traffic. Tires squealed. Miraculously the walker reached the far edge of the bridge untouched. He moved robotically toward the concrete retaining wall with complete indifference to his surroundings.

The burly trucker muttered under his breath, set his brake and swung down from the cab of the eighteen-wheeler. He looked ready for a shouting match with the blockhead who was ignoring him. But the man merely stopped at the chest high railing and hoisted himself to a standing position atop the wall.

When the trucker realized what he was about to witness, he gasped "Ohmygod". He lunged forward toward the lone figure on the railing and called out to him in breathless shock.

"Wait. Talk to me. Let me help you."

If he heard, the small man gave no sign. The truck driver reached out to him and came within inches of grabbing one arm. But there was no expression or head movement to indicate the man was aware of the trucker's presence. Barry Millwood took one forward step into the night and dropped out of sight. The trucker peered over the rail and saw nothing but inky black. He leaned on the barrier and brought a hand to his face, rubbing his eyes in disbelief. Somewhere in the distance a navigation buoy flashed its signal light.

By now there were two cars stopped behind the tractor-trailer. Their occupants were running frantically toward the spot where the jumper had stood.

"What the hell—what happened?" one motorist stammered.

"I tried to grab him but he never looked back. Didn't even look down at the water. Just walked right off the side of the bridge. Looked like a robot—like his mind was a million miles away."

The occupants of the other car stared in shock until the lady blurted out, "We have to get help or something."

A patrolling trooper skidded to a halt and placed his unit, its blue light winking, across the lane blocked by the motionless vehicles. He scanned the scene and took stock of the situation. The trucker hurried to meet him, still breathing heavily from his failed rescue effort.

"Did somebody go over?" the trooper asked the small group of onlookers.

"Man jumped. I tried to stop him." The trucker's face was ashen. His voice cracked as he spoke.

The trooper spoke into his hand-held. He notified the tollbooths to shut down the bridge and summoned the Coast Guard to commence a search of the waters below; surveyed the assembled spectators and took charge.

"Before we create a real snarl up here, let's get these vehicles off the road. The keys are still in the empty car so you, sir, take it to the south end. I'll lead everybody past the tollbooth where we can park. I'll take your statements there. We can't do any more up here."

As he drove his big rig to the south end of the Skyway, the trucker cursed under his breath. He had read that nearly forty people had ended their lives with a long plunge into the bay from this bridge. A number of would-be suicides had been talked down to safety and a handful of them had actually even survived the jump. He had seen the troopers patrolling the bridge at all times of day and night. The growing popularity of this place as a launching platform for troubled souls and the traffic hazards caused by fog must keep the police busy. On his many trips across the bay between St. Pete and Sarasota, the truck driver had learned to stay alert for problems. That fact may have made the difference moments ago when he narrowly avoided a jarring rear-ender with the stopped car.

Those who frequented the Skyway had come to accept that the tragedies would continue despite all safety efforts. This was another of those sad nights. Without word or ceremony, Doctor Barry Millwood, local psychologist, solid family man and a decent human being, simply disappeared into the dark waters of Tampa Bay and ceased to exist. The official finding would be suicide.

* * *

Nearly a thousand miles away and half a day later, another tragedy was about to unfold. George Jackson scurried around the lobby of the George Washington University Hospital in the nation's capital. His starched blue coveralls identified him as one of the hospital's custodians.

George looked up from his work to see Doctor Myron Wainwright, huddled in his winter coat and scarf, hurry by. Wainwright strode toward the entryway of the gleaming new hospital building heading for the bustling streets of Foggy Bottom. As he passed by, Wainwright spoke to the custodian.

"Need a break, George." The doctor looked at George for an instant then forged ahead toward the exit.

"Morning, Doc. Bundle up. Typical D.C. in February out there." There was something out of kilter about the doctor today but George couldn't put his finger on what it was.

"Short walk. Lunch." The doctor stared ahead into the cold day.

"Just watch those crazy drivers, Doc. Lord knows they won't be watching out for you. They'd just as soon run over you as look at you." George didn't yet comprehend the brutal truth of what he had said.

Doctor Wainwright strode out into the blinding sunlight of the frosty morning. He stepped off the sidewalk in mid-block to cross 23rd Street. The custodian watched him go and had an uneasy feeling that all was not well. The doctor's manner and the tone of his speech had been almost robotic.

Then came the screeching of brakes and the sickening thud of metal against flesh. George shouted, "Help!" and raced to the scene.

When the police arrived, the distraught driver of a steaming van stood near a limp form. "There was nothing I could do. He was in front of me before I could stop."

George Jackson volunteered his eyewitness account. He nervously stroked his balding head and looked away from the medics and Wainwright's covered body.

"It was almost like he was sleepwalking, officer. For some reason I can't explain, I felt like he was in another world. Watched him walk right into the street. Never looked in either direction."

"Not much doubt about this one," the patrolman told his fellow officer. He stood in the street in the shadow of a tall building and rubbed his ears as the cold wind swirled around them.

"Must have had his mind on something else," his partner replied. "Hell of a price to pay for inattention."

The finding was accidental death.

Elsewhere, two people went about their daily routines, unaware they were about to become involved in these two seemingly unconnected events. Before another week went by, they would both be in hot pursuit of answers to puzzling questions surrounding the deaths of Doctors Barry Millwood and Myron Wainwright.

CHAPTER 2

The day began like any other for Dan Cooper. He had just started to munch on his bran flakes and sliced banana as he opened the newspaper. His wife Ellen was reading. This was normally quiet time for the Coopers. The smell of coffee brewing brought him to the kitchen. He scouted up his own cereal and fruit and poured his freshly squeezed Florida orange juice. They rarely spoke until after coffee except for the acknowledging hum she gave in return for his customary morning peck on her cheek. It was one of those comfortable times with the ease of thirty years of sharing the breakfast table. Dan read aloud the headline in the St. Petersburg Times.

"Says here a man jumped off the Skyway Bridge last night." He sipped at his coffee before reading on.

"I thought they put up safety guards or something to prevent that," his wife remarked and turned her attention back to her book.

"There's probably no way they can guard against these things. If somebody wants to end it all, he'll find a way to outthink all the safety measures."

Ellen nodded her agreement in a detached way. Dan took the opportunity to regard his slender, brown-haired wife for a long moment. Even after all these years, watching her had an effect on him. She had trimmed off a few pounds since they came to Florida five years ago and was nearly back to the size eight she wanted to reach. At five feet four she stood at chest height on him. The liquid brown eyes behind her reading glasses could still reduce him to mush, a fact he had often tried unsuccessfully to conceal.

He read on but there were few details. An eyewitness had identified the suicide as a man with a slight build. The victim had not yet been positively identified. Dan shook his head and mumbled, "What a waste," as he turned to the sports section.

From the patio came the sound of the swimming pool pump turning on and the spa fountain began to cascade. Dan stared out the morning room window at a pair of herons. The birds strutted on their long legs past the patio screen as casually as if they were domesticated pets. He reflected on how hectic life had become for them. Then they chucked the daily grind in northern Virginia for the peace and quiet of the Florida Gulf coast. This really was the life after more than thirty years of workaday routines. They had marked time in an apartment and watched their airy new ranch home go up in a gated community. It was definitely more house than they would ever need. But by mutual agreement this was finally their time for a bit of self-pampering. His six phenomenal years in the software business had made it all possible. Now they adlibbed their daily schedules and wondered how there was ever time for him to hold a job when they both had so many interesting things to do.

Ellen picked up the remote and clicked on the television morning news. The room came alive and their attention was soon riveted to the TV newsman's words.

"The body of the person who leaped to his death from the Skyway has been recovered. The St. Petersburg police have identified him as Doctor Barry Millwood, a prominent local psychologist. There is no evidence of foul play and the police have closed their investigation and termed the incident a suicide."

Dan looked across the table at Ellen and reached out to take her hand. The blood seemed to have drained from her face. She was trying to speak but she could manage only a weak, "Oh no, Dan. Not Barry!" Ellen trembled and began to cry.

"We have to go to Susan. She needs someone now," Dan said.

Ellen heard his words but was already way ahead of him. She whirled and snatched the telephone from its wall cradle.

"Give me a minute to call her. I want her to know we're on our way." She disappeared.

He drew his six-foot, 180-pound frame away from the table and immediately rushed toward the bathroom. The gray flecks in Dan's hair compromised the otherwise youthful look of his fifty-three years. In his present state of mind, he wasn't sure whether he was setting off to shave and prepare for the frightening trip to console his best friend's widow or just wanted to vent his own grief in private. He made quick work of his shave and began to dress. Ellen followed him into the bathroom.

"No time to waste," she said. "Sue's really hurting. I should be there now."

"I'll get out of your way and wait for you in the kitchen," he called back.

They drove the twelve miles from their home in Trinity to the Safety Harbor house of the Millwoods. Dan remembered how he and Barry, unalike in so many ways, wouldn't be picked out of a crowd as close friends. Barry was noticeably shorter and had a totally different disposition—or at least it seemed that way to people outside their friendship. Barry gave the outward appearance of being severely serious, possibly antisocial. The Coopers and Barry's own family knew him as a genuinely endearing man with a quick wit and a surprising bent for humor inside their own tight little circle.

Ellen stared dead ahead, nervously twisting her hands.

"Are you going to be all right, El? This hit us both pretty hard but I know how close you and Susan are—like sisters."

"We don't have time to think about our own feelings," Ellen answered. "The important thing is to see that Susan gets all the comfort and protection she needs. Barry was her pillar of strength. Now she's all alone."

How like my gal, Dan reflected. *Talk about a pillar of strength—I'm looking at mine! She's going to be personally devastated when she has time to sit and think about what happened last night. But her only thoughts at this moment are for Susan's welfare. Ellen will protect that lady like a hatchling in the nest. Everyone should be blessed with a friend like my wife,* he thought.

"I can't see Barry purposely driving to that bridge to leap," Dan told her. "That just wasn't in his nature. He had so much to live for. There's no way he would have taken his own life. There has to be a lot more to this than meets the eye."

It wasn't a matter of Dan being in some sort of denial. Suicide was simply an impossible option for a person like his friend. Barry had been a psychologist for years and had dealt with analyzing other people's mental problems on a daily basis. Dan knew that many psychologists became so emotionally involved in their patients' problems that they harmed their own health. Barry had never given any indication that was true for him. Susan had always said he seemed to be able to maintain his scientific objectivity even with difficult cases. Dan would like to believe that he was close enough to Barry that he would have picked up on the slightest indication of a personal or health problem. The whole episode just didn't compute in Dan's suspicious mind.

"Dan, tell me this isn't real. I can't imagine him leaving her like this without a warning or a goodbye. He would never have hurt her intentionally." Ellen was as puzzled as he was.

They were nearing the community where Barry lived—used to live—and Dan had decided that the two ladies should have their time together without him. He knew that was best for the widow. That word sent chills through him. And he wasn't anxious to face Susan at the moment, anyway. Let her have some time to unload to Ellen. He'd be back to do whatever he could after a proper interval.

"Look, El, she needs you more than me right now. Let me bow out and give the two of you some time to clear the air. How long do you want me to be invisible?"

"Make it an hour. Call my cell number before you head back. By then we should be settled enough for you to see her and maybe run some errands for her."

Ellen reached for her purse on the seat. They turned into the driveway of the large two-story Spanish style home. When Dan pulled to a stop he reached out and gave Ellen's hand a reassuring squeeze. Then she hurried to the door.

* * *

His best friend was gone. It was a dizzying, deadly stroke of suddenness that couldn't be reversed. Susan had to be deeply and permanently wounded and Dan was powerless to help make her pain go away. He felt totally useless at this point. Also understood that he had to make himself scarce while the women got on with the serious matter of dealing with the shock. Dan retreated down Highway 19 to the Burger King and sat alone in a corner with a cup of very black, totally unsatisfying coffee. What he really needed right now, Dan mused, was a tall shot of bourbon and branch water—hold the water.

He was nearly ready for a second refill when his ear tuned in to two men at a nearby table discussing the morning's news.

"Yeah, took a header right off that baby into the bay," one of them said and made a wide, sweeping arc with his hand.

"Musta been bonkers," the other man replied. "I'd rather just shoot myself. Pow! No fall, no waiting."

Dan felt a sudden sting and jumped from his seat. He had crushed the Styrofoam cup and burned his hand. The two men looked at him and laughed, not knowing they were a split second away from having their noses flattened. They didn't know Barry. How could they sit there and joke about the tragic end of a decent man?

He fumed but his better judgment prevailed. He clinched his teeth and settled for fixing a wilting stare at the two insensitive buffoons. Walked to the counter, careful to keep his temper under control, and ordered a refill for his coffee. Then Dan strode to the door without looking back and stalked to his car.

In a barely audible voice he said, "I don't know how, Barry, but I *will* find the real answer to last night."

Dan sat quietly in his car for a long time sipping the hot coffee and remembering better times. He and Barry went back more than thirteen years. They had met in service about two years before they both left the Air Force. Millwood was six years his junior and seemed to Dan more a younger brother. They were stationed in the Washington area. Barry was a staff psychologist at the Walter Reed military hospital and Dan worked at the Defense Information Systems Agency in Arlington. Both families chose to live far out in the suburbs of Northern Virginia, away from the Washington bustle, and contend with the commute. The long drive was more than justified by the peace and quiet that waited for them in Loudoun County. Their wives became acquainted in the new neighborhood in Ashburn. Ellen Cooper and Susan Millwood were fast friends by the time the men got their busy schedules under control so the families could swap home cooked dinners. For the next two years they were inseparable.

Dan punched his phone and rang Ellen's cell number. When she answered, her tone was more subdued than when he left her.

"Can I show up now?" he asked.

"We're doing all right now," Ellen replied. "Come ahead."

He turned north and his mind raced backward in time. The Millwoods had moved to the Tampa Bay area first. Barry decided after ten years in uniform that he wanted to try life on the outside in private practice. Doctor Tom Sherman was looking for a partner in Clearwater and they agreed to join forces. Barry made the transition to civilian life easily and was highly regarded in the bay community.

Dan retired that same year with twenty years service and took a position with a high tech company in Northern Virginia. Later he joined with two partners in creating a wildly successful startup software company in Virginia. He and his associates eventually sold the venture for a ludicrously excessive profit.

At least four times each year they had visited, with the Coopers enjoying a taste of mild winter weather in Florida and some time on the beach in the summer. The Millwoods always managed to return to Virginia for a short time around Easter and again during the beautiful Blue Ridge fall foliage season.

Dan and Ellen had often talked about eventually moving to a warmer climate once he hung up his work clothes. Then the right day came with the company sold and their daughter Danielle in her senior year at college. He remembered vividly the day he had said to Ellen, “How would you feel about living with an old retired geezer?”

Her reply had been, “Seems like we went through this once before. You’re going to do it for real this time, huh? Promise?”

“With no business to worry about, this will be my chance to finally get serious about my dream of writing. What would you think if I carried you off to sunny Florida?”

“Thought you’d never ask,” she answered and the future was set.

So, eleven years after they left Air Force life, the Coopers were ready for a permanent change of scenery. They passed the news to Danielle who was excited about spending her last school summer on the beach. Then they contacted their good friends the Millwoods and headed south.

As Dan neared Safety Harbor and the painful chore he knew he had to face, he thought about all that the four of them had shared. He was more angry than sad by now. Wanted to strike out at something but there was no clear-cut blame to be laid. All he could do at the moment was to resolve that he would not rest until he unraveled the full story. His personal mission would be to learn how Barry came to be on that bridge.

Minutes later he followed Ellen to Susan Millwood’s kitchen and hugged their friend.

“Susan, honey, I don’t quite know what to say. If it helps at all, I want you to know I share your loss. Barry was the closest friend I’ve ever had.” The diminutive blonde smiled up at him and seemed to understand what he was unable to express.

“Thank you, Dan. He often told me how much your friendship meant to him,” she whispered and kissed his cheek. The anguish was written on her face but she was trying hard to contain her grief.

“There’s a favor I want to ask of you, Sue. I need your okay for something I feel driven to do.” He was looking past her tear-stained cheeks into those soft gray eyes.

“Name it.” Her voice quivered but she faced him squarely.

"You and I both know someone or something other than Barry is behind what occurred last night. I aim to find out what really happened. Let me do this for Barry and for you."

"Dan, I don't know how to feel about all this. I need to know the truth. It's all so confusing. Help me find out why he's gone."

Susan stopped speaking and the tears began again. Ellen went to her and wrapped her arms around her. She spoke calmly, "Just let it go, Sue. We're here for you."

Dan turned away awkwardly, chastising himself for complicating things at this delicate time. Coming back here and facing Susan had been the most difficult task he had confronted in many years. Now he had made a mess of a well-intentioned gesture to help. Old heavy-handed Dan had screwed up again. Just as he prepared to slink away, Susan reached out for his hand and gave him the lift he needed.

"Dan, I love you for understanding. Barry cared for us too much to leave without a word of explanation. Find the answer for me. Please."

He was choked with emotion when he answered, "Beginning today, Sue, that's my top priority."

CHAPTER 3

Dan and Ellen provided moral support to Susan and her children. They did all they could to keep her looking forward for the sake of her two teenagers. The Coopers seldom saw their own daughter, Danielle, who was recently married and living in Virginia. Johnny and Carol Millwood helped fill some of the void they felt with their own child no longer nearby. Barry was an only child. His parents were deceased. Susan's relatives all lived in New England, so the Millwood kids had adopted the Coopers as their extended family in Florida.

Ellen had called Danielle in Virginia and conveyed the sad news of Barry's passing. Dani, as Ellen often called their daughter, regarded Barry and Susan as an aunt and uncle. The Millwood children, for whom she had served as a babysitter, looked up to her. Danielle immediately made plans to fly to Florida. Having her close by would be a comfort for everyone.

The funeral service was one more gigantic hurdle for Susan to get past. She and Barry were devoutly religious and had brought the children up to believe in the sanctity of human life. Now she would have to face the stigma of the word suicide. The priest delivered a guarded benediction praying for forgiveness for the deceased and for the comforting of the mourners in attendance.

Somehow they all made it through the heart-rending service. There was some comfort for Dan and, he imagined, more importantly for Susan, in the number of mourners who came to honor this fine man. Barry had made his mark in his profession, his church and his neighborhood and they all responded to bid him farewell. Yet there was an aura of emptiness that overwhelmed the occasion. When the words had been said and the prayers were delivered, they endured the somber graveside gathering that, for Dan, added a note of finality to a treasured friendship.

Afterward Dan did his best to console the widow.

"Susan, those of us closest to him know he didn't act on his own. I won't rest until I prove that."

Susan managed a smile and squeezed his hand. "You and Ellen have been so wonderful. I need to go on with life for the children now. Let me know how I can help you with your search."

"We're with you every step, Sue," Ellen told her and hugged her tightly.

When they returned home, Dan felt suddenly hollow inside, drained of emotion, mentally exhausted. The void created by Barry's tragic death could never be filled. He didn't know which emotion to entertain first—deep sadness or intense rage. His promise to Susan was one he was determined to keep at all costs starting as soon as she was ready to assist. Dan walked to the den and pulled a photo album down off the shelf. He leafed through the pictures that held so many happy memories connecting the Coopers and the Millwoods. He lost himself in the flashbacks that passed before his eyes.

Danielle missed her father and came looking for him. She rapped lightly at the den door.

"You in here, daddy?"

His daughter came and stood behind his chair and put her arms around his shoulders. Danielle had grown into a twenty-two year old near carbon copy of her mother, though a bit taller.

"They'll be all right, Daddy. They have you two." She came around to face him. He looked up and marveled at how much his lovely daughter looked and even moved like the bride who had transformed his life.

"We'll probably never be as close to anyone as we've been to the Millwoods, Danielle. How are Johnny and Carol taking this?"

"I'm so glad I could be here for them. They'll be fine. If you're okay I'll get back to helping Mom fix us a bite. We've been talking about when Johnny and Carol were just little tykes."

"Yes, honey, I'm fine now. Thinking about some good times. Tell Mom I'll be along in a few minutes."

Dan returned to the photo album. He stared at the pictures of their families together and remembered the cherished times. There were the four of them at one of Barry's parties with his hospital group. Dan and Barry looked like they'd been partying hard. The gathering was the first close contact Dan ever had with the crazies Barry referred to sarcastically as his 'accomplices'. They were an odd lot, those men and women in white who were so efficient and proper on duty and a crowd of absolute hell raisers in private.

Dan remembered Barry's words when he'd looked a bit nonplussed at the medical staff's party behavior. "These people operate at peak stress. If we didn't let down now and then, we'd spend all our time treating each other. Turns into a real pressure cooker some days."

Dan replied, "Wait 'til you see the people I deal with in my business, Barry. Talk about head cases. At least we aren't allowed to use sharp instruments. That's a blessing for the world."

There was a photo of Danielle with Johnny and Carol Millwood when they were around six and four years old. Danielle had known them since Johnny was three and his sister was only a year old. The Coopers were sure Johnny had developed a genuine crush on their daughter. When they were sharing family vacations prior to the Coopers moving to Florida, the high point of their visits for the lad was seeing Danielle again. He wouldn't let her out of his sight.

She had blossomed into a truly beautiful young lady. Dani was now a college graduate out in the business world doing quite well on her first job. She had married shortly after graduation. Her devoted husband Rick made it easy for Dan and Ellen to feel comfortable this far away from the child that had been the center of their lives.

Ellen gently urged the album away from him and fixed her big, brown eyes on him.

"We're both hurting, Dan, but as you often say, it's time to suck it up and go on. Sue needs all the help we can muster. We have to pull it together for her as well as ourselves."

"You're right, Ellen, like always. But I owe him and you're my witness that I *will* pay him back."

That payback would begin bright and early tomorrow.

CHAPTER 4

The search for the truth behind Barry Millwood's death completely occupied Dan Cooper's mind. He knew there were ethics and doctor-patient relationships that would preclude his delving into office medical records or interviewing any of Barry's patients directly. Somehow, though, he had to dig for leads and gain a better perspective on his friend's state of mind in recent days.

Exactly where to begin was the question. He decided to start with Barry's office and his dedicated assistant. Marge was as shaken as the rest of them at this stage but agreed to help when both Dan and Susan requested her aid. Dan saw she needed to stop dwelling on the jolt of Doctor Millwood's sudden departure. He would involve her productively in helping him search for clues.

The tremendous emptiness he felt made Dan anxious to get started on disproving the suicide notion. But he wanted to give Susan room and time to grieve. She solved that problem by calling him the next morning.

"Dan, I'm ready to help you. Whenever you say, we'll start."

"I'll start my search at his office," Dan told her. "Marge said she would give me access to his things. I've agreed to steer clear of any material marked Patient Confidential. If you really are prepared, I'd like to come over tomorrow."

"I suppose you should talk to his partner, too. Let me call Tom Sherman and ask him to help." Susan sounded as anxious as Dan to lift the shroud of uncertainty around Barry's last night on earth.

* * *

Millwood and Tom Sherman had their offices in a multistory building on Route 19 on the north side of Clearwater. They had enjoyed a steady expansion of their clientele since Barry joined Tom. They were well into their thirteenth year of practice together. The suite of offices on the first floor of the Palmetto Park Building was tastefully decorated and crisply tidy. Dan approached the receptionist to ask for Marge, but Barry's long time assistant appeared before he could make his request. Marge's face told him that the turn of events had exacted a toll on her. She was still having difficulty dealing with the shock.

When they were alone Dan asked, "Had you noticed any changes in Barry recently?"

The tall redhead shook her long tresses vigorously and seemed totally at a loss. "He was always a joy to work with. That didn't change right up to the last day."

"I was hoping there was something about his actions, maybe changes in his behavior, that could get me started in the right direction."

She thought for a long moment then corrected herself. "Wait. There *was* something that may help. I noticed very recently that he seemed sort of detached at times." It was as if this was the first time she had stopped to seriously think about that change in Barry's demeanor.

"What do you mean detached?"

"I was used to Doctor Millwood being deep in thought and having to repeat what I said to him. He was so absorbed in thinking about his patients and sorting through how to help them. His recent lapses were a new experience for me, like his mind was so far away that I had to prompt him back. I don't know, it just wasn't him. Strangely, his drifting would only last for a short time and then he'd be normal again."

She instinctively started to straighten the items on the desk but Dan stopped her.

"Why don't I start with everything as near as possible to the way he left it."

"You're right, of course. Call me if you need anything, Dan."

"Wait a second. I appreciate that you can't get into any details about specific clients but I need to ask, Marge. Was there any reason to believe this distant manner could have been due to his concern for any particular current patient?"

"No, I can't come up with a logical answer for why he would suddenly go into those trances. I just can't explain his odd behavior."

"When did you first notice this, Marge? How long had he been so noticeably distracted?"

"Let me see," she began. "Best I can remember, it wasn't until the past week or so. I remember the first time. We were discussing the fact that he had found a new source for the antique figurines he collects. Suddenly he was somewhere else, his mind was out there in the ether. I had to tell him three times that Mrs. Thomas had cancelled out and he finally had an opening to take a breather. He'd been so busy lately that I was worried it could affect his own health."

"Okay, I'm going to look around his office and check over his computer. Doctor Sherman has agreed to take a lunch break with me and let me probe."

That seemed to please her.

"Doctor Tom is seeing Barry's patients temporarily, so the break will be good for him. He's carrying a killer schedule right now. Told me he had to lean heavily on me to help him keep his head above water."

That sounded like a smart assessment on Sherman's part. Marge had an air of ability and professional efficiency about her. Seeing her still in the office must have been reassuring to apprehensive patients. And she probably knew most of Barry's clients nearly as well as the doctor himself did.

Dan closeted himself in what had been Millwood's office, sat down behind the neatly kept desk and pondered where to begin. He had only a vague idea what went on behind this door or, for that matter, what any psychologist really did for his patients. Barry rarely talked in any detail about his work. When Dan asked, he usually said something like, "It would be pitifully boring to an engineer." He did know from reading that psychologists are trained to provide tests and counseling. They help patients with learning and behavioral problems and get them through any number of crises in their lives. A few of them, including Barry, also had the medical training to prescribe medications.

Whatever it was he did, Millwood apparently did it exceedingly well. He'd been honored on numerous occasions as an outstanding member of his profession. The photos and framed certificates on Barry's office walls attested to the respect he had earned.

Dan riffled through the correspondence in-basket and found nothing of particular interest. Barry had placed several items in a box marked Action. Among them were notices of future meetings and events that Barry apparently planned to attend.

One announcement in particular caught Dan's eye. A pamphlet touted an upcoming seminar at the University of South Florida School of Psychology campus in Tampa. Barry had circled the dates with a red pen. In the detailed program for the symposium, he had circled two presentations. The first was entitled "Clinical Research in Brain Neurotransmitters" to be presented by Doctor Jason Gernsbach of New Orleans. Neatly penned in the margin was the note 'Dinner with Jase'. A second handwritten note accompanied the program's synopsis of a presentation entitled "Behavior and the Cerebellum." That talk was to be given by Doctor Victor Krevins, Tampa psychologist and member of the USF teaching faculty. The note said 'Must Hear.' Dan wrote down these references and called Marge in. He pointed to the handwritten notes.

"Do these notations mean anything to you?"

She showed immediate recognition of the entries.

"I rearranged his schedule so he would have most of the day free for that program," she answered. "Krevins is a local psychologist. Barry said he'd known Gernsbach for a long time. Apparently it was important for him to hear both of them."

"Do you think there's a way I could sit in on the symposium?"

"If it's okay with Doctor Sherman, I'll call and tell them you'll be attending from our office instead of Doctor Millwood." She made a quick reminder note.

"Thanks, Marge."

Dan continued to scour the contents of the office for some direction to head in gathering information. Whenever he ran across a marking showing patient sensitive information he backed off as agreed. Each time he did this, Dan wondered what he was missing, but he was bound by his promise to respect doctor-patient confidentiality. So far his search was turning up absolutely nothing but he was convinced there had to be leads here somewhere. He desperately needed to confirm his conviction that Barry was not a suicide.

He investigated every scrap of data he could find, pored over Millwood's appointment calendar and office message slips. Looked through medical journals Barry had left near at hand searching for scribbled notes, dog-eared pages, anything that could get him started in his quest for clues. Dan checked the answering machine for incoming messages that may provide leads. Nothing sounded promising. His frustration was growing that nothing was going to open a reasonable path to follow. Then Marge rapped on the door and informed him that Doctor Sherman was ready to go to lunch.

* * *

Dan and his late friend's partner sat at the elegant little Clearwater restaurant. They shared a corner table by the water's edge. Cooper began the conversation.

"Wish this was taking place under happier circumstances, Tom. Thanks for giving me the time. I know you're incredibly busy."

"We're all still reeling at this stage," Doctor Sherman replied. "If I can help in any way, I'll try."

"You can understand my disbelief when I heard Barry's death was ruled a suicide, Tom. You of all people would know that couldn't be true."

"My reaction was identical, Dan. The only way I could ever see Barry dying that way would be for someone to drag him to the top of that bridge and physically throw him over the side. Murder, yes, but not suicide."

"Then you can see what I'm going through trying to track down the real reason he's dead. Susan needs to come to closure and I owe it to her to find some answers. Maybe together we can turn up a thread for me to follow."

"I wish I could give you a lead. I'm at a complete loss as to what could have happened to cause him to be on that bridge. He was as level headed and self controlled as anyone I've ever known. I don't know how I'll ever find another partner to match him. God, I miss that guy." The frustration was visible. Tom attacked his drink and withdrew, turning silent.

"Marge said he seemed somewhat detached and distant at times over the past week or so. Does that register with you, Tom?" By now Dan was pleading for some scrap of information to pursue.

"Marge was his assistant for a long time. She could read Barry pretty well. Can't say I noticed any odd behavior at all. Of course, we've been extremely busy for the past several months. We'd even talked about finding a third associate to share the heavy patient load."

"Before I started, Marge cautioned me about sensitive patient information, Tom. You can be assured that I'm being extremely careful about that. But I've done a thorough search and so far it's coming up zeros."

Sherman didn't answer. He shrugged and emitted a long sigh.

They ate in silence, stumped by the absence of clear indicators that would predict such a violent event as Barry's plunge. Dan rolled over again and again the blind ends he had encountered in Barry's office. There was still his computer to be searched. Dan had saved that for last. He wasn't exactly a fan of scouring endless files for data bits. Data surfing was a task his friend Jud Black could have reduced to an efficient hunt, but Jud was nine hundred miles away and Dan needed answers now.

Finally, Dan broke the weighty silence and spoke as they had their coffee. "I'm curious about something I found in Barry's office. He apparently planned to go to a program at USF. Specifically wanted to hear presentations by Doctor Jason Gernsbach and Doctor Victor Krevins. Do those names mean anything to you?"

"He and Jason Gernsbach were friends if I recall correctly. You should ask Susan about him. As far as Krevins is concerned . . ."

His voice trailed off and Dan could see that Tom was struggling with how much more to say to him on that subject.

Sensing that prodding was going to be needed, he nudged Sherman along. "Yes? Is there something I should know about Doctor Krevins?" His tablemate took a deep breath and continued.

"Well, he and Barry were classmates as undergrads back in Indiana. Barry was doing Krevins a personal favor at the office."

"What kind of favor?"

"Victor asked him if one of his students could spend some time observing an active full-time psychologist's office. Barry agreed to let him tag along a couple half days each week to get the feel. He's a doctoral candidate named Peter Drake. Seems to be a nice enough youngster."

"But about Krevins?" Again, Tom appeared hesitant.

"Normally, you understand, professional ethics wouldn't let me comment on an associate to anyone outside the medical field. Victor Krevins, however, presents an interesting case. Let me just say that his theories seem to fall a little outside the norm. He's not highly regarded by his fellow psychologists. I don't doubt he's an exceptionally gifted scientist but he doesn't enjoy a high level of trust. I'd rather not say any more."

"I appreciate your candor and take your words in confidence, Tom."

* * *

Dan made up his mind that he would definitely be at that session at the Tampa school. Chances were he wouldn't understand much of what the speakers had to say, but there could be other benefits. If either an old friend of Barry's or a somewhat tainted peer could aid him in his search, he felt committed to check out both of them. The day of the gathering at the university was a week away. Meanwhile, he could bring himself up to speed on the subject of psychology and perhaps be able to ask questions that wouldn't sound too dumb.

He returned to the office and dug in, anxious to make a new start.

"Now for the computer," Dan mumbled and turned it on. The screen blinked and displayed a box with the word 'Password' and a blank. He went to find Marge. She would have Barry's password.

"It's MySusie," she answered.

"I would have guessed it was something like that," Dan replied and smiled.

"You'll notice I'm keeping it turned off. No reason for anyone to look at anything in his files unless we need information for a patient visit. So I'm guarding his data."

"Sounds reasonable to me, Marge. I hope only you and Tom know exactly why I'm rummaging around in here."

"Everyone thinks you're picking up personal things for Susan, nothing else."

"Good. I made sure Sherman knows the real story," Dan confirmed. He would have expected that the fiercely loyal Marge would take this protective attitude.

He did a quick scan of the files on Barry's hard drive and saw several that were eye-catching enough to open. But each time his hopes were buoyed that he was about to make a discovery, the file at hand would prove to be routine. Dan was accustomed to spending extended periods on his own computer in the course of writing fiction drafts, but his head was already beginning to hurt. He felt a twinge of light headed dizziness. Must be his intense concentration for more than half a day on details that was wearing on him. At this point Dan resigned himself to the fact that his efforts were becoming not only non-productive but also very tiring. This search of the office would have to be continued at a later time when he was mentally sharper.

As he was leaving, Marge hailed him. "Let me introduce you to Peter Drake. Pete?"

A slender young man in his mid-twenties appeared from a side room and offered his hand. He was taller than Dan and sported coal black hair and a gaunt face. This was the graduate student Victor Krevins had secured a part-time position for with Barry.

"Glad to meet you, sir. Doctor Millwood often mentioned his close friendship with you."

"I'm sure your time watching Barry has been helpful to you."

"Very helpful. I spend the majority of my time assisting Doctor Krevins with his clinical tests at the campus. He's taught me the finer points of research and testing techniques. My time here has been particularly valuable in showing me what a practicing psychologist encounters on a daily basis. I've learned some valuable lessons I can use when I'm certified and out on my own."

He was well spoken. Peter Drake was likely far above average in the brains category or Victor wouldn't waste his own time helping the young man launch his career. Peter was tall and awkwardly thin but looked the part of a psychologist. He did, however, have a somewhat stuffy and officious demeanor about him.

Dan hoped his search of Barry's home office tomorrow would be more successful. He rang Susan and asked to come by in the morning to get started.

CHAPTER 5

The next stop was the Millwoods' house. Maybe the clues were among Barry's more personal items in his home office. Chances were that very little of his business information was there because Millwood had been sensitive to closely guarding patient data. If there were any indications of Barry's innermost thoughts in those final days before the waters of the bay claimed him, Dan may find them here. Susan had assured him he wasn't prying. Barry would have wanted him to do everything he could to remove the cloud of suspicion over his death.

"I'm so happy you're here, Dan. Let me know if there's anything I can do to help."

"Are you doing okay, Sue? Anything you need me to do? I can fetch and tote with the best of them."

Her reassuring smile let him know she was trying hard to commence the healing process. Dan was sure it would be a long journey for her.

"Made some fresh coffee and the pot's on the warmer in the office. I'll leave you alone."

She turned to leave then paused at the door. "Oh, you'll need the password for Barry's computer." Her chin trembled.

"I suspect I already know it. MySusie?" She nodded agreement and closed the door behind her.

His friend had done quite well in his practice and the Millwoods lived in a rather exclusive neighborhood of upscale homes. They moved into this house soon after the Coopers relocated to Florida. Dan and Ellen arranged a monumental housewarming party for them. One of the rooms Barry had insisted on in the builder's design was a spacious office with room for lots of bookshelves, a large cherry desk, a computer workstation and a comfortable leather easy chair.

It was in this room that Millwood also kept many of the china figurines he treasured so highly. They were ornate and elegant in their handmade beauty, miniature works of art. Dan wondered how Barry could keep an obviously valuable collection of small treasures such as these in a house with no alarm system. He had repeatedly warned Barry about the danger of theft but Millwood was a naively trusting man who refused to recognize the danger.

He set up in the office and began a methodical examination of every bit and scrap of information it contained. The records gave a concise picture of the Millwood family's finances. He felt a twinge of guilt with this part of his exploration but Susan had given him full license to scour any and all of Barry's records. Dan soon concluded that he could rule out financial difficulty as a factor contributing to Millwood's plunge. To the contrary, the man was not only one of the most mentally stable people Dan knew, he also had rock solid financial stability. For the first time he learned that Barry and Tom Sherman shared ownership of the building where they had their offices. Barry also had the titles to other valuable properties.

A copy of Barry's latest medical examination report was filed away. Dan read through it and, although he ran across terms he couldn't understand as a medical layman, the indicators he did recognize all seemed to be within normal ranges. The text summary of the report was very upbeat, finding Millwood to be in good to excellent health. He had always taken care of himself, exercised regularly and was a confirmed jogger. He was careful with his diet and sometimes even chided Dan for some of his dietary sins. The medical report was dated only five weeks ago and it essentially pronounced Barry Millwood a healthy forty seven year old male. So unless there had been some recent revelation, his leap hadn't been prompted by anything connected with his own health.

"Any luck, Dan?"

Susan had stopped in to bring him fresh coffee and sweet rolls.

The aroma of the home baked pastry brought him back from wherever it was his mind had traveled. He'd been tucked away in here for a long time and she seemed to sense that he needed some temporary diversion.

"I'm still sniffing out clues." He didn't have the heart to tell her his efforts added up to a big fat zero so far.

"You must have some things you want to ask me. I'm ready now." She took a deep breath as if steeling herself for the ordeal to follow.

"Didn't want to bother you until I had to, Susan."

"I want this cleared up as much as you do, Dan . . . even more. I can't bear the looks I get from people who think Barry killed himself. Some of them probably even think I did something awful to prompt him."

She paused and looked down at her lap. Her hands were tightly clasped, the fingers so tightly woven that the knuckles were white. Dan tilted her chin up and looked into her eyes.

"You've known me long enough to see that I can be like an old plow horse with blinders once I set my mind on a goal. I won't stop until I whip this thing."

She nodded and rose to leave. He gave her a reassuring smile and plunged back into the work at hand.

Barry's appointment book contained the usual entries—events at the high school involving Johnny or Carol that he didn't want to forget, personal appointments. He'd made notations to meet Susan on each of the next four Wednesdays for the regular lunch dates that were a long-held custom in the Millwood household. Nothing struck Dan as noteworthy until a bell rang in his head. Barry had penciled in red on the desk calendar the opening date of the same symposium at the University of South Florida. In smaller letters were the words 'Jase and Crazy Vic'. That note pretty well summed up Barry's opinion of Victor Krevins. Now the presentations were an absolute must for Dan to hear.

He doggedly tracked down every piece of written material in the home office and pored over each tidbit. So far he was no closer to answers than when he had left Barry's professional office. Dan was becoming very downcast so he sat back and forced a break in his efforts. What was he missing? Was he even going about this right? He refused to accept the suicide theory and yet there was no hint of hope so far that he would find a more logical explanation.

Cooper held his head in his hands and stroked his forehead as though it would help his thought process. If only he could discover some fragment, some path, however oblique, to pursue. He walked to the kitchen and found Susan.

"Please stop me any time I go too far. I need to know if you noticed anything different about Barry's habits, his routines, maybe unusual actions on his part recently."

Susan frowned. "He was oddly distant at times the past week or so. That just wasn't the way he normally acted around us. Barry never brought problems home from the office. Most of his time at home was ours and we knew it."

"Tell me what you mean by distant. Did he withdraw from you and the children?"

"He began to spend more time alone in here during the past ten days or so. He was on his computer more than usual. Said he was tracking down figurines for his collection and sounded all caught up in it. But that shouldn't have made him so detached from us. It was like he wasn't listening at times. Seemed his mind was drifting."

Dan recognized a pattern but didn't yet know what to make of it. Marge remarked about the same lapses of attention on his part at the office and the timeframe was about the same. Susan said he was spending more time on the computer. As much as he dreaded plodding through data files, apparently there was no putting it off any longer. That would be his next effort.

"I know Barry could go to great lengths searching out porcelain figurines for his collection. What was special this time about his compulsion toward his hobby, Susan?"

"He said there was a new source on the Internet that sounded very promising and he was trying to see how authentic their offerings were. I wondered why the sudden urgency but didn't press him."

"Let me get back to my rummaging and I'll keep you up on

my progress." Dan smiled at her and immersed himself once again in his search.

He hoped he wasn't holding out false hope to her. Some key piece of information was hiding in this office and he was overlooking it. The frustration was almost overpowering.

Dan turned to the computer and brought it to life. At the prompt, he smiled and typed MySusie. Then he set to work checking the My Documents menu of folders and files. The list was extensive and many of the files were of considerable size, so this was going to be a long process. It was time to see if Jud Black wanted a short Florida vacation. This sort of thing was much more in his bailiwick. Dan chose one folder that sounded promising and opened it to find four files. He did a quick scan of each and found no immediate leads. But he printed out the contents for further examination at home.

On an impulse he opened the read section to view Millwood's recently received email. Most of the contents were of no great interest. One message with the unusual screen name 'Secret Treasures' caught his eye. When Dan opened the attachment and looked at the text, he saw that it touted the company's ability to find hard to locate porcelain figurines for serious collectors. Barry had replied the same day and asked for more information. A follow-on message provided him with details for submitting specific search requests for guaranteed price quotes from Secret Treasures. Marge had mentioned a conversation with Barry about his hobby around the time his odd behavior started.

Dan printed the contents of these exchanges then decided to take a break from his efforts. His head was beginning to ache with the concentration and the eyestrain. He would pore over the printed files tonight and get back to his task tomorrow.

As he wrapped up his work and prepared to leave, he found Susan in the kitchen and inquired, "Can you clear up a couple of questions for me?"

She stopped her work and took a seat on one of the bar stools at the kitchen counter.

"Sure. What do you want to know?"

"I found references at his office and here at home to a symposium over at the college in a few days. He obviously planned to attend."

"Yes, I know the one you mean. He said it was a chance to hear about new work going on and to see some of his friends."

"That's exactly why I'm asking. His notes showed interest in presentations by a Doctor Gernsbach and a Doctor Krevins. Do those names ring a bell?"

"Sure. I know both of them. Jason Gernsbach and his wife are long time friends. We first met them a few years back at a professional gathering. We've kept in touch with them. They live in New Orleans. I made plans to have Jason over for dinner while he's here. Hoped you and Ellen could join us."

"And Krevins?"

"Well, he's a special case. Barry and Victor Krevins were undergrads together back in Indiana. Victor came from a wealthy family and inherited quite a fortune. Certainly didn't have to work for a living but Barry says he's always been a driven man. He's on the local college faculty and does a lot of clinical research. Also has a part time practice to keep his hand in with patients. Victor was never one of Barry's favorites."

"That sounds like a careful understatement given the fact that Barry's note referred to him as 'Crazy Vic.' I'd say they weren't close."

"It's just that Krevins always had an odd approach to his profession. Barry admitted that he's a brilliant man but seemed to think he was pretty far out with some of his theories and his chancy techniques."

"And you've met the doctor?"

"On several occasions. He's a tall, very intense man with eyes that are almost scary in the way they look through you."

"Okay, Sue. It's time for me to call it a day here. I still have some reading to do back at home." He held up the printouts for her to see.

CHAPTER 6

Outside, the February night in northern Virginia was bleak and cold. A fresh snow lay on the ground around the cabin in the Clarke County woods. Well into the dark hours there was a blue glow from the basement.

Jud Black was at work on his latest brainstorm. This one involved revolutionary improvements in home security systems. The software he was building would automatically prompt active defense measures when the host system sensed an intrusion. The beauty of the product would lie in its simplicity and low cost that would make it available to most middle-income homeowners.

He had been so busy he wasn't sure what time of day it was. The sound of sleet pecking at the basement windows told him the night was raw. But in here, in his personal domain, time and weather were of slight importance. Only results counted. Jud leaned back in his squeaky chair—just had to find that 3-in-1 oil—and regarded the computer screen. He was a study in somber concentration, fading into his surroundings in his head to toe black garb. Some would say his manner of dress was a concession to his name, but he never gave it a second thought. It simply pleased him to dress in hues that ranged from darkest gray to jet-black. And if there was one quality that stood out in Jud Black's character, it was that he always did exactly what he damn well pleased

Being a thirty-six year old retired multimillionaire wasn't the best thing in the world, though he had to admit it sure beat the hell out of most of the alternatives. Jud still needed, as he always had, the satisfaction of a challenge well met. With the need for money no longer a prime motivation, he was writing code for the pure mental satisfaction it gave him. This boy wonder bullshit was okay until you woke up one morning and asked yourself, "*What have I done lately that was really cool, that will last beyond next week?"*

A persistent nudge against his leg brought Jud out of his deep concentration. He sneered at the big, black dog that was nuzzling him for attention. The pooch was frantically wagging his tail and prancing on all four paws. That could mean only one thing.

"You sure about this, Downbeat? It's colder than the knob on the shit house door out there. Maybe you ought to go dump it in a dark corner and we'll worry about it later."

The dog wouldn't take no for an answer. He whined and licked Jud's hand.

"Okay, if you're sure. You won't stay out there long in that sleet."

He grabbed a smoke while he waited for Downbeat to make his quick circuit. Jud mulled over the two competing markets that could make Guard Dog, as he had dubbed his new product, a commercial success. One path of opportunity was to sell it to an enterprising security system manufacturer for enhancement of their existing offerings then sit back and collect royalties from their sales. The other route was for his software to be bought in total by a leading systems maker and set on the shelf. Holding the patent rights would guard the buyer against similar future software that could make present alarm systems obsolete. Either way there was a handsome profit to be reaped, although that wasn't his real driver. Most of all, Jud delighted in the thought that once again he was scooping his fellow code slingers with innovative software that advanced the state of the art. Even if it never came to market, he would know what he'd accomplished.

Downbeat came scratching at the door well and Jud hurried him in out of the nasty weather. The dog ran past him shivering and shook the ice pellets off his coat. Jud rubbed him down with an old wool blanket.

"Now go curl up and let me get back to work, mutt. I'm getting pretty foggy but I've gotta finish this."

Jud kicked back and contemplated the next instruction to be keyed into the Guard Dog program. To the casual observer he was much like so many of the computer geeks who slaved away in isolation producing little marvels of software ingenuity. Black was a handsome man on a slender six-two frame and he seemed younger than his years. But his look of innocence was deceptive. His penetrating eyes could stare down a computer screen as if it were an adversary. Behind them lurked an unconstrained mind and abilities seldom matched by his contemporaries. His long black hair pulled back in a ponytail and the ring in his pierced eyebrow tempted one to categorize him. Jud Black, however, had a hidden elegance of thought that allowed him to match wits with anyone.

Ever since his unofficial retirement almost five years ago, Jud had tried to wean himself from these creative bursts. Those surges compelled him to glue himself to a machine with code flowing from his fingertips. He wanted to spend his time with his first love, composing and recording cutting edge alternative music. The old urges just wouldn't go away. He was a software wizard at heart. That's what his hacker friends told him, anyway. If you cut him, he would bleed ones and zeros and he dreamed in lines of code.

Jud had been swept away by a creative spark and sat down thirty hours ago at his workstation. The Guard Dog program was out of the cage, raging in his brain and he had to get it down while the juices were flowing. His eyes burned and the coffee had reached the bitter-strong stage. A cloud of smoke haloed around his head as he crushed another butt into the overflowing ashtray. The odor of stale tobacco clung to his clothes. Jud knew it was time for a decision. Maybe he should crash and recharge for a few hours. Or perhaps it was time to refuel with his usual sandwich and Murphy's Ale and plunge ahead. The telephone rang and gave him a reprieve from his dilemma.

"Nekkid." Black answered with his usual greeting. Most callers were shocked into hanging up but his friends recognized it as his playful way of putting them off guard.

"If you're naked today, you're freezing your buns off in that February weather."

"Hey, howsaboy, Dan?"

Jud leaned back in his swivel chair and went into relaxed mode. He hadn't spoken with Dan Cooper since just before the holidays. This was as good a time as any to take a breather and catch up on how Dan was doing in Florida.

"Well, Ellen and I are fine, but I have another problem. Think I need your help."

"All you have to do is ask, partner. You should know that by now." Downbeat ambled over and sniffed. Jud fed him a stale pretzel.

Dan and Jud owed each other a large measure of gratitude for the way their friendship had represented a turning point in both of their lives. They shared a strong bond that went back nearly eleven years. He and Dan had totally different backgrounds and outward appearances. They were astonished to discover that their views of the world were strangely similar in many respects. Where they differed it was seldom a matter of contention, just an amusing variance of opinion they quickly dismissed as unimportant.

"We have a situation down here that has me stumped. I need a brainstorming session with you to sort out the truth. Jud, I am way too close to the problem to think straight."

"Let old Jud take a crack at it. What's bothering you?"

"A good friend of mine is dead. The police have decided he committed suicide. So far I've run into a series of blind alleys trying to disprove that. Need another perspective on things."

"Heavy. Give me some details."

"You met him when you came down here last year. Barry Millwood, my psychologist friend. You remember the three of us went to the beach with the girls and you picked up a three-alarm sunburn.

"Ouch. Yeah, I remember Barry *and* the sunburn. He seemed like a pretty regular guy for a skull doc."

"He drove his car to the top of the Skyway Bridge last Wednesday and stepped off. A witness said it looked like he was sleepwalking. I just refuse to believe he would do that on his own. He had to be so distressed he was totally unaware of what was happening."

"Health problems maybe? Financial funk?"

"He was acting a bit strange lately but I've checked out all the angles. According to his records he was in excellent health and in great financial shape, too. There's no logic here, Jud. It's driving me up the wall. I'm determined to get to the bottom of this mystery."

Jud paused and began digging through a stack of papers. He heard Dan's voice on the phone and picked it up again.

"What's that, Dan?"

"I said are you still there?"

"Hold on a minute. I'm looking for last Friday's Washington Post—you know, the paper you love to hate? There's an article I want to check again. Something came together when you used the words psychologist and sleepwalking. My instincts told me I needed to check this out before we went on with our conversation."

"Wondered about all the bumping and rustling, Jud. Of course, I can picture your basement piled high. How long have you been down there this time?"

"Oh, a day and a half or so, Dan. Got a project on the griddle. Actually, it's almost tidy down here at the moment. Week's worth of old newspapers, couple of full butt cans, a few leftover snacks, and half a case of Murphy's Ale bottles—all empty."

"Sounds about par for the course." Dan laughed aloud.

Jud found what he was looking for and said, "There you are, you little beauty."

He announced to Dan, "Here it is. *Doctor Myron Wainwright, noted psychologist at George Washington* University *Hospital. Fatally injured in a traffic accident on 23rd Street at noon on Thursday*. Seems he walked out of the hospital like he was sleepwalking. Got himself squashed by a delivery van."

Dan remarked, "That's eerie. Barry's fall happened just a few hours earlier. Two robot-like victims a thousand miles apart. Do you find that a little odd, old buddy? I mean, the circumstances are strangely similar. Or am I just grasping at straws here?"

"No, let's pursue that," Jud answered. "Occurs to me they were in a profession that's not exactly routine. Wonder if they knew each other? Is there some reason they both checked out the same day? Is the strain finally getting to the head docs?"

Jud was cruising now. Sometimes you just had to think outside the box. Dan would approach the problem logically and apply his engineer's mind to the situation. Jud tended to blue sky and see what came to mind. Together they could be a pretty effective problem-solving duo as they'd proven many times.

"What else do you know so far?" Jud asked him. "What makes you think this was something other than him diving off the bridge on his own?"

"I have to be honest. I have no proof to the contrary. My conviction is based solely on my knowledge of Barry. After being as close to him and his family as we've been for all these years, I know there has to be something more sinister than Barry just copping out on life. Both his wife and his assistant mentioned he was going off into trances."

"Okay, I can accept that. You're a pretty good judge of character. You picked me as a business partner. Have you been able to get access to his personal items and records?"

Jud reached down and retrieved a slice of cold pizza from a paper plate. He held it out to Downbeat who sniffed, turned away and returned to his spot in the corner. Jud tossed the pizza, plate and all, into a wastebasket.

"Working on it, Jud. I'm talking to his wife. She's Ellen's best friend. I've quizzed his partner and his office assistant. Checked his records at his office and home. So far I'm coming up dry, but I have to be missing some key."

"What about his computer files? Anything out of the ordinary there?"

"You know I'm no expert in that arena, Jud. Sort of a hit or miss approach for me where you'd have a well laid out plan for scouring his files."

Jud sat back and thought about that. He shook his head in agreement.

Dan went on. "Haven't finished exploring the files yet. I have some printouts. Understand he was a doctor and I have to be careful about what confidential information I run across."

"What did you print out?"

"Just some information in one folder that sounded interesting and a couple of email exchanges. I haven't finished looking through the printouts yet. Felt a little burned out after scanning his home machine. There's obviously a better way to go about this."

"How do I say this, Dan. Oh, what the hell. You and I aren't touchy about what we say to each other."

"Spit it out, bithead. You're going to tell me I need a guardian when I use a computer, right?"

"Well, I like to think I've taught you a few tricks over time. You're still a bit of a ham hand where machines are concerned, though. We wouldn't want to lose any data before we can analyze it. Sometimes even attachments to emails can hold surprises."

"What do you mean, Jud? What kinds of surprises?"

"I don't want to sound too far out here, but people have been known to send an email message with an attachment that contains hidden software. Then the sender can use that routine to remotely access your computer later. He can even install files called daemons on your machine. They do tasks in the background you don't even know are taking place. How weird is that?"

Dan went silent so Jud lit another smoke and inhaled deeply, waiting for a reaction. The response came in the form of a request.

"That's exactly why I need you down here, Jud. You'd come at this thing from totally new angles. How about taking a break for some winter sun in Florida? It's important to me that I finish this matter and put my mind at rest."

"Okay, give me a few days to finish up what I'm working on. I want to check out this incident over in D.C., too, with the other dead doc. You've tweaked my curiosity. We may stumble onto a connection."

"Just talking to you makes me feel a lot better, Jud. I'll hold off on the computers. Wouldn't want to horse up anything."

"Great. I'll see you soon, Dan. Take care."

"Phone me your flight information and we'll pick you up at Tampa International. Ellen and I will both be looking forward to seeing you."

* * *

How about that? Dan Cooper. Man, does that take me back, Jud thought.

Eleven years ago, he had met Dan at AllTech. Dan was brought in to run the major program Jud was assigned to for a government client. The work force for the program was a major element of the small company. More than fifty computer and communications specialists were assigned. Most of them were degreed but Dan always seemed to gravitate toward Jud when he wanted important technical advice.

Jud took pride in being self-taught and non-degreed. He had something that most college grads could never touch. Computer programming came naturally to him. You just had to jump in and not put boundaries on your imagination, he contended. Jud refused to believe there was any computer problem he couldn't solve given enough time. The skills were something he honed by grinding it out at the gut level since his early teens. By now Jud knew most major hardware platforms from the inside. That spanned from his original Radio Shack TRS-80 to the advanced machines he had access to in his government contract work.

Instant mutual respect between Dan and Jud grew into a high level of trust. Their bond made the differences in their ages and backgrounds irrelevant.

Jud took a long drag on his smoke and remembered the day that had changed his life forever.

* * *

Dan, Jud and their pal Pat O'Leary were having a beer at happy hour. Jud came right out and said what he knew all three of them had been thinking.

"Hey, we're three pretty savvy guys. What the hell are we doing working for somebody else when we could have our own business?"

He was obviously right. Dan looked at Pat and they both shrugged as if to say *what took us so long?*

"I can write software and a lot of my friends have solid programming talent," Jud had pointed out. "Dan knows how to manage and he markets like a pro. Pat has the knack for handling people and technical solutions. His people would walk through fire for him. Sounds like a winning team to me."

"All that's stopping us is money—lots of money," Pat had replied.

Dan had chimed in. "Well, we're not totally without funds. We can each ante up some money and borrow the rest. Don't even have to quit our jobs—just double up and moonlight. After all, if we're not serious enough to take a chance, this conversation is just so much BS."

He had laid down the challenge they were waiting to hear. Why not?

The software packages the new company planned to offer would be elegant in their utility and beautifully straightforward in their composition. Dan suggested, "Our marketing approach is rough as a cob but we'll give the customers what they need."

Jud smiled at Pat and said, "You heard it here first. That's the name we're looking for. Cooper-O'Leary-Black. COB Software."

Armed with a simple corncob as their logo, they got down to the business of writing, testing and packaging their first product. What followed during the next six years was truly phenomenal. The decision to go for broke had been made at a most opportune time when the computer industry was exploding into the home market. Dan worked the financial plan. He determined that with a small investment from each of them and one million dollars in seed capital, they could launch COB as a nights and weekends endeavor. The three men took a flyer and came to market with an initial software product that stood the industry on its ear. After that the successes built. No problem was insurmountable to the talented group of programmers who gravitated to the new company under Jud Black's urging.

Their solutions in software and Dan's down to earth marketing approach caught the fancy of the army of home users looking for efficient user-friendly aids. Early on they had agreed that COB products would be affordable to encourage wide distribution. This strategy helped them capture a large customer base.

Big software companies began to take serious notice. COB was costing them potential sales of their more costly packages. By the fourth year of operation, the three entrepreneurs were being courted by most of the big software houses. The competition to buy out COB was intensifying. This had been a fantastic ride but by now Dan, Pat and Jud could see an even better alternative without the stress of running to stay ahead of the industry. Then came the decision point they all knew had been facing them for months.

"I don't know about you two, but I've had enough of working every day," Dan told them. "This was great fun but I'm ready to enjoy our good fortune."

"Been looking at a nice home place over in Maryland," Pat countered. "Playing around with the idea of buying an Irish restaurant in Frederick and being a barkeep."

"Sure wouldn't be the same without you two nut cases," Jud told them. "Half the fun has been that we don't take ourselves too seriously. Still know how to have fun while we're doing something we can make a profit on."

Jud liked to boil things down to the essentials. Running COB was no longer the fun it had once been. Time to move on.

"Why don't we hang a big price tag on COB and see if anybody bites?" Jud had asked them. He was just as ready to make the jump as they were.

So, a mere six years into its meteoric rise as a brash new company, COB sold for more cash than any of them would have dreamed possible. They ensured that their employees were well provided for with stock and long-term contracts with the buyer. Then the three men took an early retirement to pursue more mundane endeavors. With several million dollars in each of their bank accounts, Dan, Pat and Jud had become, respectively, a semi-retired writer in Florida, a pub owner in Maryland and a composer/ recording artist in Virginia. Jud still kept his hand in by doing some consulting and writing software from time to time. Basically they were free to do exactly what they wanted and it was time to enjoy life. They owed no one except each other and that was a huge debt they were all happy to repay.

Now Dan needed his help. Would he come to Florida and lend a hand? Damn right he would.

CHAPTER 7

The newspaper account of Doctor Wainwright's untimely death left too many questions unanswered. What could have caused him to walk directly into the busy traffic of 23rd Street without looking for a safe opening? What had held his attention so completely that he would ignore or fail to heed the obvious danger? There was something too eerily similar about this incident and Dan's account of his friend's plunge.

Jud read and reread the Washington Post article but there was too much lacking. He did a bit of surfing for information on Doctor Wainwright then drove to the offices of the Post on the chance that the on-scene reporter would be available. Luckily, he was able to grab a few minutes of the young reporter's time. On a precautionary impulse he introduced himself not as Jud Black but as 'Jud Green'.

"So I take it no one found a reason for the accident other than inattention. No clue why Wainwright was blind to his surroundings in those final moments before he was reduced to a grease spot. Seems odd to me. He'd probably spent years playing dart and dodge with the D.C. motorized assassins. Just doesn't compute in my suspicious brain that he would be that careless."

"Certainly seemed odd to me, too, Mr. Green. Mid-block jaywalking in this town gives you a life expectancy roughly equivalent to a spirited game of Russian roulette. George did say Wainwright was a bit glassy-eyed when he left the building."

"George?"

"George Jackson. He's one of the custodians at GW. I talked to him only minutes after the accident. He spoke to Wainwright before the doctor left the lobby and he also witnessed the accident."

The reporter began to shuffle papers on his cluttered desk. He clearly had nothing of substance to add and considered the matter closed. This death was a minor occurrence to him in a town with daily incidents of mayhem and murder. That was probably all the time he could spend on Wainwright's fate. Too bad, Jud thought. Wainwright had a few minutes of notoriety he never asked for and it was time to move on. The world could be uncaring.

Jud thanked him and set out for GWU Hospital to find George Jackson. Maybe it would be wasted time but his intuition told him something more than a momentary lapse of judgment was involved in this tragic event. Besides, he had definite plans for his visit to the hospital.

* * *

The new GWU Hospital facility had recently opened next door to the Foggy Bottom metro station. It sat directly across the street from the former hospital. Jud was admiring the shiny new structure's lobby when a man in blue coveralls walked by with a half full trash bag. The man's nametape read George. Jud took the precaution of introducing himself once again as 'Jud Green' and engaged the custodian in conversation.

"Gave me a creepy feeling. The doctor was always upbeat and had a good word for everybody. He just wasn't himself the last time I saw him." George shook his head. "No sir, something was wrong."

"What makes you say that? Was it what he said or how he looked?"

"A bit of both, I'd say. He liked to stop and chat. That day there was a purpose in the way he walked. Like he didn't have any time to chat—had to get somewhere right away. Just said hello and hurried out." George turned back to his work and dusted a tabletop. "Never saw him walk like he did that day, either. Sort of acted mechanical if that makes sense."

"Anything else that caught your attention?"

"Only that he spoke kind of choppy—like his thoughts were someplace else. Now that I think about it, his eyes were different. When he looked at me, his eyes were sort of blank."

"And you saw the van hit him?" Jud queried.

"Doc just walked straight across the sidewalk and off the curb. He must have been staring at the other side of the street. Didn't even bother to turn his head in either direction. Couldn't have seen that van coming."

"Can we get a cup of coffee or a soda and talk in private, George? I have an important question to ask you."

"Sure. I can take a short break, couple minutes, and we can talk in the snack bar."

When they had found a quiet corner, Jud continued. "George, I can tell that you liked Doctor Wainwright. You're genuinely upset over what happened to him."

"He was one of the better people on the staff here. Wouldn't want it repeated, but there are a lot of these high-powered doctors that are first grade asses."

"But Wainwright was an exception, I take it."

"He was an okay fellow. I owed him for some help he gave my wife when she was having health problems a while back. Didn't even charge us."

"Then you'd want to see his death solved? If somebody had a hand in causing him to die, you'd want the whole story to come out, wouldn't you?"

"What are you saying, Jud? It wasn't an accident?"

"Humor me, George. It's a theory at this point but I need to check it out." Jud lowered his voice to a barely audible whisper and leaned closer to George.

"Can I get to his computer?"

The custodian straightened up and looked at Jud in shock. "Whoa, there. That's dangerous. You could get me fired for talking about such things."

Jud reached out and touched his shoulder. He looked George squarely in the eyes.

"It's not my intent to get anybody in trouble—except for whoever may have caused Myron Wainwright to be run down. I only need a few minutes of access to his computer. We can do it after hours. Call it an opportunity to repay your debt to him."

He carefully rolled over Jud's words. Rubbed his slightly balding head. Jud had clearly presented him with a dilemma. George could be in serious trouble with his employers for helping Jud do what he was proposing. He was counting on the fact that George felt indebted to Wainwright and would want to revenge a good man who met a violent end before his time.

"Oh, jeez, this is scary." George looked all around to confirm that no one else was listening. "I'm almost afraid to ask. What exactly do you want me to do?"

"Simply look the other way, friend, while I explore a bit. Then I'll be out of your hair . . . so to speak." He had paused when George rubbed the thin gray fuzz on his pate and beamed broadly at Jud's choice of words.

They set the plan and Jud was given 20 minutes—no more—to examine Wainwright's office. He reassured George that he would go about his search quickly and quietly then be gone. The clock would be running as soon as George gave him the high sign and unlocked the office door.

Jud had already resolved to get access to Wainwright's office one way or another. He'd brought along a pocketful of diskettes. George's cooperation made the job a lot easier. Now he would be less concerned with being discovered trying to find the right office and force his way in. The goal was to be in and out within the allotted time and download as much information as possible.

Jud had to do a rapid attitude reset. He had never cared for the antiseptic, medicine feel of hospitals and doctors' offices. Probably had something to do with a forgotten childhood experience. Surroundings like this always made Jud feel threatened. He tried not to think about it. Too much work lay ahead of him tonight.

George hurried Jud to the broom closet and held out a set of blue coveralls with a patch that said 'Herbert.'

"Here, put these on. Anybody sees you, they'll think you're part of the crew."

Jud felt awkward in the oversized clothes but slipped them over his own. Hopefully, no one would notice the ill fit and his oddly mismatching boots. George obviously knew how they must deal with the security folks. Jud just wanted to get into that office and down to work.

"Thanks, George. You won't be sorry."

"Don't know why you convinced me, Jud. Something tells me you really are trying to help. Just don't get me fired in the bargain. Remember, twenty minutes."

* * *

Hurrying to Wainwright's workstation, its monitor dark and lifeless, Jud withdrew the diskettes from his pocket. The first order of business was to guard against leaving any fingerprints in case there were difficulties later. How he hated typing with latex gloves but it was a necessary precaution.

Gaining access to Wainwright's hard drive was easy. Before his trip to the newspaper office he had taken the time to explore the hospital's computer security system through a 'back door' network access. He wanted to know more about Doctor Myron Wainwright. Jud already knew the password for this machine since it was mandatory that all passwords be stored on the security server for emergency use. The system administrator had made a decent attempt to mask the password file. The sysadmin's efforts presented no obstacle at all to Jud. He wondered if the patients realized how vulnerable their personal information was to an experienced hacker. And it was no knock against this particular hospital. Hell, he could break probably 90 percent of the networks in hospitals, banks, businesses. He knew tricks that made them all easy targets.

In his head, Jud had a precise sequence laid out. He had to make the most of the limited amount of scan time a nervous George had allotted him. Wouldn't need access to the hospital's network, only Wainwright's computer. That would present one less chance that his presence in this office tonight might be detected after the fact. He did a screen dump of files listings to a thankfully quiet stand-alone laser printer. Then Jud began downloading selected files to a diskette. It was a relatively smooth operation and he was finished with time to spare. Then he turned his attention to a mental checklist of standard tests.

Jud almost spooked when the door quietly opened. But then George appeared.

"You okay in here? Got ten more minutes then we got to get you out."

Jud replied, "I'll be out by then."

Almost as an afterthought, he performed a quick search for the presence of data that may be hiding among the computer's many files.

Bingo! He was able to view digitized video messages in the background. If only he had the time to inspect this finding more closely. Maybe there was a connection between the messages and the doctor's strange actions. His time was running out and he was certain George would soon be after him to vacate. This discovery could warrant a return visit to appease his curiosity—with or without George's assistance. He wrapped up his work and shut down the station just as the door slowly opened.

"Time's almost up, Jud. Have to sneak you out." George at first started into the room then withdrew. Jud heard another voice in the hallway.

"Just finishing up in here, Doctor Prentice," George called out. "Be out of your way in a few minutes."

Before Jud could find a place to hide, George stepped back and the door opened wide. A buxom redhead hurried past him and regarded Jud with alarm. She stopped short and quizzed the custodian with her eyes. Then she turned on Jud.

"Who are you and what are you doing behind that desk?"

George swung the door closed. He held up his hand to preempt her outburst.

"It's okay, Doctor. He's here to help." George told her.

That bit of reassurance wasn't about to appease her rage at finding a stranger in here after hours posing as a member of the cleaning crew.

"You know this could mean your job, George. What in the world were you thinking?"

Jud walked toward the redhead and began as calmly as he could under the circumstances.

"Let me explain."

He had definitely been caught with his hand in the till this time. If wits and charm didn't carry him now, he was in deep trouble.

"My name is Jud Green," he said, still playing the name game. "I'm looking for clues to explain Doctor Wainwright's accident. I believe somebody was messing with his head and drove him to walk into traffic. Want to find out who it was before they try it again."

"But we can't have people breaching hospital security. You should be arrested and George should lose his job."

"Don't blame George. He let me in here out of loyalty to Doctor Wainwright."

"Obviously, you aren't aware who I am," she scolded. "Myron and I were very close and I object to anyone rifling through his things."

Jud read the woman's badge. Doctor Janine Prentice, member of the hospital staff. She looked to be in her early thirties and had cherry red hair. Janine was a wee bit on the plump side, but she showed possibilities. He couldn't help it. This was something Jud always did, take stock of any interesting new woman and build his own little fantasies about her. Unfortunately, at the moment, the jaw of her potentially pretty face was rigid and her blue eyes were boring holes through him.

"I have only the best intentions, Doctor Prentice. I know you wouldn't want to leave a cloud hanging over the doctor's death. If I'm right, there's bad business going on here. If I'm wrong about this, I won't bother you again."

"You remember when Doctor Wainwright helped Netta and me when she was having those bad headaches," George said. "If there's anything to this, I have to help Jud. I owe Doctor Myron. Please, let him try."

"Tell me why I should trust you," she challenged. "What's your real interest in Myron's death?"

Jud needed a believable story and it would have to be manufactured on the fly.

"I have a thing about unsolved deaths. There was something in the newspaper story that struck me as being out of kilter. It was all too clean and final. I started to wonder what was going on that could have made them describe him as detached and robotic. Now it's a bit of an obsession for me to find the answer. Guess you could call me an amateur sleuth."

"Then you have no direct involvement, no connection with Myron or with the hospital?"

"Lady, it's strictly a gut feeling at this point. They just wrote him off and that bothers me."

Janine was slowly beginning to calm down as the two men reasoned with her. She settled into the leather armchair facing Jud and stared at him for a long time. He was content to wait while she sorted out her feelings about his intrusion. Jud wondered whether 'close' was the proper term for her relationship with the deceased. There seemed to be a deeper commitment to maintaining Wainwright's posthumous security.

Finally, the fire in her eyes began to subside and she nodded toward Jud. "All right. I'll go along with you for now. But if I don't like what I see, I'll have security in here stat."

"Fair enough." Jud said. "Now let me show you what I' m doing."

Janine came around the desk and leaned toward the computer screen as he explained what he had found so far. He unfolded the story of the hard disk files and some unusual content he wanted to explore more deeply. Janine's manner softened. Jud pointed out there was a hidden video message he needed more time to analyze. Her eyes sparkled with new interest and she asked him pointed questions about what he was learning.

"I also saw a couple of odd email messages in his download file that refer to dressage. Doesn't that have to do with horses?"

"Yes. Myron and I both love horses. We both rode in dressage competitions. In fact, we were in the process of buying an estate in Loudoun County where we could keep horses."

Hmmm, we were buying? He peered at her and she smiled.

"Myron and I live in the same condo development; we've been very close for some time. He convinced me it was time I moved in with him and an estate in the horse country seemed to be the perfect answer."

"The interesting thing about this particular message," he said as he called up an email from Dressage Edge, "is that it has a lengthy attachment. When I read the text it seemed way too wordy. Now let's see if there's more here than meets the eye."

His fingers danced over the keys and Janine watched, her attention on the rhythm of his hands. *She should see me at full speed,* he thought. *These awkward gloves slow me down but 'Jud Green' has to be careful about leaving prints behind.*

"The attachment contains a hidden digitized video file. The extra text in the attachment could have been there to allow more time for the video file to be installed while Wainwright was reading. I'll need a lot more time to slow down the video and parse it to understand what it does We could be onto something here."

"You'll have to explain what you just said in layman's terms," Janine said.

"Back in the fifties there was a scare concerning the use of a technique called subliminal persuasion by advertisers. You and I are obviously too young to remember the flap first hand. A lot of folks were apparently afraid to watch movies for fear they were being manipulated in some way to buy products. They believed messages were being flashed on the screen so quickly that only the subconscious mind saw them."

"I'm aware of the subject," Janine said, "and the attempts over the years to either debunk SP or prove its viability. This is a recurring topic in my profession. We're divided in our opinions as to whether there even *is* such a thing as workable SP."

Jud nodded and continued.

"That's right. The so-called experts proclaimed there was no such thing as effective subliminal persuasion. But fifty million dollars worth of SP audiotapes are still sold every year. The tapes persuade people's subconscious to eat less, stop smoking, any number of behavior modifications. Using the technique over the Internet is strictly against the law but we may have an example here of an attempt at visual subliminal persuasion. Don't know what end game the sender is playing but it raises a number of possibilities."

Now he was rocking. Janine was totally drawn into his speculations. Her expression left no doubt that he had sunk the hook and was rapidly reeling her in.

"And where do *you* stand on the SP debate?" he asked. She was having trouble with that question. He could see the wheels spinning.

"I guess I have to plead to being undecided."

Jud hurried on to derive as much as he could from Wainwright's computer. He worked hard to convince both of them that he should have a second chance at the machine later. Janine wouldn't commit to that just yet. No matter, he thought. I'll find a way to get a longer look at that video with or without her permission.

Then he asked her, "Can I have a turn with his home computer?"

Janine wrinkled her brow and started to speak but thought better. She merely offered a shrug of resignation.

"I have the key and I'll let you in. But it's on the condition that I stay and observe. Myron's still entitled to his privacy. Out you go if you pull any tricks."

She appeared to have come to grips with the fact that Wainwright was gone. Jud knew she dealt with harsh realities and disappointments every day in her profession. Somehow, though, she seemed to be recovering too easily. He did hear a definite note of uncertainty, perhaps suspicion, in her voice. Jud had turned on all the charm he could muster but there were mixed signals in her response. He recognized he would have to be very cautious in dealing with her.

CHAPTER 8

Janine Prentice answered the doorbell and led Jud into her condo. She no longer had her antiseptic, white-coat look of the previous evening. In fact, she had undergone a rather tantalizing transformation. Jud was taken aback at Janine standing there in a black silk jumpsuit, her red hair drawn back and her attractive face glowing. Was this really the somewhat frumpy, irritated woman he had encountered last night?

"Wow! Excuse me, miss. I'm looking for Doctor Prentice."

She gave him a mocking smirk then laughed. "Stop in for a minute then we'll go up to Myron's condo. How about a drink?" She motioned for him to sit and retreated into the kitchen.

"Maybe a beer. Nice digs, Janine. Is it okay to call you Janine?"

"Considering what we're about to undertake, I'd say we should be on a first name basis, wouldn't you, Jud?" Silk had a way of moving in a very interesting manner.

Nice condo on the upscale side. Janine knew how to live all right. Early American with burnished woods and rich fabrics. He settled onto the large red-patterned sofa.

Janine returned with a bottle and a glass. She poured him a tall, frosty glass of Killian's Red and then retrieved her own tumbler and knocked back the remainder of her drink. She poured herself a refill from a half-full carafe of a strange orange liquid. Jud speculated he had a clue as to why she was acting a bit flighty.

She stood directly in front of him and stared down intently. Jud wondered if she was still debating how far he could be trusted. Okay by him, he thought. Gave him more time to look her over and he was beginning to like what he saw in that jumpsuit.

"You sound convinced that Myron's death was more than an accident, Jud. But what other explanation can there be? I'm surprised we haven't had more accidents on that busy street. The people drive like maniacs and the pedestrians defy them."

"Well, what I've seen so far on his office computer piques my interest. Could be another reason Myron was daydreaming. Now I have to keep going until I get some answers. Guess it's the computer geek in me."

"Meaning your theory about SP, I suppose." Her comeback seemed to indict his whole approach.

"I may surprise you yet, Janine. Don't discount it until we see what's on the computer in his condo." Jud took a long pull on his brew.

She cuddled up beside him on the couch. He had the uneasy sensation that there was something else going on here and he wasn't in control of the situation. Janine downed the remainder of her drink and leaned over the cocktail table to set down her glass. Was it his imagination or had she managed to discreetly lower the zipper at her neck? Fascinating span of cleavage on display. When she straightened up, her face was a little too close for comfort. He stood and drained his beer as he walked toward the kitchen.

"Better get started on the computer in his place, don't you think?"

She slowly uncoiled from the couch and followed, snatching a key from a wall peg.

"If you insist," she replied in an irritated tone. Once again she hovered near enough for him to fully appreciate her subtle perfume. "My, you're in a hurry," she cooed.

Jud immediately concluded that comment was best left unanswered. He came here with a purpose in mind and he wasn't going to finish this way. Janine's goal, whatever it may be, apparently had little to do with the machine waiting in the condo on the next floor. He admonished himself to keep his priorities in order. This was no time to be thinking about diversions. He managed to walk ahead of her, feeling a bit self-conscious about how he was reacting to the surprising change in her. Wondered if it showed enough for her to notice.

Janine hovered over him at first at Wainwright's place and asked questions about his keyboard manipulations. But after her third interruption, he fixed her with an annoyed stare that caused her to back away.

"It's all a mystery to me, Jud. Guess I'll take a seat and let you work on your own."

She fanned her face with one hand and tugged at her top, lowering the zipper another inch. By now she was more than a little unsteady on her feet and he agreed she needed to find a seat. Her hips twisted their way into the living room while Jud buried himself in thought in the small bedroom Wainwright had converted to an office. After a few minutes he saw her peer in on him then slip out the door. That suited him fine because he needed some quiet time to ponder what the machine was revealing to him.

Sometime later Jud heard the door open and Janine reappeared with a new supply of the curious orange mix she'd been pouring. She sashayed into the office and lifted the decanter and two empty glasses. She moistened her lips and made an attempt at a sultry smile.

"Have a drinky poo with me, Jud. Ish great stuff."

Whoa, he thought—she's rapidly getting snockered on whatever she's been sucking down.

"What is it?" he asked and the corners of her mouth turned upward in a sly grin.

"Lil'mix of mine. Call it Orange Revenge. Soothes the nerves and clears the sinu . . . . sinuses. Need it after listening to poor slobs spill their guts to me. God, you can't believe the drivel I hear from those whiners."

"What do you put in it to get that weird color?"

"Lit'l o this, lit'l o that. Vodka, rum, whiskey, orange juice, coupla special ingre . . . ingredi . . . other things." She kicked off her shoes and held the container between her ample breasts.

"Just a taste, Janine. I'm on a roll here." With all the drugs that must float around the hospital, Jud was afraid to speculate what 'special ingredients' might mean.

Janine poured two generous portions and handed him a glass, toasting with her own.

"Drink up, handsome."

Jud took a tentative sip. Actually, it was pretty tasty, but he'd play it safe just in case.

"Thanks. Now I need about half an hour totally alone to digest my findings." He had to keep reminding himself to stay on target here.

"Can do. But my timer's running. You know what they say about letting a three minute egg cook for five minutes."

Janine toyed with her jumper top and Jud wondered why her words sounded like an ultimatum. If she tugged that front down any farther the whole damn thing was in danger of gathering in a heap around her feet. Then where would they be? With some difficulty, he erased the image from his mind.

She tapped her watch, picked up the supply of Revenge and carried it to the couch. Her gait was more nearly an ungainly wobble now. Janine looked in at him briefly while she emptied her own drink. Then she curled up on the couch and drifted off to sleep.

Thanks for that, he thought. He could only handle one challenge at a time.

A few more key sequences and he had uncovered an interesting visitor on Wainwright's machine. He was certain Myron hadn't invited this hitchhiker. There in the background flashing across the screen in lightning fast repetition was a video. Jud was able to slow it down to a manageable speed. It alternately presented visual images in a center segment of the screen that read HURRY THERE and then projected a view of a building front.

Jud noted an unusual swimming sensation in his head and tried to remember why it reminded him of an earlier experience. He finally made the connection to an incident several years back and increased the volume to search for a low frequency sound file. His instincts were correct. There was a low level tone warbling along with the video and the combined effects were stupefying. The sound was so far down the scale that he felt more than heard the sound. Jud forced himself to crank down the sound and avert his eyes from the computer screen.

After a short break to clear his head, he opened the Internet email section and located the source of both files. They had arrived attached to the same message from Dressage Edge he had seen at the hospital office. A check of the files' source code told him everything he needed to know about this clever installation. They were programmed to run every time the computer was activated, drumming their repetitive messages into the user's head. The combination had a degree of elegance that Jud had to appreciate as a veteran programmer. Taken together, the audio/video combination presented interesting possibilities. But exactly how could that result in the glassy-eyed behavior of the late Myron Wainwright? And did they hold any significance in the matter he would soon be looking into in Florida? Maybe he was stretching to make a connection between the two psychologists' deaths.

"It's awfully quiet in here."

Janine had slipped silently into the small office and stood across from him with the zipper of her jumpsuit still at half-mast. Her snooze seemed to have done wonders for her. She may be a few pounds on the upside of svelte but what was peeking out at him was looking better all the time. One beer and a sip of Revenge couldn't be responsible for that. No, Jud admitted, she had real potential. He tried to stay focused.

"I found some very absorbing stowaways on the machine. Looks like someone was messing with Myron's mind. They sent the files to both locations to be sure he saw them over and over. Look at this."

Just as he realized he should be cautious about inviting her closer, he realized she was already standing behind him. Janine placed her hands on his shoulders and slid them down his ribs as she bent nearer. She appeared more alert, even purposeful, after her snooze. This little job may have unexpected side benefits.

"Show me, Jud." She pressed her breasts hard against his back. Jud found the room warming up and his attention wavering.

"Woops. Pay attention, Janine. Watch the screen. Tell me what you see."

She backed off for the moment and followed the video with him. By the time the building front painted she was blurting out, "That's 23rd Street coming out the front entrance of the new hospital. It's the old hospital building directly across the street. We see it every day."

"Then Myron would have recognized it. If he saw this view repeatedly when either of his computers was turned on, his attention could be fixed on that point across the street. Maybe the repetition conditioned him to focus on the spot any time he came out the front door of the hospital. Damn, this is ingenious," Jud marveled.

"You're back on the SP kick again, aren't you? Who said SP works?"

"Think about it, Janine. You may have just seen the first proof of workable subliminal persuasion. There's also sound in the background that enhances reception of the visual message. The possibilities are frightening. Someone may have unlocked a code for instructing the brain to perform unconscious acts."

"Gimme a break, Jud. You sound like some of the eggheads I deal with at the hospital every day. Where do you come up with this stuff, anyway?"

"You're an intelligent woman. The brain works on minute electrical impulses much like a computer. What if I found a way to steer and control those impulses to send tailored instructions. Behavior modification and controlled response would be the next logical steps."

"You're a fascinating man, Jud Green . . . and brainy, too. Now see if you can guess what I'm thinking."

Once again he felt her pressing into his back. The hair on his neck stood on end when she traced his ear lobe with the tip of her tongue. He told himself this was no time to get distracted. But what the hell—the night was young. This machine wasn't going anywhere. He swiveled the chair to face her and looked up into her mischievous eyes.

"So you want to admire my mind or what?"

"It's not your brain that interests me right now." She leaned nearer and tugged at his shirt.

Oh, well. It seemed to be a curse that followed him. The females just had to know if he was real. Maybe it had something to do with the myth about men with big feet. Maybe it was that little boy innocence he could project.

"Okay, baby, you win," he mumbled. He scooped Janine off her feet and carried her into the bedroom.

There would be no more playing around with computers tonight.

CHAPTER 9

"Dan, my man, we may be onto something. Can't wait to get to Florida and check out those two machines."

The morning had been routine until now but Jud Black was changing that in a hurry. Dan carried the telephone to the coffee pot and poured a refill.

Ellen telegraphed a quizzing stare.

"Jud." Dan replied to her silent question.

"Ellen says hi. What's the big news?"

"Progress, pal. Progress," Jud announced. "I spent some quality time with Doctor Wainwright's computers—not to mention his former girlfriend. But that's another story."

"Not again! You crazy bithead. Every time I think you prefer computers to women, you re-earn your nickname."

Jud laughed aloud. Dan had taken to referring to him as Studley when he observed that Jud's disarming charm and his intelligence were like magnets to the women. Most guys tried hard to be smooth and convincing to females while a few had that something natural that drove women up a wall. Jud was blessed with those qualities though he professed it was as baffling to him as it was alluring to the ladies.

"Okay, now get your brain out of the gutter, Cooper. This is serious shit."

"All ears at this end. You saved me a call, anyway. Fill me in."

Jud assumed a serious, almost instructive tone.

"I hope you took my advice and stayed away from those computers down there."

"Oh, I knew better than to fritz with them after your warning. I asked Marge to be sure no one was allowed to turn on Barry's office computer until you got here. Susan keeps the home office door locked, too."

"Good, because there's an even better reason for you to avoid those machines. They could be like ticking time bombs and I'm not sure what effect they could have on you."

Dan made a scribbling motion with his free hand and Ellen scouted out a pencil and pad.

"What's that all about, Jud?" he asked nervously.

"There's hidden video and low level audio on Wainwright's workstations. I believe the combination of messages was repeated over and over until he was prompted to walk out of the hospital lobby with his attention fixed on the building across the street. He had no idea he was stepping into traffic. Wainwright's whole world at that moment was the front of the building across 23rd Street. He was staring at it and never saw the cars."

Dan scribbled on his pad furiously; his voice cracked when he spoke. "That's scary as hell! You think Barry was coaxed onto the Skyway Bridge the same way?"

"Entirely possible. Hang in until I can wind up my business and get there next week."

"Well, I haven't been entirely idle since we talked, Studley."

"Just had to turn the screws again, didn't you, Cooper?"

"What are friends for if they don't tweak your nose now and then? Anyway, I've been reading and talking to some knowledgeable people. There could be brain-related reasons beyond his control that caused Barry to flip out."

"Boning up on the brain? Did you read anything about subliminal persuasion?" Jud asked.

"A little. Wanted to ask Barry's partner to tell me more about it. Why?"

"Let me tell you what I found on Myron Wainwright's machine before I was so rudely interrupted last night."

"Yeah. Interrupted. How many times?"

"Later, hoss. Lay in some cold Murphy's and I'll tell you all about how us swinging singles live. Anyhow, there was digitized video on his office computer and both video and audio on his home machine."

"How did you get into his office? You mean at the hospital? On second thought, don't answer that."

Dan signaled to Ellen for a refill and sipped at his coffee while Jud continued.

"As I was saying, I found subliminal messages that were sent to him as attachments to an email and installed on his computer. Every time he turned it on the messages would be played over and over and impressed on his subconscious. That's how subliminal persuasion works if I can believe what I've heard. Somebody was tinkering with Wainwright's noodle. If we find Barry's workstations have been played with the same way, we have an ugly bucket of snails on our hands, friend."

"You're scaring the crap out of me, Jud. What if this *is* son of SP? Is there somebody out there smart enough to do this twice with success within twenty-four hours? It chills me witless what they could be planning for their next victim—or maybe for us if we get in their way."

"Yeah, we could be a problem for somebody, Dan. So far we're turning out to be either a couple of totally wigged out dreamers or a damn cool pair of sleuths. I'm booking a morning flight to Tampa on Wednesday. We should know soon if we're smoking something rotten or onto the find of the century."

"Won't be the first time we stuck our booties out in the breeze and hoped for the best, Jud. I have some other angles to work before you get here, too."

"Just don't touch those machines. I don't want you taking a header off a bridge; at least not till I get some free beer and a dip in your pool."

"Message received. See you soon."

Dan settled back and stared out the window. His conversations with Jud were always interesting and thought provoking. But this one had gone completely off the scale. What had they gotten themselves into?

He couldn't be sure how closely Ellen had listened to their conversation but her worried expression told him she'd probably heard too much. Dan didn't offer an explanation and she didn't ask.

* * *

He immediately reissued his warnings to both Susan and Marge. First he called Susan at home.

"Sue, you're keeping the computer turned off, aren't you?"

"Just as I said I would, Dan. The computer is off and I locked the door. Don't know why it's necessary but I take your word."

"Trust me. I don't want you or the kids looking at that screen until Jud checks everything on the computer. He'll be here this week."

Now to make sure no one was tampering with the machine at the office. He hoped Marge's iron clad shut down was still in effect. Had to catch her before they started another workday.

Marge sounded excited and a bit nervous when Dan reached her.

"I've only had the computer on briefly to pull off some essential bits of information for Peter and Doctor Tom. But I did snoop just once. Found a file you're going to be interested in seeing."

"What is it, Marge?"

"Barry was keeping notes on his own strange feelings during recent days. Guess it comes under the heading of 'physician heal thyself'. He was so used to analyzing other people, he was trying to diagnose what was happening to him. I made a printout of his computer file and have it in my purse for you. Nobody else knows."

Two breaks in one day, Dan thought. *Finally things were going his way*. He pumped his arm to signal at least a small victory had finally come his way.

"I'll be there to pick it up right after lunch, Marge. You're a doll. And keep that computer off, off, off. We can't trust anybody. Tell them it's broken and you're waiting for the repairman. That should get us through until Jud can inspect it."

So far he'd felt like he was running to keep up with Jud in cutting through the fog surrounding the two tragic deaths. Now maybe he would finally have something important to relate to his pal.

CHAPTER 10

"I'm too stoked to relax," Dan told Ellen after breakfast. "Jud wants me to soft pedal for a few days until he gets down here, but I have to stay busy. Think I'll go to the library and do some research. I want to learn more about the fascinating organ called the brain."

"Why the sudden fascination with brains, Dan? You're always soaking up information on new subjects but this is casting a pretty wide net, even for you."

"You know I want to be a serious writer, so I have to do all sorts of reading for pleasure *and* information. That's why I've been going through books at an incredible clip since we came down here. It was always easy for me to say I didn't have the time for anything but technical reading. That was a cop-out. Now I have a lot of years to make up for when I was too lazy to read."

"But the brain? Come on." She looked puzzled.

"That has to do with the symposium at USF. The one Barry was showing such an interest in attending. It may be a dead end, but I have to be there. And if I hope to understand a tenth of what those doctors say about psychology and the mind's secrets, I have to study up."

"Just remember to take your cell phone. At the expense of disturbing the other folks in the library, I'll probably have to ring you to remind you to eat. I know how absorbed you get when you're writing or doing research. You'd probably miss lunch lost in a book."

"Once again, you have nailed me, madam. Do I have no secrets from you?"

"Not since the day you gave me this, big boy." She fingered the small gold band and gave him that sly little smile that said *your ass is mine, big fellow. Admit it.* And his sheepish grin answered *gladly, heart o' mine.*

* * *

The stacks at the local libraries had become very familiar to Dan by now. He spent time there at least twice a week. Dan had logged many hours in the reference section pursuing whatever the subject of interest may be for a particular day. Must by now be firmly established in their high volume customers file as many books as he'd taken home. His office was full of notes and hints from all the books he'd checked out and devoured. Two of his three writers' workshops met at the Hudson and New Port Richey libraries weekly. Dan worked hard honing his writing skills with the insights and helpful hints the workshops provided. He was determined to write for both the sheer joy of crafting words and for the pleasure readers could derive from them. It was a thoroughly engrossing change after years of running hard in the business world. Now things proceeded at his own pace and every day was a new writing challenge.

He waved toward Pamela at the front desk and hurried back to the reference section. Called up the search workstation screen and located a number of books and reference volumes with information on the brain. Wrote down their locations and set out to find them. Dan set aside two books to take home and began his perusal of the scientific journals and reference books. What started out to be a chore soon became a compelling quest for more and more information about the brain.

He read about the billions of nerve cells in the human brain that transmit and receive electrical signals, impulses that are generated by sights, sounds or sensations of touch. At each junction between the nerve cells a chemical reaction moves the encoded information to the next nerve cell. The process repeats many, many times for each output response such as moving a leg or arm.

Dan quickly made the connection with his electrical engineering background. The brain actually functions as a complex computer. Automatic life-sustaining functions and all of our bodies' voluntary actions are driven by these tiny electrical signals. He was intrigued until a frightening thought crept up on him. What if there was someone out there who could crack the encoding format for brain instructions. That person could use the knowledge to control an individual's movements, thoughts, even his behavior patterns. The implications made him shiver and his palms began to sweat.

The cell phone on his belt rang. Well, she was right again. He was so immersed in his reading that the noon hour had come and gone and food hadn't entered his mind. Dan retrieved the phone quickly to silence it.

"Yes. I know. But I'm on my way."

Her chuckle said *told you so* but her words were "Love you."

"I'll call you from outside," he answered. Dan gathered up his notes and headed for the checkout desk.

On the way down Little Road he mulled over the impact of what he had been reading. There could be positive aspects to mind control as well. What about the brain related diseases that had resisted all attempts to solve their exact origins? How might a breakthrough in encoding instructions to the human brain affect cures for Alzheimer's, for multiple sclerosis and any number of other brain related maladies? Possessing the keys to cerebral information exchange could bring new miracles in medical progress if that knowledge was properly used.

Dan punched in his home telephone number.

"Thanks for the reminder, baby. What would I do without you to remind me to eat on time?"

He was only mildly diabetic but he had too much living to do to let carelessness with his health get in the way. It was time for his midday fix with some food and that big horse pill.

"That's my job," Ellen told him. "By the way, I went to see Susan again today. She's not doing well. Sue's a great mom and a wonderful housekeeper but Barry was the one who kept things organized. The sheer weight of taking care of the family finances and all the day to day details are smothering her." Ellen was worried and it showed in her voice.

"All you can do is offer moral support and let her know how much we both care for her. If she can use my help with the chores I can get her organized. You know what a details nut I am."

"I hoped you'd say that," she told him.

"What, that I'm a nut? Haven't you figured that out by now?"

"No, smart ass. That you'll show Sue how to keep her records in order."

"I'm shocked. You didn't learn language like that at the wives' club."

"Don't get me started, buster."

"Hon, I need to go to Clearwater. Marge has some information for me. Then I'm going to try to corner Tom Sherman for whatever time I can grab. Want to follow up with him on some things I've been reading this morning. I should be back home well before dinner time."

"First you eat, Dan Cooper."

"I know. Turning into Checkers right now. Got my pills at the ready."

* * *

"Thanks, Tom. I know how busy you are and I'll try to be brief." They sat in Tom Sherman's office between his appointments. Dan was happy to have even a few minutes to use him as a sounding board.

"If this will help you find what or who caused Barry's death," Tom told him, "I'll take all the time you need. We may have to do it in segments, though. My dance card is kind of full this afternoon."

"I've been doing some reading," Dan said. "I'm struck by the similarities between how the human brain works and the way computers process information. You'd be aware of research findings on things like brain control, behavior modification and the like."

"Dan, I'm impressed. Most laymen think such things are mundane. The brain is the most fascinating and challenging organ in our bodies. We know so little about how it really works. I see patients every day that desperately need a medical breakthrough somehow to release them from serious illnesses but we don't have the tools to help them."

"I see references to something called the 'small brain', Tom. Seems a number of researchers think it's the secret to finding cures for brain related diseases."

"You've done your homework. Yes, some refer to the cerebellum as the small brain. We know it controls and coordinates our motor systems to move all our limbs and joints. And the more we learn about it the more convinced some psychologists are that it's the heart of thinking that may control memory, mood and even language." Sherman walked over to the bookcase and withdrew a book.

"The symposium coming up at USF, Tom—I mentioned that Barry had planned to attend—will I be able to learn more there or will it be over my head?"

"Marge asked me about putting you on the list and I told her to send in your name." Tom reached for a note pad and began writing.

"I'm jotting down some good references on information exchange and the cerebellum. That's where most of our memory resides. There are those who say if we could steer the cerebellum, say with commands below the level of consciousness, we could program behavioral actions. This book has a thorough discussion of the cerebellum." He offered the hardbound volume.

"Thanks, Tom. Goes to the top of my reading list this afternoon."

"Take a crack at these other books and articles. I've given you a starter list if you have time. They could help you follow a good bit of what the lecturers will be saying."

Dan looked at the titles and authors' names. He was surprised at how legible Tom's note was with the reputation most doctors have for scribbling. He couldn't resist taking a jab. "Gee, another first for me. A doctor's note I can actually read. The pharmacists must love you."

Tom grinned. "You may not be aware that unless a psychologist has specific medical training, he isn't allowed to prescribe medications. That's been a continuing debate in our profession. Never wrote a prescription in my life, but Barry often did. He had the credentials."

"That would explain it," Dan replied and folded the note into his shirt pocket. "Oh, about controlling behavior, does that have something to do with this subliminal persuasion I've read about?"

"You really are into this, aren't you? Okay, I have an appointment soon, so let me give you my quick take on SP. Many of my associates say if you can't prove it's there it must not exist. I believe we just haven't been clever enough yet to confirm SP's true nature. But I believe it's possible we'll eventually be able to manipulate the way brain instructions are issued. What a medical miracle it would be to turn cerebral processes on and off to treat brain deficiencies and anomalies. We'd be well on our way to treating, maybe preventing, Alzheimer's disease, multiple sclerosis, epilepsy; even internally repairing brain abnormalities and injuries."

Dan had evidently raised a subject on which Tom was passionate. "Whew! I believe I hit a hot button."

Tom had already taken down another book from the shelf and was writing. "Hope you're an avid reader. Here are some good references on SP."

This had been a productive day but Dan's head was swimming with facts and overwhelmed by the possibilities they presented. What if he *had* stumbled onto a case of true genius in behavior manipulation? But then the question would be why it was being used for such destructive ends when it could be a boon to mankind. At the very least, he needed to sleep on this and try to reach Jud tomorrow. He wanted to hear what progress he was making with his probe of the GW Hospital incident. And he needed to tell Jud that his far out questions had led him to pursue new avenues with eye-opening results.

For now, there was the matter of that information Marge had for him. He took her aside and they talked where no one could overhear them.

"Dan, I don't understand what I read in that file on Barry's computer, but it's all here on these pages." She slipped an envelope to him.

"I'll read it later. Please watch yourself, Marge. And don't tell anyone, not even Doctor Sherman, about this."

She stared at him but he just nodded. At this point he couldn't trust anyone.

CHAPTER 11

Saturday morning arrived. Time for the Coopers' weekly pilgrimage to the Oldsmar Flea Market. From February through the summer they made a habit of shopping for fresh fruits and vegetables at the vendor stalls.

This was the first time since their friend's death that they had taken time out strictly for themselves. Their time and energies had been devoted to Susan and her children and to Dan's pursuit of leads.

The notes Marge gave him from Barry's computer were disturbing. From Barry's self-analysis of his confused thoughts and loss of focus, Dan now understood better what Jud was trying to tell him. If there were hidden files on that machine working on Millwood's mind, urging him to go to the Skyway Bridge, they had stepped into a dangerous muddle. But if he was to be of any use to Jud when he showed up, Dan had to clear his head and unwind, however briefly.

Ellen spoke with a note of concern.

"Dan, I hesitate to bring this up, but you haven't been yourself the past three or four days. I know you're preoccupied with helping the Millwoods. Is there anything else I should know?"

"Didn't realize I was off track, hon. Sorry, just can't seem to concentrate."

"That's what I mean. Like your mind was wandering. You've never had that problem."

Dan turned down a gravel row in the flea market's grass-covered parking lot and looked for an empty spot.

"Well, today is for fun. It's a beautiful day and I think we beat the crowd. Think happy thoughts and let's goof off. We'll cover the flea and have a late lunch somewhere. I want to chill out and give my brain a breather. It's been a fast and furious week."

For the next two hours they wandered up and down the rows of vendors searching for bargains. Dan modeled sunglasses for Ellen and hunted for buys he usually ended up using once and filing away in a drawer. Ellen homed in on the kitchen gadgets and things to make little decorator touches around the house.

The pungent aromas of the food court were tempting. Normally he would have coaxed Ellen to stop with him for his usual grilled sausage with onions and deep-fried potato spirals. Dessert would be ice cream and antacid. Dan fought the urge to settle for a Polish and mustard. Now that he had his lady out he wanted to take her somewhere with a modicum of class, feel the Gulf breezes and sip wine. They'd been so caught up in the events around them that he hadn't taken her out to eat in nearly two weeks.

"Let's hurry and round up our veggies to take home. Then we can swing over to The Beachcomber and unwind."

They worked their way through the growing midday crowd toward the fruit stands near the front exit. Carefully compared and selected cherry red Ruskin tomatoes and plump Plant City strawberries. Dan loved this time of year when he could overindulge in the tart-sweet berries at their peak. Ellen added enough fresh produce to stock up on salad fixings for the week. They wound their way to the exit, arms full of brown bags, and emerged into the bright sunlight.

Not five minutes down Tampa Road Dan's cell phone rang.

"Catch that, will you, El?"

Ellen listened then said, "Hold on. He's right here." She handed the phone to him. "It's Marge. She sounds really upset, Dan."

"What is it, Marge?" Dan quickly pulled to the side of the road when he heard her heavy breathing. "Where are you? How can I help?"

"At work. I'm hiding." She was panting as she talked, as if she had been running.

"What's wrong?"

"The door's been forced. Barry's computer is on. Somebody's in there." She was trying to keep her voice low and he was having trouble catching all her words.

"Lock yourself in. Call 911. I'm heading to you now."

Before she could reply, Dan heard noises that seemed to be drawing closer. Marge whimpered. She apparently dropped the phone and he could barely make out her next words.

There was scuffling and Marge's muffled voice shouting, "Please. No."

"Dial 911, El!' Dan barked. "Tell them a woman is being attacked. Palmetto Park Building on Route 19. First floor doctor's office."

He swung out and sped toward Route 19. Ellen reached the emergency dispatcher and gave her the address where Marge needed them.

Dan hurtled around and between cars on Tampa Road, hoping he'd be pursued. Where was a policeman when you needed one?

* * *

By the time they arrived on the scene, Dan expected to see patrol cars sitting in the parking lot. But there was no activity in sight. He slammed to a halt and vaulted out of the car, hurtling across the pavement.

"Call again, Ellen. Lock the car door. Stay there till the cops arrive."

Barry and Tom didn't keep Saturday office hours but other tenants were in the building and the outside doors were unlocked. He shoved the door open and rushed to the suite of offices on his right. Dan wasn't sure what he may encounter or how he should be prepared to react, but he'd ad lib something. Marge was in danger and she was depending on him.

Oddly, the entrance door to the office suite was ajar. That surely must have alerted Marge that something was amiss. If only she'd called first and not gone inside. Dan surged in expecting to be met by someone or something out of the ordinary but all was quiet. He rushed to Barry's old office and found the room silent, the computer dark. Then he turned his attention to the other rooms where Marge may be cowering in fear.

Unfortunately, he found her. Marge was lying on her back in the middle of Tom Sherman's office. One hand was raised and turned palm out over her eyes in a protective gesture. Her legs were drawn up under her motionless body. Dan tried to check for a pulse but it was already evident to him that he had arrived too late. Her vacant stare and the crimson stain on the carpet told him more than he wanted to know.

Dan stifled his instinct to move her, knowing the police would be arriving soon. The look of her eyes staring emptily at him was unnerving. He took off his windbreaker and covered her face just as a policeman burst in, weapon drawn, and shouted, "Hands up!"

He stepped away from Marge's body and raised his hands high in the air. Ellen was close behind the officer yelling at him, "That's my husband. We were trying to get to her." The cop wasn't impressed; he continued to draw a bead with a weapon that looked to Dan at the moment as big as a cannon.

Minutes later a paramedic looked up from the still form and shook his head.

"She never had a chance. Somebody hit her with a heavy object. It was a vicious blow and death occurred quickly."

The policeman grilled Dan about the reason he was here. He wanted to know why he'd been standing over her lifeless body. A rather impatient Dan tried to explain.

"My name is Dan Cooper. This is my wife Ellen. Marge phoned us for help. We rushed here from Oldsmar. Just didn't make it in time."

"Tried our best to summon help," Ellen added. "I talked to the 911 dispatcher twice. It all happened so fast."

She looked down at Marge's body and shuddered. The medics gathered and repacked their equipment.

"There was nothing you could have done," the medic said. "Whoever attacked her wielded a strong hand. She was gone in seconds."

Dan turned to the policeman and asked, "How could her attacker get in here without being noticed?"

"We run into some pretty clever burglars, Mister Cooper," the officer replied. "They can even beat cipher locks and alarm systems. This was a simple key lock door. Looks like the only things really secured in here were the patient records. What puzzles me is that nothing seems to be disturbed."

"Marge said when she called that the computer was on in an office down the hall and someone was in there."

They walked to Barry's former office and the policeman did a quick sweep but found nothing unusual. He turned to Dan and looked stumped.

"The new class of high tech criminals is scary, Mister Cooper. If there's something they want off your computer, they can get it remotely. Why would they take a chance on a clumsy break in?"

"Marge was keeping that computer turned off at my request. It belonged to the doctor who fell from the bridge last week. My guess is somebody wanted the information on it bad enough to risk forcing their way in."

"We'll have the experts inspect the whole area and see what they come up with. In the meantime, you have to come with me and answer some formal questions for my report."

Poor Marge had chosen the wrong time to go by work on an off day. She had interrupted someone in the process of searching Barry's office. The fact that his computer had been turned on today told Dan that the unauthorized visitor was looking for something specific. Could it have to do with the hidden files Dan was sure by now were on that machine? Or maybe Barry's description of what those files were doing to him?

The most baffling part of all was why being discovered in the act was so threatening that the assailant had reacted by killing Marge. Could be that he had miscalculated the force of the blow and made a terrible mistake. Or was there a deeper, more threatening reason?

He took the arm of a visibly shaken Ellen and they followed the policeman to the station.

CHAPTER 12

The day of the USF symposium was finally here. Dan felt as prepared as he would ever be. For the past four days he had absorbed all his mind would take on the subject of how the brain works. The pros and cons of whether subliminal persuasion actually existed swam in his head. The technical terms and medical language were daunting at first. Dan was accustomed to using the specialized language of engineering but some of this was pretty deep. However, the more he read the more comfortable he became with at least the basic concepts and the words took on a degree of familiarity.

Dan certainly wasn't ready for an extended dialogue with the psychologists who would make up the majority of the symposium audience. But hopefully he wouldn't be left at the starting gate when the lecturers began their presentations. The auditorium was nearly full by the time he arrived. He located a seat near the back next to a young blonde woman and settled in to take copious notes.

The nearly new psych building was impressive. This appeared to be an up and coming institution in the field of psychology. Dan concluded there must be something to be learned here today. The auditorium held, he estimated, nearly two hundred intense looking individuals—and at least one medical neophyte who could be in water over his head.

The first speaker had little to say that interested Dan, so he occupied himself drawing doodles on his pad. He sketched some of the anatomy from his reading. Then he labeled the drawings unconsciously with electrical signals and engineering notations that gave them more meaning for him. When the speaker finished and was taking questions from the audience, a distinctively feminine hand appeared over the pad and pointed to one of the symbols.

"You must be an engineer—not one of these psychologists," a pleasant voice whispered.

Dan looked up from his scribbling to see the sparkling blue eyes and lovely face of the blonde seated next to him. The way they were packaged was tantalizing.

"Afraid so. Name's Dan Cooper. I've been accused of being an electrical engineer."

"Paula Taylor. I'm a EE/computer science grad myself so I tend to scribble that way, too. Did you come to hear any particular lecturers?"

"I'm mainly interested in the next one, Doctor Gernsbach, and the last speaker before lunch, Doctor Krevins."

There was something about her movements that made Dan think he had prompted a reaction with those names, but that could have been just his imagination. He was fascinated by this stunning blonde who was, wonder of wonders, also an engineer. Where was she when guys in two-day old beards and week old socks filled all his classes?

"What's your attraction to today's program?" he asked her.

"Psychology has always been a side interest of mine. Along the way I managed to work in a few psych courses to break the tedium of my normal studies. I audited a course at MSPP up in Minnesota and it whetted my interest. Then I took some classes right here this past year."

"Strange. Most engineers would welcome breathing room for an occasional no-brainer course and an easy grade. I wouldn't think psychology falls into that category."

"Depends on your personal preferences. I'm not your run of the mill EE or computer geek."

He was thinking to himself, *Young lady, you couldn't be a run of the mill anything. I'd say you're probably quite the opposite.*

Doctor Jason Gernsbach, the Millwoods' friend, was introduced as a distinguished member of the staff of St. Mark's Teaching Hospital in New Orleans. He had earned an international reputation for his clinical research into neurotransmitters. Gernsbach was studying how they were activated and passed their signals throughout the brain. He would enlighten his peers about recent advances in tracking two types of neurotransmitters and their interactions with receptor proteins.

Gernsbach described how the outcomes of these actions had been observed in laboratory animals as he alternately stimulated and inhibited their brains' electrical impulses.

"One of the substances, acetylcholine, has been found to be important in the study of Alzheimer's disease," the speaker said. "In fact, a deficiency in the natural production of this chemical may well be a major cause of the onset of Alzheimer's."

The doctor's stage presence was impressive; Dan read that he was in his mid-forties. There was a touch of gray hair at his temples that added to his overall appearance as a scholarly professional. Dan listened intently to his explanation and found he could follow most of what the doctor was saying. He thought how fortunate Jason's students must be to study under him. All the while he was writing down notes Dan wished he'd had professors that made his note taking in thermodynamics or mechanics this straightforward. And those were physical sciences that one should be able to touch and feel, not the often arbitrary world of biological processes.

Gernsbach concluded his lecture and prepared to answer questions. Dan looked over at the young lady seated next to him.

"That's a real teacher in action, Miss Taylor. I don't see anybody in the audience that looks like they're being talked down to." Dan couldn't help thinking again what a stunning woman Paula was.

"Exactly what I was thinking. He has a talent for clarity. Isn't your hand tired by now?"

Dan had been so absorbed he had filled two pages with notes and his hand was beginning to cramp, a fact he hadn't realized until Paula asked.

"Didn't want to miss anything. Think I'll take a break and come back to hear Krevins, though."

"Sounds good to me. May I join you?" she asked.

When she stood, she was at eye level with him in her heels. This divine creature was an oasis of beauty among all the balding and bespectacled psychologists. She had a natural beauty in a classy, non-obtrusive way and legs that went on forever. In fact, he was already starting to feel guilty about his obvious reaction to her.

They walked quickly and quietly to the nearest exit.

Over coffee and muffins she inquired of him, "So how does a EE get interested in what the brain doctors are doing? Some of these psychodocs are way over the line."

"Oh, I was an agriculture student long before I was an engineer. Didn't get involved in chasing electrons until the Air Force agreed to send me off to their school. I've always said I was a guinea pig. If they could retread an old aggie like me, they could teach anybody."

"So you started out in the biological sciences?"

"Sure did. Human and animal biology have always intrigued me. Guess I'm rediscovering that fact since I have lots of time on my hands. I'm retired and trying my hand at fiction writing."

She sat up and looked keenly interested in the way this conversation was going. Then she tossed out playfully, "Holy cow, Dan. Aggie, engineer, writer. When are you gonna decide what you want to do when you grow up?"

"It's been an interesting ride. But now I'm content to lie back and enjoy Florida and put pen to paper—or fingers to keyboard—and see what happens."

"So what did you actually do in the Air Force?"

"I was a communications officer. Led a couple of squadrons handling comm and air traffic control. It was a great opportunity to work with radio and landline systems and run computer networks. Even managed to get in a bit of research and development work. Led into a nice second career in industry, too. How about you, Paula?"

"Oh, I work with software development in a small company up in Gainesville. It's not exciting but it's a living."

Dan chuckled. "There's nothing routine about the software business. I've been there. Jumped in over my head with a couple of partners and started our own company. Had some dumb luck producing software."

Now her curiosity was noticeably aroused. "What's the name of your company?"

"COB. Maybe you heard of us. Sold out to the big boys and moved on a few years ago."

She almost came out of her chair and leaned in toward him. "You've gotta be kidding. COB is a legend in our business. What you guys did for the reputation of small houses was phenomenal. There was a time when I would have sold my soul to join the group of gurus you had on your payroll. I even sent a resume and applied for a job."

Dan glanced at the time and cut their discussion short. "We'd better get back in there if we're going to catch Doctor Krevins' spot."

"Only if you promise to have lunch with me. I have to hear more about your software exploits. I'll buy."

"Not on your life. I'd love to treat you to lunch, Paula."

They walked back and took their seats just as the moderator was about to introduce the next speaker.

"Ladies and gentlemen, we are indeed fortunate to have the next presenter with us today. He's taken time from his extremely busy teaching and clinical research schedule here at USF to bring us some exciting news in behavioral research. I'm pleased to present Doctor Victor Krevins, who is a University of South Florida faculty member and a practicing psychologist in the Tampa Bay community. His topic is "Behavior and the Cerebellum."

A smattering of applause followed. Then a voice drifted to Dan from the seats behind him. The caustic comment wasn't even well concealed.

"This must be the entertainment segment. Crazy Vic and his off the wall visions."

Smothered snickers rippled from nearby seats and someone chimed in, "He's always good for a laugh or two."

For the first time the dead serious mood of the room of intellectuals had been penetrated. Dan realized these professionals could be every bit as sarcastic and cutting as any other group. He glanced over at Paula and, oddly, she wriggled in her seat as she appeared to be doing a slow burn. He touched her arm and sent her a quizzical expression. She returned his unasked question with a steely look and jerked her head from side to side.

Victor Krevins more nearly fit the mold of what Dan had expected to see here today. He was certainly not height-challenged, a term Dan liked to use to tease his late friend Barry. The speaker was well over six feet, perhaps six-four, and had to lean forward to reach the microphone on the podium. Barry and Victor must have been the long and short of their class at Indiana. But Barry made up for his lack of stature by being a giant among gentlemen.

Dan felt like he was a kid in the Saturday movie house about to watch a tall, gaunt John Carradine in some dark horror flick. The small tuft of beard on the doctor's chin heightened the effect as did a pair of the coldest eyes Cooper had ever seen. If he could believe the comments by both Tom Sherman and Susan Millwood, Krevins was every bit as far from the norm as he looked.

The doctor set his piercing eyes on the audience before beginning. He scanned his listeners and his frigid stare swept the rows. Then he homed in and Dan had the queasy feeling that the doctor was looking directly at him. A strange transformation took place as the once cold eyes mellowed and the hint of a smile crept across Victor's face.

"Good morning, colleagues and guests. It's a pleasure to be here to tell you about our work with cerebellar prompting and behavior control. I'll try to stay on schedule, but there's so much to tell you."

A mumbled reply came from the next row. "And now his imitation of the kiwi bird."

Dan stifled a laugh. He was well aware of that term from his engineering school days. They used it as a derogatory comment about someone who waffled or was unable to clearly state a concept. The saying was that he was like the kiwi bird that screeched and flew in ever decreasing concentric circles until he flew up his own ass crying *ki-ki-ki-criminy, it's dark in here!*

For all of his preparation over the past week, Dan found that Krevins quickly lost him in his convoluted discussion of that mystical part of the brain known as the cerebellum. The presentation was so cluttered with technical terms and acronyms that Dan repeatedly lost the point the speaker was trying to make. Perhaps the doctor needed teaching lessons from Jason Gernsbach who had been a stellar presenter.

Through the fog of stilted language and jargon decipherable only by other psychologists, some highlights did get across to Dan. Krevins had been conducting research here at USF into the functions of the cerebellum and how it communicated with other parts of the brain. Dan remembered Tom's description of that brain section and how it appeared to be central to motor functions, memory storage and possibly other vital processes.

"Our clinical research has confirmed the viability of eliciting conditioned responses from both common laboratory animals and lower level primate subjects through controlled prompting of the cerebellum." Victor Krevins droned on and on.

The clinical work he detailed involved observing responses in lab rats and speculating about new possibilities for steering their behavior. He discussed follow-on research with a chimpanzee. The doctor had used direct communication with the chimp's cerebellar region to preprogram and later trigger specific actions. Unfortunately, the chimp had taken a fatal fall from its cage and the results were inconclusive.

That brought another half-muffled outburst from the same heckler behind Dan.

"Fall, hell, old Vic drove that chimp bat shit with his experiments. Anybody know the sentence for monkey murder?" Another murmur of giggles followed.

As the question and answer period started, Dan decided his own brain needed a rest from the punishment Krevins had dealt it. He gave a head nod to Paula and she bent to retrieve her purse from the floor. It was time for an early lunch.

"Were you as lost as I was in that last topic?" he asked her when they were settled in at the restaurant bar.

"I gathered he was saying he was developing a way to send encoded messages directly to the cerebellum to steer subject behavior. He claimed to have had some encouraging results. It made sense to me if, in fact, the cerebellum is like a computer. It can turn electrical impulses on and off to control other brain parts. You know, it's kind of like he's trying to create software for the brain."

"Now why couldn't Krevins just say it that way?" She had a knack for transforming doublespeak into pearls of wisdom. She was quite a remarkable woman.

"Interesting concept but isn't it a bit far fetched?" he asked.

"Who's to say? Everything worthwhile that was ever accomplished seemed out of reach and reason until one day the big breakthrough came along. Maybe he's stumbled onto something. What I really want to hear about, though, is you and COB." She sipped her beer.

"Oh, there's not much to tell. We were just three very fortunate guys who exposed our fannies in the hope of making a go of a small business. Then, before we knew what was happening, the venture took over our lives and it was like being yanked through a cheese grater by the gonads. Sorry about that."

"Don't apologize. I hear worse than that every day, particularly if the coding on the latest product isn't going well. Code slingers can be pretty temperamental people, you know. What made you hang it up after such unbelievable success?"

"All three of us announced at the outset that we'd work only as long as it was fun. Setting up the business was a challenge for me. I enjoyed serving as the management figurehead for some really creative people. There was always a generous amount of marketer in my soul and I got to practice with great products to hawk. But the growth was so fast that the pressure was just more than any of us wanted. We said let's dump it and let somebody else have the worries of staying on top."

"From what I heard, the payoff wasn't all that bad, either."

"The big outfits had a bidding war. They all lost and we won. At least we have the option of doing whatever we want in our 'golden years'."

"Horse muffins. You're still a young man. Young, interesting and rich is a great combination."

Watch it, Dan. She's an entrancing beauty, but you've got a pretty tough little sweetie of your own at home.

Before he could dwell on that his attention was drawn to an outburst outside the bar.

There was some sort of heated discussion going on in the hallway. Dan could see that Jason Gernsbach and Victor Krevins were apparently having a disagreement. They must have missed something spicy with their quick departure from the lecture hall. Gernsbach seemed to be trying to calm down his associate and placed his hand on Krevins' shoulder. The taller man lashed out so violently he nearly struck Jason in the face as he swept the hand away. At that point, Jason shrugged and turned toward the restaurant.

Their table for lunch was ready. Dan realized the doctor was alone and walked over to greet him.

"Doctor Gernsbach, I'm Dan Cooper. We have mutual friends, Susan and Barry Millwood. Would you join me for lunch?"

"Jason," he answered and thrust out his hand. "I'd be delighted."

The newcomer was slightly flustered. His face was red. That must have been quite a confrontation out there in the hall, Dan reflected.

After introducing Paula, Dan told Jason how much he had enjoyed his presentation and she echoed the compliment. As soon as they ordered, she rose and excused herself.

"Our lunch should be a few minutes arriving. Time enough to 'wash my hands'."

Dan turned to Jason and said, "Couldn't help noticing the outburst. You look like you could use a calm down—maybe one of these?" He pointed to the martini he held.

"Good suggestion. Victor can be a little hard on the nerves. He took offense to my question after his discourse."

"From here it looked like he was about to turn physical on you."

"Oh, he just has a quick temper. I questioned his insistence on doing research with human subjects when the possible effects are so uncertain and possibly dangerous. Victor is truly a brilliant man but he drifts a bit off course at times."

"Sounds to me like you asked a fair question," Dan told him.

"Are you in the profession?" Jason asked. "You said you know the Millwoods."

"No. We were Air Force buddies and neighbors back in Virginia. They're the main reason we retired to Florida. We've been close friends for years."

"Then you must be as unnerved as I am over the terrible news about Barry. Tell me what happened to him."

"We don't really know much, Jason, except that he fell to his death from a very high bridge. I never thought of him as suicidal and I still don't."

Gernsbach reached into his pocket and withdrew an object that he turned over and over in one hand almost as if it was an absent-minded habit. Then he laid it on the table by his plate. A small silver penknife with the engraved initials JG.

"I'm going over to see Susan for dinner but it's not a reunion I particularly relish," he said and nursed his martini.

"My wife and I will see you there. Sue wanted us to meet you, but it looks like you and I have already taken care of that. I'd like to get your opinion about this whole matter but that's something we'll have time to talk about later."

Dan and Jason sipped at their drinks and the food arrived. As if on cue, Paula reappeared.

The food was surprisingly good but Gernsbach picked at his lunch. Appeared to be still a bit on edge after his encounter with Krevins.

Paula drew him out. "I found your lecture fascinating, Doctor."

He responded, "Please call me Jason, Paula." Then he asked, "Are you a psychologist?"

"Just an interested student of psychology, Jason. Your research is so interesting." She turned on her charm.

"Had me worried," Jason said. "Too pretty to be one of us." For the first time, Gernsbach almost managed a smile.

Dan felt they needed to pay more attention to their lunch companion. He turned the conversation to her by telling Jason she was one of those computer whizzes as well as a practiced dabbler in psychology.

"So this is your hobby? How interesting." Jason was clearly also ready to change the subject to something lighter than Barry's accident.

"We all have our quirks. What's your hobby, doctor?"

Gernsbach remembered the small penknife that still lay beside his plate, picked it up, opened the blade and made patterns in the air with it.

"Oh, I'm a whittler of sorts. I build model ships. Find it takes my mind off things medical and brings me back to sanity. My current project is a finely detailed paddle wheeler." Jason closed the knife and put it away.

"Now there's an interesting hobby," Paula remarked.

* * *

"Caught you at home after all. I was worried another dolly had run you down, Studley."

Jud Black answered in an annoyed voice. "Give it a breather, Dan."

That set the tone. Dan was getting under his pal's skin with the nickname and one more warning was enough.

"What I called about is I'd like for you to try a search for information on somebody."

"Try? What do you mean try? When did you ever know JB to fail to find anything he set out to capture?"

"Looks like it's not my day, Jud. Now I've pissed you off twice."

Jud roared and made a raspberry sound into the phone. "Hey, wake up, Dan. It's Jud. You sounded so serious the last time I talked to you, I figured it was time I loosened your reins. What's up?"

"There's a real oddball down here that has me curious. His name keeps coming up and I saw him in action today. He spoke at the psychology symposium on his laboratory tests with conditioned behavior responses. This guy is a real creepy looking individual.

I'd like to know more about him and you have ways of finding out."

Black went into his musical imitation of the old Twilight Zone theme and answered, "We aliens have our methods." Now that was more like Jud.

"His name is Doctor Victor Krevins, He's a practicing Tampa psychologist and a member of the University of South Florida faculty. You're a fan of old movies. Picture a tall John Carradine with a goatee and laser eyes. He's around his mid forties. A psychology grad from Indiana, classmate of my friend Barry Millwood. What else can I tell you that will help?"

"That's plenty. Give me overnight to, shall we say, visit some data banks? Let me give you a wakeup call about four AM."

"You do and Ellen will have both our hides! How about eight o'clock?"

"Can do easy," Jud quipped.

"Oh, I spent some time with a very interesting young lady at the lectures, too, Jud."

"Whoa. Her name better be Ellen."

"Nothing like that, fellow. She was just an intriguing person. Maybe a bit younger than you, a EE/computer science grad. Works in Gainesville at a software company."

"Really caught your eye, huh, Cooper?"

"You know me. A certain old pal of mine came to mind and I thought I might try my hand at match making. Trying to steer you away from a life of sin as a marauding bachelor. Her name is Paula Taylor. She's done some course work in psychology at USF and a school in Minnesota. Don't know where she got her degree. This is one sharp cookie and a looker to boot."

"Opportunities missed, old buddy. I'll be in touch. Got my Murphy's Ale cooling for the weekend and the pool heated?"

"You bet."

CHAPTER 13

"Hello. Dan Cooper here."

"Are ya nekkid?" Just as he suspected, Jud was already cruising at eight o'clock in the morning. His friend detested drugs and what they could do to razor sharp minds like his, so Dan guessed he was just always on a natural high. He wished he could bottle that enthusiasm because it was priceless.

"The missus doesn't allow belching or nakididity at the breakfast table," Dan retorted. "I save that for the patio."

"Whooee. Heat the pool, man, I'm on my way."

"I assume you're calling with some feedback, Jud." He looked at Ellen but by now she didn't need the name. There was no doubt who was on the other end of the line. She grinned and busied herself at the sink.

Jud went into his Lily Tomlin nasal telephone operator impression. "If this is the party to whom I am speaking, I have a hot flash for you."

"Wait. Let me get something to jot this down." Dan searched for writing materials.

Jud lowered his voice and told him, "Just relax and listen. I'll have all of this to you by email shortly."

"Sounds like you had some luck."

"You toot, we tote. Man, I'm information central this morning. Here's the quick and dirty version. Subject is Victor Ernest Krevins. Born 1956 in Urbana, Illinois. Earned his BS degree at Indiana University. Got his MA and PsyD degrees in Clinical Psychology at Minnesota School of Professional Psychology, where he also did some teaching. Looks like he bounced around for several years after that then lasted awhile at a school down south. He left before gaining faculty tenure. Then he returned to MSPP and rode it out to tenure there. From reading their records, I don't think he left on the best of terms. Had to dig pretty deep for that tidbit—but nothing's safe from us alien beings from Hackerovia, you know."

"So when did he show up at USF?"

"He's been there for the past six years teaching and doing clinical research. He's also in part time practice and accredited to at least three local hospitals as a visiting psychologist. This guy is deep into behavioral research."

"Very interesting. I don't suppose you have any indication of how he's regarded in the profession?"

"Funny you should ask. The confidential . . . *ahem* . . . evaluation profiles indicate some problems for Krevins. I read real concern in them over the radical views he holds on mind control and memory manipulation. Seems to be on a crusade to use human subjects for experimental tests. I'd say he's not the most popular member of the staff. His genius is apparently well recognized but the way he channels it sounds suspect."

"That's beautiful work—and fast. I can't wait to see your email."

"Nothing to it, dude."

"No, really. You're smoking, Jud. Must have been up all night."

"Nah. Bowl of pudding when you know a couple of tricks. Maybe you can return the favor and introduce me to that bombshell you ran into over at the college. What's her name, Paula?"

"If we sort out this mess I'll do the honors and tell all the lies you want about what a genteel citizen you are. That's a promise, Jud."

"You cut me deep, my man. I *am* an upstanding citizen. I almost never lie down under the bar."

"We'll talk about it after we take care of business."

"She does sound impressive."

"She's even more impressive in person."

Dan knew from Ellen's expression as soon as the words were out of his mouth that he should never have said that.

"Hurry on down and let's go full bore on this thing, Jud."

"Hang in there, pal. I'll be in tomorrow afternoon," Jud said. "United 231 at five o'clock. And don't lose your head and touch any machines. Remember I told you they could bite."

"Got it. Have a good trip and we'll see you at the airport."

Dan's mind was racing ahead but Ellen sat down across the table and brought him back with a question.

"What did you mean, *she's* even more impressive in person?" Out of that whole conversation she had apparently homed in on that one unguarded statement.

"Someone I met at the symposium yesterday. Remember I said Jason Gernsbach and I had lunch together. This young lady joined us". *That sounded a whole lot better than saying* he *joined* us. "But you're much more impressive in person, babe."

He stood up, swooped down and planted a big kiss on her. She answered with a skeptical, "Uh-huh."

* * *

The tense moments of condolence from Jason Gernsbach were behind them and the evening at Susan's was progressing more comfortably. They listened with interest to the exploits of Johnny and Carol at high school. Dan made a mental note to be at Johnny's next basketball game and catch Carol's gymnastics meet. Susan had done her usual outstanding job of entertaining even under the stress of her loss. She and Ellen went off to police up in the kitchen and the teenagers retreated to their rooms. Dan and Jason found themselves together on the patio.

"My wife wanted to come along and see Susan but she's also a doctor and her schedule wouldn't permit it. We're both so fond of these folks. Just doesn't seem possible he's not with us."

"I know," Dan echoed. "It leaves a big hole in our lives, too. But I'm trying my best to find out what was behind our losing him."

Gernsbach looked confused and asked, "You don't agree with the police that he took his own life?"

"Not for a second. And the more I search the more I'm convinced. Nothing concrete yet but a lot of unanswered questions."

Jason leaned back and inhaled the fresh night air. "Not quite as muggy as New Orleans." Then he asked, "Any way I can help?"

"As a matter of fact, I would like to ask you about Victor Krevins. Not that it has anything to do with Barry—I'm just curious about Krevins."

"You've seen him, Dan. He's a genius but definitely a loner. I heard some of the comments his appearance prompted. My colleagues can be pretty caustic at times but Victor invites criticism with his radical views."

"I understand he's a bit on the periphery with some of his research ideas. I wouldn't normally ask you this, but it's important to me to learn all I can about Barry's state of mind. Do you know if the two of them were at odds about anything, particularly in the recent past?"

"Are you aware they were classmates as undergrads?"

"Yes, Sue told me they were."

"Well, I heard Barry say on more than one occasion that he was worried about some of the things Victor was trying to do in behavioral research. Barry wanted to believe the best of him for old times' sake, but the indicators were there. Victor insisted we should take wide license with laboratory procedures that could possibly be destructive to test animals. And he even advocated applying some of the same techniques to human subjects but was always sanctioned from going that far."

"Krevins seems to think almost anything is possible in behavior steering if we crack the instruction code that drives the cerebellum. Do you agree with that theory, Jason?"

"I'd like to think we could work miracles with the proper prompting of brain functions. But I'm not willing to bend my ethics and seriously endanger human test subjects to succeed. I'm afraid Victor doesn't share my reservations. In fact, that's a large part of why we were having the heated discussion you saw yesterday."

There was apparently a lot more beneath the surface that Jason wasn't saying but Dan had pushed him about as far as he could at this point.

"He did look extremely agitated. I was worried he would start swinging at you."

"I asked what I thought were fair and logical questions about his experiments and he went ballistic on me. He doesn't have the medical training to permit him to prescribe medications. That doesn't deter him from insisting natural and herbal drug equivalents can be used on volunteers. I cautioned that he had to exercise a great deal of care. Reminded him I had written my views in a recent medical journal article. He accused me of trying to undermine his work with that journal piece. That's when he turned really ugly on me. But then I knew he was short tempered."

"Something tells me you don't trust this man at all. I sense you have good reason to believe he's already pushed the envelope . . . maybe broke some rules?"

"Well . . . maybe we should leave it at that for now," Jason replied nervously and squirmed a bit in his seat.

Apparently Jason could have said much more but Dan had stopped as good judgment dictated.

"May I ask a favor of you, Doctor? I believe Barry was driven to his death by something beyond his control. I won't rest until I prove it and exact revenge for him."

Jason was listening to his words with an expression of disbelief. "What makes you come off the wall with something like that?"

"A friend and I are chasing the possibility that subliminal persuasion through his computers may be responsible. Can I call on you if I have questions?"

Jason looked shocked and took a long moment to reply. "That's . . . interesting but a bit far out." He appeared to be mildly amused once the shock wore off.

"Only time will tell. I'm serious about this. We already have some positive clues in that direction and they're hard to discount."

Dan's tone and determined look apparently got through to the doctor. He sat up and frowned.

"The impact of what you're saying could be earthshaking, Dan. It's not something I can believe without a lot more proof, but if you've run onto a breakthrough of that magnitude, I don't want to be left out."

Gernsbach could be another piece of the puzzle falling into place. If he and Jud could get enough minds working on the leads they were finding, they may yet clear up the mystery behind his friend's death. His efforts just might prevent future heartache for others. Jud would be here tomorrow and they could launch their investigation full tilt.

CHAPTER 14

The aircraft's monotonous drone was getting on Jud's nerves. He sat back with his headset and turned on the MP3 player. May as well use the lag time to pore over the track he'd recorded in his home studio this week. Jud was his own harshest critic and the album wouldn't go to market until he was satisfied it was as close to perfect as he could make it. Jenny's Riddle had a reputation and he refused to compromise.

He was sooo looking forward to a break for sun and warmer temps down in Florida. The overnight low in Clarke County, Virginia last night was 17. Snow predicted later today. Dan's timing was right on with his invitation to thaw out on the Gulf coast. Surely they'd have this whole mess with dead doctors and mind games wrapped up before the St Patrick's Day bash at Pat O'Leary's bar. He'd talk Dan into joining Pat and him for the celebration.

Jud wondered what Dan thought of the information he had gathered on Krevins once he'd had more time to absorb it. From all accounts, Victor was considered a brilliant, if somewhat quirky, expert in his area. But electronic mind prompting? Where and when would a busy psychologist have time to master the complicated technology involved to pull that off? Jud admitted to himself that people in the computer field with an abundance of talent often dabbled in some offbeat pastimes to keep their minds challenged. Those endeavors were, however, usually direct spin offs from their computer skills.

A number of his acquaintances fell into that category. They were engaged in computer hacking for fun and curiosity. Such energies could also be channeled into destructive actions when hackers turned into what were referred to as crackers. At that stage they began maliciously interfering with computer nets. The results were downright scary at times.

The image of a genius psychologist running amok in a lab with live test subjects left a big frosty lump in Jud's gut. With or without outside help, Victor Krevins may be into something that had to be stopped now. And if someone was messing with minds over the Internet, Jud took that personally. He'd nail them at all cost.

He sat back and sipped his beer while he listened for flaws on the newly cut track. This domestic swill the airline passed off was only a cut above holding your breath and enduring the thirst. But it would have to do for now. He lost himself in the music.

Somewhere in his dim consciousness Jud felt a tug on his arm and looked around. The old lady in the window seat was pointing toward the aisle. The stewardess was about to reach across him with two miniatures and a cup of ice for his neighbor.

"Here, let me help you with that," he said.

Grandma had been slugging scotch straight up ever since the bar rolled by for first call. She smiled sweetly at him.

"Must be some great tunes on that thing," she said. "You were in another universe."

"One of my favorite groups," he replied. "Helps pass the time. I get mighty bored flying." He had returned to his music when she again tugged at his sleeve.

"Mind if I ask what kind of music? I'm quite a buff myself."

Sure. Had to be at least in her mid seventies. Probably a fan of some rocker like Bach or Chopin.

"It's alternative. May not be your kind of entertainment."

"Are you kidding?" She sat up and beamed. "You're talking Lil's favorite vibes. Is it industrial tinged alternative or traditional rock oriented alternative?"

That set Jud back. He stared at her and felt his jaw drop an inch. Her amused expression was an unspoken gotcha.

"Well . . . uh . . . more the rock variety," he managed to respond.

"I see. You mean, sort of Neil Young-ish, not of the Skinny Puppy legacy, huh?" A sly grin lit her lips.

He was floored. Had to see what she thought of the new cut. She knew her music. This was his first chance to hear an unbiased opinion on the new tunes.

"That's too cool! Take a shot at this and tell me what you think." He handed her the MP3 and she donned the headset.

Jud watched her intently. She closed her eyes and concentrated. Something had grabbed her right away because Lil actually gave her overworked elbow a rest. The refills sat unopened and she was lost in his tunes. He watched her and chuckled to himself. This old gal must have been some rocker in her youth. But she was totally expressionless so he had no way of knowing what her critique would be.

She handed the player across and smiled that sweet smile once again.

"I'd recognize the sound anywhere," she told him. "Complex Zappa harmony structure and bluesy guitar like Vaughn or Hendrix. Has to be Jenny's Riddle."

He swallowed hard. "It is, Lil. What do you think?"

"Totally prime. How did I miss this one? Thought I'd heard all the Riddle's work."

"Oh, it's just been released," Jud lied. He wasn't comfortable with praise from fans. He wouldn't tell her that the group Jenny's Riddle was his own creation.

Jud had a fan from the senior set and she was the first critic of his latest cut. Lil was also having a blast watching the shock she'd generated.

"Hey, I've got a few years on you but my ears are as keen as ever. This momma's been around the block a few times. Recognize talent when I hear it. Have to get hold of a copy and perk up my vacation."

Lil opened a new bottle and poured. Once again it was time for cloud watching and her liquid lunch. He liked her style—strictly no BS, tell it like it is then move on. Take away about forty years and he could go for this gal.

Jud couldn't sleep. He always had trouble sleeping on airplanes. The cramped seating for his six-two frame didn't help and he just wasn't quite at ease until he was back on good old mother earth. Something about the whole atmosphere implied life suspension. Why didn't they have a travel class where you could be sedated and brought around when the whole ordeal of wasted time was past?

Maybe he could catch his friend Sam at home. He checked his address book and reached for the airphone.

Jud's first instinct was to do some spur of the moment phone phreaking. When they were coming up in the computer world, he and his friends had delighted in tapping Ma Bell for free calls with a variety of tricks they carried off either with their wits or with clever little electronic devices. He looked at the phone and thought how amusing it would be to hook a free call to his friend in Ocala on a system the telephone company deemed secure. But it seemed sort of minor league now with the degree of sophistication he had reached. And he'd never miss the money, anyway. Hell, the earnings on his COB profits were building up faster than he could spend them. So it was back to the trusty platinum card.

His friend answered with a large helping of sleepy in his voice.

"Man, it's afternoon and you're still in lala land?" Jud asked.

"That you, Jud? Yeah, had a late night at the machine."

"I can call back another time. Just had a quick question for you."

"Shoot, stick. I should be up and at 'em by now, anyway."

"I'm on my way down to Tampa and I remembered you live near Ocala. That's fairly close to the Bay area, isn't it? And how close are you to Gainesville?"

"Two hours at most up I-75 from Tampa to Ocala. And Gainesville's another few miles north of here. Is that all you need to know?"

"No, actually I wanted to ask you about somebody you may know. There's this dynamite blonde that writes software in Gainesville. Her name is Paula Taylor."

There was a low whistle. "That one is a real piece of work. She's a living doll. Her IQ must be off the scale. So smart she's scary. Works at Craft and Brown in Gainesville."

"Friend of mine met her in Tampa, Sam. Any chance I could get an introduction? You know, as an out of town dude looking for fun and sun?"

"Not a problem. But she can be a bit weird, so it's your nickel from there. I've seen her cut up guys pretty bad with her putdowns. She's a master ball buster, if you read me."

"I read you. A domineering female, huh? I hear she's a code slinger. Maybe also a hacker?"

Jud was walking a fine line. He and Sam had been close back in the metro Washington area before Sam moved to take a new software job in Florida. They had swapped a lot of ideas and shared many evenings penetrating security systems, always for fun and enlightenment, never maliciously. At least half a dozen companies had stronger security systems because the two of them had found flaws and informed the firms how to fix them. Neither one of them could abide the hackers turned crackers that delighted in bugging and crashing networks.

Hackers had an unwritten rule that, unless you were both in the same tight group, you never let someone connect a face or a name with a precise location or your hacker name. So Sam's answer would be guarded at best.

"If I had to guess, I'd say there's a good chance she's smart enough to be an experienced hacker. Don't know first hand how those people operate, though."

Sure. And Sam believed in Captain Marvel and the tooth fairy. His pal was waiting to give him the straight word when they were face to face. You never knew who may be listening.

"Give me a call and we'll manage to get together. I'll even hook you up with the delectable Miss Taylor if that's possible."

"Stay loose, babe. Be talking to you." Jud cradled the airphone and settled back in his seat.

This could be an interesting trip on multiple fronts. Jud passed his empty can and got his things together for their landing in Tampa.

At the terminal Liz walked up the ramp ahead of him. Despite her considerable scotch intake her gait was steady. As she bounced along, Jud could detect a low hum. She was still enjoying one of the tunes on his new Jenny's Riddle work.

They left the jetway into the terminal. Lil turned and gave Jud the peace sign. She sang out, "Rock on, Jenny."

"Enjoy your visit, Lil," he threw back.

What a savvy old babe. Can't always read people just by looking at their wrappers.

Jud could already feel the Florida warmth chasing away his winter chills. Now if he could find his way to the shuttle train and the baggage area, he and Dan could get on with some serious pool dwelling and share a couple of cool ones. The puzzle of bridge jumpers and traffic victims could wait one more day.

CHAPTER 15

Dan and Jud shared a bear hug at the airport baggage claim.

"Great to see you again, Jud. "You and I have strict orders to head straight home. The pool's hot and the brew's cold and Ellen has some prime steaks for the grill."

"Damn, hoss. I feel like I'm having a midwinter dream. Left 25 degrees and snow flurries back at Dulles Airport and it feels like spring here. Must be 75 out there."

"I keep telling you this is the place to be. If I want to see snow and ice, I'll have somebody send me pictures from Virginia."

"Need one of those tinfoil contraptions the guys on MASH used to put around their necks to reflect the sun's rays. Maybe I could get some color back." Jud chuckled.

"Don't worry. A few minutes outside will do wonders for you, pal. Weather's great. Makes me want to get up and going every day."

"So how's Ellen liking it?"

"Couldn't be happier. For us it's like an extended second honeymoon. We do exactly what we want when we want. She's into crafting and reads even more than I do. I'm knocking out novels and writing magazine pieces. Best of all, pretty soon it'll be beach weather again."

They picked up Jud's bags and hurried to Dan's parked car. Rode back from the airport with an unusual hush hanging between them. Normally these two weren't known for being quiet around each other. They would find a multitude of subjects from the mundane to the technical to the downright whimsical to bounce off each other. It was that kind of relationship. They were constantly challenged by each other's intellects and inquisitive approaches to everything going on around them. But on this day there seemed to be a whole menu of unasked questions dangling out there. Neither one of them seemed to be willing to make the first probe.

"Okay if I smoke, Dan?" Jud watched for a head nod then dug out a pack of smokes.

"Your funeral, man, not mine."

Jud lit up and they both fell silent again.

After long minutes of awkward silence, Jud ventured, "Earth to Cooper. This mess really has a hold on you, doesn't it, Dan?"

"Sorry. I'm a bit preoccupied the past couple weeks. Trouble concentrating. I'm so baffled by what happened that it's working me over."

"By now I would have expected half a dozen jabs, Dan. You're not even a challenge today. Where's your wit, your sarcasm, your digs? How am I going to deal with you without your usual cantankerous side?"

"Hey, I may be a few years your senior, buster, but I'm far from being a cantankerous old fart."

Jud took a last drag and crushed out his cigarette. "Now that's more like it. Had me scared to death you were wigging out on me."

"Seems like I've been drifting away like that the past few days, Jud. Don't know what it is, but it's frustrating when I lose my train of thought." Dan nervously rubbed his brow.

"One thing for sure. I'm not letting you near any bridges until I see what's on that computer you plodded through the other day."

Dan caught his breath sharply. "Do you really think . . . ?"

"Let's not rule out anything until we know what we're dealing with here."

Dan let that roll around in his head for a bit and he didn't like the implications. What had he stepped into here? Puzzling deaths, a wild-eyed scientist and a beautiful blonde mystery woman. Too much too fast.

"I read the info on Krevins, Jud. Raises some intriguing questions. I'd say he bears further study."

"Well, you piqued my interest in your Miss Taylor. May have a line on her through a mutual friend. If you think it's worthwhile, I'll try to meet her up in Gainesville."

"And check out a dynamite babe as a bonus, huh, Studley?"

Jud gave him his best lecherous grin. "That, too. But we may even have a more technical side interest in common, according to my contact up there. Could be a foot in the door to learn more about her."

Dan would leave that alone for now. He surmised Paula's computer smarts would have logically spilled over into the world of hacking. That was a subject Dan and Jud had an agreement about not broaching between them. It was Jud's other world and Dan didn't belong in it.

Cooper admitted it was high time for him to come out of his fog and clear his own single-track mindset. Maybe he was dwelling too much on Millwood's death when backing off for a while could give him a new perspective. Tonight they'd catch each other up on the news and tomorrow they could get serious.

"So how's life treating you? he asked Jud. "Any new little Studleys running around or are you still leading a charmed life?"

It was like an invitation to a verbal sparring match. They were off and running. It had been entirely too long since he'd had a good mental workout with the likes of Jud Black and tonight was for fun.

* * *

The next morning they set out for Safety Harbor to see Susan and continue the work in the home office. She seemed to Dan to be emerging slowly from her depressed state. He hoped that was due in some part to his efforts to untangle the mystery of Barry's death. But it remained to be seen whether he would succeed in his search even with Jud's help.

Susan bussed Dan on the cheek and took his hand. "I really appreciate what you're doing."

"Don't thank me yet. I'm still baffled. But I'm not giving up."

She looked at Jud and Dan realized he was remiss.

"Sorry. Let me reintroduce you two." Dan addressed Jud and squeezed Sue's hand. "Jud Black, Susan Millwood. Maybe you remember when he was down to see us a while back. He's the smartest computer maestro you'll ever meet, so I've asked him to help me. He ain't a bad guy to have for a friend, either. We made a few bucks together in the software business."

"Oh, I remember him. He's not exactly a forgettable character. Good to see you again, Jud. I recall the tales about how you, Dan and Pat whipped a whole industry."

"Gad, did I lay it on that thick? Anyway, Jud and I are going to pry all the secrets out of that computer in there. Then we're going back to Clearwater and check out the computer at the office."

"Here's the door key," she said. "Ellen's coming by in a few minutes and we're going to make a run on some local stores. Probably have lunch out."

"Do me a favor, Sue. Keep her in the bargain aisles and don't let her hurt me too bad with her plastic."

"Fat chance. Can't tell what we may come home with," she said with a twinkle in her eye.

"We'll get to work now. Enjoy yourselves."

* * *

They dove into the computer scan. Dan was once again fascinated by the speed with which Jud coaxed it to spill its contents. He estimated that the Cooper method, even if he had one, would have taken on the order of days rather than the minutes Jud's speeding fingers required.

"There it is," Jud blurted out and plunged ahead with no perceptible pause. Moments later he pointed to the monitor with one hand and rapped the table with the other. "Exactly what I expected to see. Digitized video."

"I see it." Dan said. "Looks like a . . . that's the Skyway Bridge!"

"And what do you see now?" Jud inquired as the scene on the screen changed to a second view.

"First I saw a message with the words SKYWAY BRIDGE MIDNIGHT on that same part of the computer screen. Then something like a section of the bridge retaining wall and what . . .

a view out over the water? It's spellbinding the way the sequence keeps repeating."

"The light in the distance. What would that be?" Jud pointed to a pinpoint of light that blinked in the very center of the screen and seemed to dominate the scene.

"Couldn't be much out there on the water but ships. Wait, could it be the light on top of a navigation buoy?"

"Now listen to this," Jud said as he increased the volume setting. A low hum was emitted from the speakers. "That's way down in the lower frequencies barely perceptible to the human ear. It seems to have a pulsing rhythm of some sort."

"This is incredible, Jud. It's like I'm there on top of that bridge, going to the wall then looking far out across the water. And something about the sound is compelling but unnerving. And why the blinding light?"

Jud stood up and beamed. "My friend, we just solved the puzzle of Millwood's long fall. He was coaxed onto that bridge by this video. Sent a message to his subconscious that steered him over the side of the Skyway Bridge. By the time he fell, his attention was fixed on that beam of light. No telling how many times the messages were drilled into his brain while he was on this computer. And I'll bet we find the same thing on his office machine."

"I believe we have our tie between the two accidents, too." Now Dan was excited. "This sounds like your description of how you thought Wainwright died staring at a building across the street."

"Exactly," Jud said. "Now there's no doubt we have a serial killer on the loose. He's also a very smart assassin. Those two doctors were murdered by remote control. Whoever sent them to their deaths could have been a great distance away when the fatal incidents occurred. No physical connection was needed and there was no trail back to the source except for the hidden video and audio prompters on their computers. Slick."

"Couldn't Barry see those same images when he was on the computer?"

Jud shook his head and looked impressed by what he'd just seen. "That's the beauty of the idea. I had to slow down the video and enhance the audio for us to even be aware they were there. At normal speed and volume they sneak up on you and drill their message into your brain and you never even know what's happening."

"So this is the subliminal persuasion you mentioned before? It really works?"

"Lots of people out there still buy subliminal persuasion audiotapes, so they believe it works. If those things can make folks stop smoking and eat less, think what a visual image might be able to do. Gives me the yips, Dan."

"Makes my flesh crawl. Now I *have* to continue. I won't rest until whoever did this to Barry is behind bars or worse. Point me in the right direction, Jud."

Jud went back to his keyboard stroking and called up a download file. He did some inspection and sat back with a muttered, "I'll be damned. Do you realize the bullet you barely dodged, Dan? Could explain your mental lapses."

"What?"

"You spent time, thankfully not too much time, on this computer searching for files and doing downloads. There's a daemon installed on Millwood's machine that automatically called up the video and the low frequency audio to play repeatedly any time the computer was on. Those same prompters were being drilled into you all the time you were searching his files."

"Then when you joked about keeping me away from bridges, it wasn't so far fetched after all."

"Hell, I *was* joking. But I'm glad now you took my advice and stayed off the computer. In fact, I'd wager whoever put those daemons there has tried by now to access this computer and delete them. Fortunately, this machine has been turned off since we talked on the phone."

He shut down the computer once again. "We want those files to stay right there for the time being. Can't take a chance on any outside meddling."

"I think it's time you gave Barry's office computer a thorough scan, Jud. Let me call Tom Sherman and tell him we're coming over."

* * *

Doctor Sherman was more than happy to have them come by and take a pass at the workstation. It had sat silent and off limits at Dan's request for ten days. After Marge's death over the weekend, Dan had made sure Tom knew the critical importance of the computer staying down.

"The police have been back asking questions," Tom told them. "Peter and I and the rest of the office staff have all been grilled. Any progress on your end?"

"We have theories but nothing I'd want to say out loud yet because they're just that—theories. Jud wants to take a crack at Barry's computer to see what rears up at him."

"I hope we can get back to normal soon." Tom gave a weary shrug. "I have a possible new partner lined up but the office has been in turmoil over the two deaths. I'm running to keep up with the patient load."

Dan took a closer look and realized how strung out and exhausted Tom was beginning to appear.

"We'll try to be quick and get out of your way." Dan showed Jud to the right office.

Jud played his staccato tune on the computer keyboard and it offered up the machine's secrets. However, he found no daemons and no email messages from Secret Treasures. They had apparently also been deleted from the trash folder so not a trace was left. Whoever had been in this office over the weekend and killed Marge had ensured that no incriminating evidence remained. Even the file Barry created to describe his mental lapses was gone.

The absence of the files was even more revealing than if they had found them present. Marge had passed Barry's notes to Dan and they confirmed something new and eerie was happening to his thoughts. The emails and daemon files were captured on his home computer. Jud said he thought he could track the path of those incoming messages to determine their origin.

"Jud, you know I never got around to looking through Barry's computer on my first trip here. There could be other email exchanges of interest. Now that we're safe from having our heads screwed over we can spend some time searching for more clues."

"That's what I'm looking through right now. There is one here that puzzles me. It's pretty blunt but maybe it means something to you. I just sent it to print."

Dan snatched the printout and read:

Subj: no thanks
Date: 01/16 18: 40:30 PM Eastern Standard Time
From: *vickren@skybox.com*
To: *milldoc@netwise.com*

Don't patronize me! Get lost with your sympathy. Some day all of you will pay.

"Looks like he teed off somebody. And the date is exactly three weeks prior to the night he died. We need to find out who has that screen name and dig out Barry's message that set him off."

"Check the printer. I've already found it."

Dan held the outgoing message Barry had sent only days before the terse answer and stared at it for a few moments. Then he looked up with a pained expression and tossed it onto the desktop. It read:

Subj: Let's Talk
Date: 01/13 10: 32:10 AM Eastern Standard Time
From: *milldoc@netwise.com*
To: *vickren@skybox.com*

Have tried to reach you without success. We need to talk about forestalling possible ethics inquiry. Owe it to you for old times sake to help out. Please contact me.

Barry

"My guess is that Vickren is Victor Krevins' computer screen name," Dan said. "He keeps showing up at every turn. I think it's time we did some further investigation of Dr. Krevins."

"Sounds like your friend Barry had something important to tell Krevins and he was being ignored. You did say they were classmates. I gather he felt an obligation to help Krevins dodge an investigation into his professional ethics. We know what Victor thought of that, don't we?"

"Maybe he realized Barry knew too much about him from all the way back to the days in Indiana," Dan said. "That made him a real threat if there was an inquiry about to be opened. Maybe even enough of a threat for Krevins to take drastic action."

"Strange, though, that the killer didn't erase that email exchange with Victor," Dan posed. "Must not have been Krevins himself in here on Saturday because he would have known to look for the messages. But being discovered was serious enough to cause the intruder to do in Marge either intentionally or in panic."

"Scary thought. There could be others involved. You're actually starting to sound like me, Dan. Think the worst and trust no one. You could be spot on this time."

"So what do we do about it?"

"Well, I crashed hospital security and survived. Maybe we should do a little after hours scouting at this wierdo's house. I'll get an address and you find your sneakers."

CHAPTER 16

The sun was barely up and already she had been busy at her computer for two hours. Long sessions through the night and bursts of creativity before dawn had become routine for Paula Taylor. She was in her element sitting alone in this cluttered room, leaning back in the big chair with her fingers gliding across the keyboard in her lap. Faded jeans and a worn sweatshirt covered her long limbs and her glistening blonde hair lay in a careless tousle about her shoulders.

Soon she would have to drag herself away and get ready to depart for her day job. It was a shame she had to make a living when there were so many more exciting challenges to be met right here. Paula liked to have the room dark with only the glow of the computer screen to draw her blue eyes totally into her work. She stretched her long legs and flexed her bare toes against the credenza top. Paula nestled closer to her electronic lover while it winked its approval.

That's the answer, she mused and keyed a comment line into the program sequence on the screen. *I'll add that to the next transmission and give it the smoke test.*

Well, there was no avoiding it. She would grit her teeth and spend the day at her mundane job at the software company. They regarded her as an innovative employee who was admired by the young programmers that came to her for guidance. At thirty-two she had progressed to the position of senior programming manager with a substantial salary. But her employer was unaware that in reality she didn't care a whit for the company or its goals. Her work was merely a means to collect a paycheck. The job was bearable only because of the extracurricular fun she was having. Some of the deep magic she had installed in their software products could lie dormant for months or years until she was ready to access and manipulate it through back doors she had carefully imbedded.

Paula reluctantly tore herself away from the computer and headed for the bathroom.

No, she thought as she showered and readied herself for the commute, *they don't know the real me. I'm not just plain old Paula Taylor, dutiful and loyal coder girl. I'm Athena, the hacker queen, Greek goddess of wisdom. I can kick all their asses. Those arrogant male execs would have a testosterone overload if they knew I could blow up their software at any client site I choose and shred the company's reputation.*

As she emerged from the shower, the telephone rang. She padded from the bathroom, leaving a wake of puddles behind her.

"Paula, honey, it's me. Wanted to catch you before you left."

"I hope this is really important, stick man. I'm standing here bare and dripping wet."

She could almost hear him panting through the phone line. Self-important slug, she had him right by the short hairs. He was like a slobbering trained pooch when she turned him on.

"Just wanted to hear your voice, Paula. And to say thanks again for helping me pull off our little experiments. You don't know how much this means to me."

"Oh, I know all right, and I'll be sure you return the favor. You're good at what you do but you're nothing without me and my special knowledge. Don't you forget it, Ernie."

"Do you have to call me that? You know how I hate that name."

"What do you prefer? Dork? Fido? You may not like my nickname for you but you can't resist coming back for more, can you?" How she did love pulling his string.

"I wanted to ask you if you could come down and spend the weekend, Paula, before the conference. Monday is so far away and I ache to see you. Please say you will."

"No dice, Ernie. I have more important things to do here. My world doesn't revolve around you."

"But you'll at least stay over Monday night?" He was pleading.

"We'll see how the day goes. Maybe if you're on your best behavior, I'll think about it. But that will be strictly my decision, so don't badger me. I'll let you know at the proper time. Understood?"

"Yes," he whimpered. He was thoroughly beaten down at this point as surely as if she had lashed him with a whip. She tingled all over with the excitement of renewed conquest. What dunce spread the myth that the male was the dominant sex? Ha!

"Now say it."

He knew exactly what she wanted to hear. There was a long silence and she repeated, "Say it!"

"I live to do your bidding, Athena."

"And don't forget it. Now say good bye."

She slammed down the receiver and laughed aloud at the subservient dolt she enjoyed dominating. He flew high all week and enjoyed basking in the awe of youngsters who admired his superior mind. How jolting it must be to have her remind him that she could squeeze him with her taunts and make him like it. The feeling of power was intoxicating. She stopped in front of the bathroom mirror and dried off while she gave herself a lingering once over.

Paula spoke to her reflection.

"After all, what's not to adore, girl? You're five feet nine inches of dynamite with a quick fuse." She touched her firm flesh and beamed approval. Men were such twits. She knew exactly how to handle them.

As she drove the short distance to work, she reflected on how her relationship with Ernie had matured into something quite unexpected while he groped and chased after her. Together they made an unbeatable team with their expert knowledge of two seemingly diverse fields. And they hadn't really clicked until she ran across him again here in Florida. Well, she didn't know where he thought he was going with this chase, but she would soon be on her own. Her quick mind had absorbed all she needed from old Ernie to make her new plan a success. It was foolproof and undetectable. The considerable profits she would reap were hers alone. Ernie could go to hell with his egghead notions once she set her net and snared her first clients.

"You have no idea who you're dealing with, Ernie," Paula mumbled.

She parked and locked her car and steeled herself for another mundane day shift.

* * *

Paula checked her watch and breathed a sigh of relief. Three o'clock and her boring day at good old Craft and Brown Software—or Crash and Burn as she called it in private—would soon be history.

The boss walked by her glass-enclosed office and waved.

Paula smiled sweetly and returned his greeting. Then she turned away toward the wall and muttered, "Good thing you can't read my lips, shmuck. Can't wait for the day I can flick you the bird and depart this place for good."

All it would take was a couple of paying clients for her ingenious new enterprise and she could put this behind her. With few exceptions, her work force was a collection of lightweights destined to slave away for the rest of their careers to enrich this or some other parasite company. But she was about to rise above that dead end route and take her rightful place with the great hacker wizards of all time.

She dialed out and let the phone ring several times. Her friend was almost surely on the Internet looking for something worth exploring. Next to her, she admitted, he was just about the slickest hacker she had met. They had never talked about why he had so much time to surf for trouble to get into but he was on line no matter what time of day she tried to reach him. This called for a quick person to person dialogue, so she'd wait him out.

On ring number six, the answering machine picked up.

"Sam here. Leave a message or leave me alone." The message was delivered in an almost musical tone, but it covered everything in, as they say, ten words or less.

"Hey, stud muffin. Quit spanking the monkey and pick up the phone. It's Paula."

A brief silence, then "Howdy, cowgirl. Ready to saddle up?"

"You wish. What I want to know is, are we still on for poker at Connie's?"

"Bet your pretty little hump we are. Six for poker at eight. But you're a week early. It's not this coming Monday. Have to wait another week to give me your money."

"And Fred? Will he be there?"

"Of course. Don't forget to bring his bag of pork skins. Should be your turn to slop the hog. Nobody else will touch those things."

Good. Fred was an integral part of her plan. It was a poorly kept secret that Fred was well connected to some decidedly shady characters on the murky side of the law. That seemed a perfect starting point for mining potential clients for what she had in mind.

"Now I'm jealous, Paula. Why the sudden interest in Fred?"

"Just curious. Last couple of sessions have been profitable with him feeding the pot."

Good. Fred and Sam were integral parts of the plan she had hatched but she had to be careful how much she told Sam. No one in their poker group other than Sam, whose hacker name was actually Armadillo, knew she was Athena. They had a strict pact that it would stay that way. They left their hacker identities at the door and guarded against using the jargon that would raise suspicions. As far as any of the players were concerned, Paula was a code cruncher of pedestrian ability. Sam was supposedly employed at some second rate software outfit in Ocala. The truth was even Paula wasn't sure exactly what he did for a living.

"Now what do I do in the meantime to break the boring routine at this toilet hole company?" she sighed.

"I could make some exciting suggestions."

"All having to do with me giving and you receiving, I suppose," she shot back.

"Cut me some slack. You can't blame a guy for trying. Okay, how about a certain goddess and a small animal getting together for some stimulating mind games and keyboard tunes?"

"Now you're talking, Sam. My place? Noon tomorrow?"

It was just what she needed. Athena and Armadillo together for a challenging weekend of swapping hacker tricks and finding new targets to probe. Resist as he might, she'd teach him yet to get into networks and wreak havoc.

CHAPTER 17

Victor Krevins lived in a large townhouse in an upscale section of Tampa. He was a lifelong bachelor, a fact that came as no surprise to either Dan or Jud. The doctor apparently had an ego too big to share a house or even a life with another human being.

They had carefully checked Krevins' schedule to find a time when he would be away from home. Saturday night seemed to be the best window of opportunity. The university was holding an awards dinner downtown and all the psych faculty would be in attendance. Jud had cased the neighborhood mid-morning and decided they should enter through the rear patio. The two men felt like amateur cat burglars but their options were limited at this juncture. Either they would be able to make a positive connection between Krevins and the death of Barry Millwood or they would have to search for new suspects.

"There he goes, Dan. It's six thirty. Should give us at least a couple of hours to make our foray. Let's drive down the street a couple blocks and come in from behind."

"Hope you know what we're doing because I sure don't. How do we get inside?"

"Not all my friends are straight arrow family men like you. I've picked up a few tricks from them. Let's hope these work."

Jud produced a small leather wallet that Dan assumed contained tools to get them past door locks.

"This makes me downright queasy, Jud. Are we crazy or what?"

"Not a lot of choice, old buddy. If we're gonna nail this slippery fish, we need something concrete; a motive for going after your friend and Myron Wainwright. Just hang in."

They both scanned for people on adjoining terraces but found no one out on this somewhat brisk evening. The sun had set and they were depending on the darkness of an overcast night to cover their movements. A neat row of large townhouses loomed above the tall wooden perimeter fence and all was quiet. Only one porch light a couple of units away and no lights visible in the fenced courtyards.

"Good to go, Dan. Wait for my signal."

Jud motioned for him to stay put as he crouched and skirted the perimeter. He stayed as close as possible to the trees and shrubs of the common grounds. Once he reached the six-foot fence at the rear of Krevins' unit, Jud hoisted himself over and into the courtyard. Dan saw fingers extend above the fence and motion him to follow. He began to slink along the tree line toward the fence. The terrace light went off down the way and Dan was alone in the dark.

One end of a rope curled over the wall and flopped toward him. Dan seized it with both hands and felt a strong tug lift him upward. He dug the toes of his sneakers into the planks and hoisted one leg over top.

"Good thing you thought of the rope," he whispered to Jud. He had rolled unceremoniously onto the ground with a thump he imagined everyone in the neighborhood could have heard.

With a finger aside his mouth, his amused partner reached down and stayed Dan from rising. They listened intently to see if there were any neighbors stirring but there were no voices and no lights above. At least for now they appeared to be safe from prying eyes.

"These gymnastics are for you young studs." Dan checked his various parts and caught his breath.

"I'd give you a six for form on that hurdle, Cooper. Damage anything?" Jud asked under his breath.

"Only my pride. Let's get inside." Dan rubbed his hip vigorously.

The back door was no challenge for the magic tool kit. Jud donned a pair of latex gloves and went to work. Apparently one of his less than stellar acquaintances had taught him well. That made Dan wonder where and when Jud had practiced jimmying door locks before tonight. No doubt there was much he didn't know about his pal. So far they hadn't done badly for a couple of rank amateurs, though. Or maybe one amateur and one practiced guide?

Victor was apparently doing well for himself between his inheritance and his job. They found themselves in a huge kitchen. Dan flicked on his flashlight and played it around. From what he could see of the room, it was impressive, outfitted to please a gourmet cook.

"Turn that thing off." Jud jerked at his arm.

"Not much light in here. Ouch. I've already bumped my shin twice," Dan whispered.

"Can't take a chance on throwing light around. Be careful with the flashlight."

Jud had taken the precaution of taping over the lenses of two flashlights so they would cast narrow, low intensity beams. He flicked on his light and Dan followed him toward the living room. From there they found a hallway and what looked like an office. There were blinds at the window. Jud made sure they were tightly closed. Then he nodded to Dan to hit the wall switch.

They were in a sizable office with walnut bookcases and a massive walnut desk. The line of bookcases was broken on one wall by a high credenza with a computer and on the other wall by a wooden file cabinet.

Jud turned to Dan and motioned toward the file.

"Okay, see what that thing holds while I get this machine working. Turn your flashlight on but keep it pointed toward the floor." He handed Dan a pair of latex gloves and said, "Almost forgot. Put these on. Remember, no fingerprints."

Dan went about a systematic search of the three-drawer file while Jud turned his attention to the computer. He brought it to life and probed and tested.

"Yo, baby, attagirl. Gimme." Jud coaxed and his digits pumped at the keyboard in rapid-fire style.

Dan was deeply engrossed in his trip through the files, being careful to leave them exactly as found. Doctor Krevins had some very interesting material stored away. Dan found himself wishing he were more knowledgeable about psychology and the brain so he could absorb what the documents had to say.

They worked quietly and thoroughly. Dan was intent on scouring the written accounts of Krevins' research. Only the sounds of keys softly clacking and paper crinkling punctuated the stillness of the room.

A long time later Dan looked up from his reading and said, "I see a disturbing trend here, Jud. Looks like he's been using volunteers as test subjects. Doesn't appear they were students or regular patients. Could be he's surfing the back streets for vagrants. That could mean he's less than careful about how they're used for testing."

"Take some snaps with that camera," Jud said and kept on stroking the keyboard. "I found a lot of test data on his machine. Dumping it to disk as I go. If this is university sponsored research, I'd expect his records to be kept there. Maybe he's doing some moonlighting only he knows about."

"Damn, I hope I'm not reading this right," Dan exclaimed. "Shows he found a drifter a few weeks ago and administered some drug I can't pronounce. Tom Sherman says most psychologists aren't even authorized to give out drugs. I'd swear this indicates he lost him."

"Lost him?" Jud asked.

"I mean the subject died! What kind of monster are we dealing with here, taking chances like that with another human in the name of science? Barry used the moniker 'Crazy Vic' for him. That doesn't begin to tell the story if this is true." Dan took the small camera from his pocket and snapped an image of the page.

"There are all sorts of gems on his computer," Jud remarked. "I see references to some important tests underway with a partner but there's no name given for whoever's working with him."

"Interesting. How about email? Anything spicy there?" Now that they'd made the plunge, Dan was warming to his task.

Jud continued to call up messages then suddenly stopped and exclaimed, "Touchdown!"

"Sounds like a choice find."

"Hold onto your hat, Dan. There's a message from Myron Wainwright dated the middle of last month. I copied it to disk—now let's get a printout." Moments later he took the sheet from the printer and started to read.

Jud didn't finish his task. Dan saw lights flash by the window and heard a car engine.

"Hold up, Jud. That could be Victor."

They heard the garage door activate and Jud blurted out, "Douse the lights and lie low."

He popped his diskette from the computer, stuffed the sheet of paper in his pocket and shut down quickly. Dan slid the file drawer closed and turned off the lights. They dropped behind the desk none too soon. There were sounds of activity in the kitchen and the hall light went on.

Now they had an immediate problem. If Victor found them their game was compromised before they escaped with the information they needed. They may have to get physical to get out of here. Dan felt like the proverbial trapped rat with nowhere to run.

Krevins unwittingly did them one huge favor. He strode directly from the kitchen to a bathroom down the hall and they heard water running. That meant they had an opening and it was now or never.

"Shag ass, Dan. Head for the kitchen. I'm right behind you."

They worked their way into the kitchen and headed for the back door. Dan's pulse was working overtime. He wasn't so sure this had been a good idea after all. They managed to exit into the rear courtyard with no one in hot pursuit and hurried across the grass to the privacy wall.

"Oh, no. The fence. I'm dead, Jud." Dan was never going to be able to scale that wooden wall without raising a ruckus and bringing somebody down on their heads. This could be their downfall.

"No sweat, pal." Jud reached out, flicked a latch and swung open a gate in the wall. Dan scowled and hurried through the opening. Moments later, the latch clicked and the agile Jud vaulted across and hit the ground running.

When they were safely across the common area and out of the alley, Dan turned and said, "How's come you let me break my tail on the ground when I could have walked in through the gate?"

"Didn't know it was there till we were both inside. Sorry 'bout that." Jud laughed and Dan decided his partner was enjoying this too much.

"Wonder how many trails we left?" Dan was having real reservations about this caper. "He could be after us and I don't want to think what his twisted brain might dream up to get even with us."

"Too late to worry about that now. The gate's latched and hopefully neither of us left anything in the office. I know I didn't. His back door is unlocked but maybe he won't notice that tonight. We got what we came after."

"Roger that," Dan agreed. "I took some snaps that should be helpful. I think this jasper is into some strange stuff. Hope we can nail him before he hurts anybody else."

Jud held up his diskette. "Believe I caught some hot material on this baby. We may have taken a long-term lease on the doctor's ass."

Dan laughed, mostly in nervous relief. "I could never do this for a living." He rubbed his sore backside.

The rest of the evening they did some bar hopping and mulled over what the outcome of this interrupted foray might be. Neither of them could think of any clue they may have left to indicate anyone had been in the townhouse during Victor's absence.

"There's a wealth of information for us to analyze on the disk. That's going to take some time," Jud told him.

"And I must have a dozen shots of documents that were real eye openers," Dan countered. "Have to drop it off on the way home at the all-night drug store. They have quick turnaround so we can pick it up in the morning."

They agreed on a first stop on their way out of town—a bar. The rush of their hurried escape was over and they both wanted a quiet spot and a tall one to settle their nerves. Jud drained his mug and leaned across the table.

"From our very fast readings, I'd say things don't bode well for Victor. He's into some murky activities and we may now be able to make positive recent connections between him and the two psychologists that died."

"Most important, I may be on the verge of a breakthrough in sorting out my friend's death—no, his murder." Dan was mad now and he wanted to go after this crazy madman who he was convinced had a hand in killing Barry.

"A step at a time, Dan. You know how hard it is to nail somebody unless you've got him dead to rights. We need to turn the screws so tight he can't get away."

"I hear you, Jud. But what I'd like to do is take care of the bastard myself."

"Then I'd lose a pal, too. Don't want you sitting in jail somewhere for ripping him apart. Just give it time. I promise I'll help you put him away if he's as guilty as you think."

"I feel like I need to pour this brew on my joints instead of down my gullet," Dan groaned. "Boy, do I hurt. That fall was bad enough, then my shins got acquainted with half the furniture in VIctor's place. Next time we do this, I'm gonna let you go ahead and find all the latches and clear paths first."

Jud laughed and held his glass high to signal for a refill.

They cruised around Ybor City and worked their way back toward the suburbs at a late night hangout. The mood Dan was in, Jud's goal now was to get him home reasonably coherent and without having to fight his way out of a bar. He'd feel sorry for any tall, skinny boozer that walked in looking the least bit like the creepy Doctor Krevins. Dan would probably be on him on all fours.

Best of all, they had made a breakthrough in stalking a killer.

CHAPTER 18

Jud looked around the patio and said, "Ellen, I'm impressed. This is the way to live."

Ellen had decided that, since it was a mild morning, she'd serve the fellows their breakfast poolside on the patio. She had set sweet rolls and coffee on the patio table and was about to take Jud's order.

He slumped back in his chair. "I was wondering if maybe I could rent a room for, say, two or three months till the cold weather's gone up north."

"You know you're welcome anytime, Jud. What can I get for you? Want some eggs and bacon, maybe sausage?"

He sipped at his coffee and fixed his attention on the column of water cascading in the spa.

"Let me soak it all up for a few minutes first. Maybe I'll just catch some sleep right here. Couldn't get much better than this."

Ellen set a pitcher of cold orange juice on the table.

"Must have been quite a night for you guys. Dan was still sawing away in there last time I looked. He's usually up by sunrise and in the office writing no later than seven thirty. Hope you two didn't leave too much damage in your wake."

"Pretty tame night, actually. We made a visit to a friend and kicked around town a bit."

She gave him a look that said, *What a shameless liar you are.*

They both turned their attention to the sliding door as Dan stumbled onto the patio. "Morning, glories. Should my ears be burning?"

"No. He was just telling me what a quiet evening you two gentlemen spent until the wee hours. Would you care to elaborate on his fairy tale or do we leave it at that?"

Dan searched Jud's face for some clue but Jud shrugged. He was on his own. Ellen certainly didn't need to worry about such a chancy adventure as last night's disorganized assault on the townhouse.

"Well, we did close down a couple bars," he told her. "Tastes like the Chinese Army marched through my mouth barefoot. But isn't it a beautiful day out? How about some scrambled eggs, bacon and toast, hon."

Jud nodded agreement. Ellen put half a grapefruit in front of Dan and set off into the kitchen.

"You're not having grapefruit, Jud?" Dan dug into the juicy pink fruit.

"Man, that's a foreign fruit to me. Get past apples and peaches and you're beyond my menu."

"This little yellow wonder is nature's gift. Gotta introduce you to fresh squeezed grapefruit juice and vodka, what we call a greyhound in Florida. Puts zing in your whistle and zip in your hard drive."

"Thought that was oysters," Jud chuckled.

They dug into breakfast and the only sound on the patio for a long while was the pool fountain. Dan could see Jud was chewing on something besides his toast and bacon. Finally, Jud pushed back his empty plate and took a deep breath.

"We have some work to do here before we move on. Need to collect our thoughts and see what we know so far."

He was right, of course. There was plenty of raw data but they had to be sure they hadn't jumped to some hasty conclusions. This was a time for sober reflection and putting it all together. Had they really seen some of the things they imagined were there? Then they needed a plan for how to proceed.

Dan stood and cleared the plates from the table.

"You get on my computer and pore through those disk files, Jud. I'll swing down to the drug store and pick up my film. Together we should be able to make some sense of all this."

* * *

When Dan returned from the drug store Jud had a stack of printouts for him to read but he thrust one crumpled page under his nose right away.

"This is the message from Wainwright we never got around to reading last night when mister sunshine almost caught us."

The email read:

Subj: Urgent
Date: 01/11 7:18:25 PM Eastern Standard Time
From: *Wainhome@lightbeam.net*
To: *vickren@skybox.com*

Owe you the courtesy of a heads up. Ethics board may meet to run inquiry on you. I could be called. Hope you can defend your actions in test lab. Please delete this message after reading.

Myron

"Another warning from a colleague. From my searches through Myron's machines, I recognize that as his email address. Victor certainly didn't follow advice and dump this message. I couldn't find any outgoing traffic to Wainwright, either. Maybe Myron had his answer when he tangled with traffic out there on 23rd Street."

"So now we know Barry and Myron both had warned him of trouble ahead," Dan said. "They were offering a hand to a colleague despite his spotty reputation. It's no big surprise, but mad dog Krevins seems to have chewed on both hands."

Dan produced the snapshots, a couple dozen clear images of documents from Victor Krevins' files. He turned to the task of inspecting each photo under a magnifying glass and proceeded with the tediously slow reading word by word. The two men sat quietly, Jud at the computer and Dan in his overstuffed easy chair. The silence was broken only by the sound of recurring keyboard activity and exclamations under their breath as they uncovered interesting items. Dan took copious notes on his observations. Once he looked up and saw Jud doing his version of highlighting on the screen.

"At the expense of having my head snapped off, I think it's time I checked in on you two." Ellen stood in the doorway.

"Pretty lady, you can interrupt any time. Always brightens my day," Jud replied, momentarily ceasing his pecking.

"Hey, charm boy. She's taken, remember?" Dan admonished.

Ellen grinned. "Never thought I'd see you two together when you were this quiet."

"Serious sh . . . stuff going on in here, Ellen," Jud shot back. "Old Sherlock and Watson are hot on the trail of the bad guys and that sound you hear is both our brains humming."

"I have some brain food ready if you gents would like to take a break and reenergize. Did you realize it's already after noon and you haven't budged from this office? If we let Dan go much longer without food, his blood sugar's going so low one of us will be doing CPR."

"Well, I sure don't wanta kiss him, so I guess we'd better eat." Jud stood and stretched.

Dan dropped his pencil and the magnifying glass and rubbed his eyes. There was so much to read and it was beginning to seem like labor.

"May be a good time for us to swap info, anyway, and see what's new. We'll be right along, El."

They sat down to sandwiches and salads and Ellen placed a mug of Murphy's in front of each of them.

"Enjoy your lunch. I'm going over to see Susan." She came around and gave Dan a peck.

"Man, you two are going to domesticate me yet." Jud stretched and enjoyed a long gulp of brew. "Makes me think I'm missing an awful lot by kicking around on my own. Just don't know how I'd find a gal that would put up with me. You know, one with the patience of an Ellen."

"Had to nip at me, didn't you?' Dan sneered. "You won't have any trouble finding a girl. Any number of women would stand in line to snare someone with your animal charm. The trick is to find the right one."

"That's what I mean. Maybe I'll just have to keep plugging along on my own. No commitments in just spreading myself around."

Reluctantly they agreed it was time to get back to the task at hand. They prefaced this with a recap of their findings for the morning. Jud pointed to the printouts he had offered before lunch.

"You've seen the exchanges between Victor and his colleagues, Dan. Krevins made some notes on his work that tell me why both of them were so anxious to reach him. This fellow is into some weird doings. I don't know a lot about how doctors muck around with people's brains, but I was under the impression that psychologists don't cut on patients and they don't prescribe medicines. Maybe our Doctor Krevins doesn't understand the rules."

"The documents I snapped tell me he definitely didn't understand or just plain refused to conform," Dan said. "If the psychology ethics cops had this information, they wouldn't just call a hearing, they'd crucify him."

"Got that right," Jud answered.

"Okay, so what do we do with what we've found?"

"First we make sure there's no wiggling off the hook for our man Victor. Then we go for the jugular. There's still the matter of how he translated all his medical smarts into a computerized scheme. Has to be somebody else involved here and we want to make a clean sweep when we pounce for the kill."

That made sense to Dan. If Victor had a partner—and there surely must be a pretty slick computer whiz in this mix somewhere—they had to get both criminals off the street. He needed to be patient as badly as he wanted to prove Krevins the culprit and put him away.

* * *

The jangling of the telephone broke Dan's concentration. He bolted toward the kitchen to answer. Dan insisted there would be no phone in his office to break his focus during writing sessions. That did, however, occasionally make for some impromptu sprints to reach the kitchen wall phone if he was alone in the house. Jud couldn't contain his amusement as Dan bounced off furniture and plummeted out the office door. His stumbling was akin to a replay of his uncoordinated entry into Victor's townhouse last night. Jud couldn't resist the urge. He called after Dan, "Got your shin guards on?"

When he returned to where Jud was working, Dan's appearance had undergone a drastic change. He wore a distinctively ashen look.

"What's wrong? You look sick, man."

"That was Ellen on the phone. Susan had a call from Jason Gernsbach's wife in New Orleans. Jason's dead."

"Run that by me again, Dan. The doc you talked to at the Millwoods' the other night is dead?"

"The same. Drowned in New Orleans. He stepped off the wharf right into the Mississippi River. No one saw him until he floated up next to a paddle wheeler excursion boat. By then he was beyond help."

"I feel like we stepped off something ourselves, like the tip end of the real world," Jud remarked and rubbed his head. "Now we can't get home from wonderland. At this rate we're going to have a serious shortage of psychodocs. What do we know about Gernsbach?"

Dan still appeared to be in shock. "Only that he was a highly regarded doctor and researcher. Fluent lecturer. From my two short encounters with him, a pretty decent guy."

"Any other connections we need to make?"

"Absolutely. I saw him and Victor Krevins in a serious and very public disagreement at the symposium. Krevins was shouting at him. Jason voiced a difference of opinion on clinical procedures but Krevins took it personally. Jason likely had his number, though. Must have known Victor was dancing on the fine edge of professional ethics. I got the notion from our conversation that Jason may suspect old Vic had landed heavily on the wrong side of the ethics line."

"So Krevins had an ax to grind with him?" Jud asked.

"He has a nasty temper. I could see him holding a grudge against Gernsbach for questioning his theories and his methods—but murder?"

CHAPTER 19

Susan Millwood insisted she had to go to New Orleans to comfort her friend Karen Gernsbach. There was no one in the world at the moment that could empathize with what Karen was going through better than Susan.

Ellen convinced Dan that Sue wasn't emotionally ready to take this trip alone. Ellen offered to fly to the Big Easy with her. Susan's parents would come back down for a few days and take care of the Millwood children while she was gone.

"I have an idea," Dan told them. "I'll fly to New Orleans with you. Want to see for myself what took place down there."

Ellen gave him one of those *here we go again* looks, but he knew she would give in.

They picked up a rental car in New Orleans on Tuesday afternoon and checked in at a hotel in the French Quarter. Susan directed Dan toward the Gernsbachs' house. This was going to be another tearful encounter and he wasn't happy about the prospect. He had important plans for the following day, though. When the sad reunion was over he suggested that he and Ellen make a stop for some travel needs. They excused themselves and left Sue and her friend alone.

"Ellen, I'm not going to the funeral with you tomorrow. You can handle those gals a lot better without me tagging along. I'll get another car at the hotel if I need it and strike out on my own. I have a couple of places to go including the police station to read the official report."

"You won't let go of this theory about a conspiracy to kill the doctors, will you?"

"Honey, it's gone far beyond that. Jud and I think we know who's behind at least two deaths and possibly this one as well. I can't stop now."

She registered surprise as if wondering how much he hadn't told her. "What are you two messing around with? Please be careful, Dan. If there's someone who's already killed three men, he wouldn't hesitate to do you and Jud harm."

"We'll watch our step. I'm convinced it's only a matter of time until we'll have them nailed."

Ellen looked uneasy and unconvinced.

* * *

Dan left the hotel the next morning and walked toward the wharf. With the anguish the ladies were facing they deserved to sleep in and start slowly. He wanted to see the accident scene first hand before he read the police version. And the news account indicated Jason's body had first been seen sometime after eight AM. Dan's watch showed seven thirty. This stroll would give him a feel for the dock at this hour.

On the way to dockside Dan made a stop. He wanted one of those sinfully good beignets and some coffee to carry along with him.

The man behind the counter asked, "Coffee light or dark?"

"Uh—dark, please," Dan replied. The counter man grinned and handed him his goodies.

He turned and headed toward Toulouse Street. His first sip of the dark brew told him the mistake he had made. Dan forgot that dark coffee in Louisiana means with chicory. Bitter and strong. The beignet made the taste bearable and there was no doubt he'd be wide awake when he reached the wharf.

He found his way past the benches in the park and onto the pavement dockside. Just ahead lay the Dixie Princess paddle wheeler, tied up and nearly motionless in the low tide. The police barrier was gone after three days but there was an unnerving red X on the wooden plank atop the dock wall. Dan surmised that was the investigators' best estimate as to the point of entry of the drowning victim.

"Terrible thing, what happened here, huh?"

Dan was startled. He'd been standing alone at the water's edge a moment ago. When he wheeled around, a thin, scruffy man with a beard stood beside him staring into the water. Dan had briefly toured the French Quarter last night with Ellen and Susan, up and down Bourbon and Royal Streets and through Jackson Square. Ellen had remarked how many vagrants seemed to be on the streets looking for handouts from tourists. This poor, shaggy man appeared to be one of that army of drifters.

"Yeah, too bad," he managed to reply. "What did you hear about the accident?" Dan decided his question was wasted but why not at least ask?

"Not many folks down here this time o' mornin," the man offered. "Most that is are still sleepin. That's how it was Sunday, too."

"Were you here?"

A knowing grin crossed the derelict's face. "Fer a fact, mister. It was me and my friend seen him walk off that wall. He stopped and emptied his pockets. Then he just stepped right toward that paddle wheel and went under."

"Walked over the edge toward the boat?"

"'Peared to be headed straight fer the big wheel only that first step was a doozy." His drooling giggle sent shivers through Dan. "Come up bobbin like a cork next to the dock couple minutes later."

"So you actually saw him go into the water?"

"Yep. We's worried someun'd think we done him, so I stopped the first gent come by and hollered 'lookee there'. Then me and Pete hightailed it out o' here. Din't want no police askin us questions."

"Did you notice anything odd near this spot? Was anybody else hanging around?"

"Well, they was a wallet layin 'bout where you're standin. We won't 'bout to touch it and get involved. I may drink a bit but I ain't crazy."

Yes, Dan could attest to the fact that the man 'drank a bit'. The odor of alcohol was all around him and there must be vultures with sweeter breath.

The pitiful man looked up at Dan with sad eyes and asked, "Got somethin' for a hungry man?"

He had already anticipated the reason the stranger would approach him and own up to having been on the scene. The vagrant was hurting for a drink and Dan was probably the first potential donor he'd seen this morning. His story could be a totally bogus line he'd manufactured to milk the tourists. But Dan was a soft touch for hard luck cases. He fished out a twenty and pressed it into the man's hand. That would buy him and his friend their daily supply of wine and, maybe, a bite to eat.

"Thanks. Get some breakfast and take care," Dan said. Then as he turned to go, a scrawny hand with ragged fingernails tugged at him.

"Here, mister. He dropped this 'fore he went in. No use to me. Jus' caught my eye."

Dan looked down at the ring the street dweller passed to him. It was a college class ring from a Michigan university. He held it up to the morning light and read the inscription inside—Jason Gernsbach.

* * *

The nearby police station was already buzzing with activity. Looked like they'd hauled in an assortment of hookers and troublemakers on their nightly rounds. Dan approached the desk sergeant and inquired, "If I wanted to see a police report, who would I ask?"

"You'd ask me. What report and why?" The sergeant reached for an antacid and chewed. He clearly had started the day off with an upset and Dan was going to pay for his aggravation.

"There was an accident dockside on Sunday morning. A man drowned next to the excursion boat. I'd like to see the official report."

"Like I said, WHY?" The luck of the draw had sent Dan here at a bad time but he couldn't leave now.

"The victim was a friend of mine and I'd like to see what the officers concluded. I understand the investigation is closed and I assume the report is now a public record."

"Let me see some ID first." The sergeant scowled down from his perch over sagging glasses and belched his dyspeptic impatience.

"Sure." Dan produced his driver's license.

"Says here you're from Florida. Thought you said you was a friend."

"Came in for his funeral, sergeant. The report?"

The policeman's scowl turned to annoyed resignation and he called out, "Hey, Antoine. Get this man's signature and show him the report he's askin' for."

Under a gooseneck lamp, Dan perused the incident sheet and noted that the time of the investigation was 8:20 AM on Sunday, February 24th. A tourist jogging along the wharf had summoned the officers to the accident scene. He stated that two men, possibly vagrants, had hailed him and pointed to the floating body. He immediately called 911 and asked for help. The emergency medical team could get no response and pronounced the victim, a white male approximately 45 years of age, dead at the scene. A large bruise to the temple seemed to indicate the victim had struck one of the pilings where the boat's mooring lines were tied. The blow would have rendered him unconscious.

Items were found strewn on the ground at the sidewalk's edge. The articles included a wallet with documents identifying the individual as Jason Gernsbach, New Orleans address, member of staff of St. Mark's Hospital. There was a gold watch, some change and miscellaneous pocket items. The investigators assumed the victim had purposely placed the articles on the ground before plunging into the water. This fact pointed to a deliberate act of suicide. The low tide and the boat's paddle wheel had blocked the body's path and kept it close to the dock wall. Time of death was estimated to be sometime between six and eight AM. All personal items were returned to the victim's spouse including the open silver penknife inscribed with his initials that he was clutching tightly in his hand. The police closed the case on the coroner's finding of suicide.

Dan returned the report and thanked them for their help. The desk sergeant managed a half-hearted wave as he left the station. Well, Dan thought, they may think it was suicide but I'd bet somewhere there's a computer video file that drove Jason down here. Probably a shot of that dock wall, maybe even the paddle wheel, for him to focus on as he took that fatal step.

* * *

Later at the Gernsbachs' home, a large group met to pay their respects and to celebrate Jason's life. Karen Gernsbach was holding up well under the tragic circumstances. Dan was glad Ellen and Susan could be here to get her through this difficult time.

Ellen eventually broke away from the crowd and cornered Dan on the patio.

"The funeral was a lovely tribute," she told him. "So many of his fellow professionals were there, some from far away. And you see how many people have been in and out here at the house. He obviously was a highly respected man. I can see why Barry and Susan liked both of them so much."

"Must have been a trying day for Jason's wife and Susan. Sue's had more than her share of agony lately. The whole world's turned upside down for her. Why the odd expression, El?"

"I was looking around for someone Susan introduced me to at the service but I don't think he's here. He was a really eerie sort. She said he lives in Tampa. His name is Victor something."

That brought Dan upright in his seat. "Tall fellow that looks like John Carradine?"

"Kung fu? No, this one was creepy."

"Not kung fu. That was David. I mean his old man from the horror flicks."

She mulled that over. "Oh, him. Not a bad description. How did you know?

"Because it must have been Victor Krevins. I've seen him in action."

"That's the name. Krevins," she replied. "Said he was going from here to Kansas City to address a group of psychologists. What do you mean you've seen him in action?"

"He was a speaker at the symposium and he's every bit as odd a duck as you may have thought."

He left it at that. No need for her to dwell on why he had reacted so quickly to her identification. It would only bring up worrisome facts that he didn't want her concerned about. He and Jud would map out their moves and he'd read her in when and if it became necessary. His sidelong glance was met with a probing stare and he was sure the wheels were turning in that pretty head.

Booking as they did at the last minute, they were locked in to an afternoon flight back to Tampa the following day. That wasn't all bad. Maybe Dan could help the girls come down temporarily off their emotional highs of the past few days.

There was time to do justice to the sights and sounds of the French Quarter tonight and have a leisurely outdoor breakfast in the morning. Surely they could sample the blues at Preservation Hall and hear some zydeco music in one of the bars along Royal. May even be time for a ride on the Streetcar Named Desire that ran through the dockside park.

They drove across town to the hotel to prepare for some quiet time and to dress down for their outing.

Before they went sightseeing, though, Dan had an important phone call to make.

* * *

"What's shaking?"

Jud Black seemed momentarily stumped by the voice on the line.

"Oh, it's you, Dan. Found any N'awlins hot spots?"

"No, but I did pick up some interesting information about Jason's alleged accident. Can't get to Gernsbach's computer but I really don't need to. I ran into an eyewitness down at the wharf and I'm convinced this is another standoff murder."

"Tell me what you learned. Then I'll give you a choice bit of info in return."

"The suicide, as the police termed it, took place along the Toulouse Street Wharf early in the morning when it was practically deserted. A jogger saw the body and called the police. Gernsbach was dead before they arrived."

"And the jogger saw him fall in?"

"That's the ironic part. I ran into a wino that said he had gotten the jogger's attention and pointed out the body. It was the derelict that saw Jason walk over the wall and drown. Just like the others Jason was sleepwalking but there was one difference. He stopped to empty his pockets first."

"What makes you believe the so-called eyewitness?"

Dan withdrew the gold ring from his pocket and fingered it as he continued. "He handed me Jason's class ring. On instinct he had picked it up before the jogger came by."

"Sounds as if the score is three to nothing in the assassin's favor. But he could be in for a large surprise. Janine told me she and Wainwright had discussed Victor Krevins on more than one occasion. Wainwright was afraid the ethics board may have credible evidence of wrongdoing by Victor."

"Janine? Is she the doctor's girlfriend you never got around to telling me about? Got something going on there, Studley?"

"Real man eater, that one. But we scientists are sometimes called upon to make heroic sacrifices."

"Yeah, sure. So there's more evidence of Victor bending the rulebook?"

"I'd say shredding it would be a more accurate term. According to Janine, Wainwright was worried that he had let his emotions overshadow his better judgment. He had given Victor a heads up then heard from Barry Millwood. Together his two associates concluded that Victor was beyond their help and deserved whatever sanction was handed out by the ethics board."

Dan rolled that over and shed his shirt, already limp and sticky from the Louisiana heat.

"What else has been going on up in cold country, Jud?"

"I've tried all the tricks I can think of to track the email messages from the computers down there back to their source. Keep hitting dead ends in the routing. There has to be a pretty slick user involved in sending the hidden files. We could be dealing with a clever computer guru. I need some help on this one from my friend in Ocala but I can't get back there until next week."

"Guess who was at the funeral?" Dan asked. "I didn't see him because I was down on the wharf and the police station, but Ellen met Krevins. If this psycho has done what we think he has, Jud, he must be supremely confident he can't be caught. Takes some real gall to bring about a death and then show up for the funeral. Chills me right down to the marrow."

"I think we're agreed whoever did this is a cold, calculating maniac capable of just about anything."

"What do you think about my trying to make contact with the doctor himself and fish for clinchers?"

"Sounds pretty dangerous to me, Dan. From what we've learned so far, he doesn't appear inclined to hold back once he's been crossed. Three men seem to have made that fatal error."

"But we need to nail him to the wall and soon. Who knows what plans he may have for other poor souls. As we speak he could be experimenting with more human test subjects."

"Just be cool, Dan, if you have to do this. Don't overplay and set him off. You've seen his temper."

"I can handle it. This will be a low-key interview as a writer interested in exploring his revolutionary research in behavior control. He'll eat that up. I'll feed his ego and see where it takes us."

"Okay. I'll be there as soon as I can break loose from some unfinished business. Have to get the latest Jenny's Riddle release wrapped up and on the market. Then I can concentrate on cleaning up this other business you and I have uncovered."

"You need to bring me up to speed on your music. We've been so busy chasing our butts in circles, we haven't sat down and just had a relaxed conversation about your recording."

"That's gonna be a long story. Maybe three or four beers long. When things cool a bit I'll fill you in on how us independent artists spread our music message."

"Ellen and I get back to Tampa tomorrow. Can't corner Krevins for a few days since he's supposed to be out of town at some gathering in Kansas City."

"Then let's work both sides of the street, Dan. I'll fly down on Tuesday and spend a couple days. Then I have to go up to Gainesville to see if Sam and I can crack this Internet dead end. When I get back to your place you can fill me in on the results of your encounter with Mr. Wonderful."

"Sounds fine."

"Oh, before you go, get a pencil and copy down some instructions."

"Instructions for what, Jud?" Dan looked for something to write on.

"We forgot one loop in our search of Barry Millwood's office computer. What if he saved email messages in his download section that we haven't seen? Normally, no one, including me, would think to look for goodies there. Let me tell you how to find them and make copies. Just don't stare at the screen for long."

The procedures Jud dictated all sounded like they were in a foreign tongue but he was very precise. Dan thought he could follow the sequences and capture anything they'd missed before. That would be one of his first actions after they reached Tampa.

"We have each other's cell phone numbers so let's stay in touch, Dan. Could be we're on a fast track now. Give my love to Ellen. See you Tuesday."

A new surge of adrenaline coursed through Dan.

CHAPTER 20

All the way back to Tampa Dan's head filled with conflicting emotions and annoying questions. He wanted this affair settled. On the one hand he wanted to personally exact revenge on whoever had masterminded the assassinations. But he also needed to be sure no one else was ever put in jeopardy by the criminal minds that had hatched this insidious scheme.

There had to be payback for Barry and Marge and for the others who had been hurt. Dan understood, though, that wouldn't put it to rest unless the technical mind behind the computer tampering was collared. He would just keep telling himself to have patience in the face of his almost unreasonable rage. Had to stay busy chasing every possible avenue for resolution.

By the time their flight landed Dan had decided on his next step. He found his parked car and loaded their bags, then turned to Ellen and handed her the keys.

"You drive and drop me at Doctor Sherman's office. There's something I need to check. I'll catch a cab home."

She looked perturbed as if to say *give it a rest.* But she must know by now he wouldn't stop pressing until he had all the answers he needed. No point in arguing with headstrong Dan in his present state of mind. He was hell bent on wading his way through this dilemma.

"When you talked to Victor Krevins, did he say how long he would be out of town?"

Ellen shook her head but Sue answered. "The meeting in Kansas City runs through tomorrow. He should be back in town over the weekend. I only remember because Barry had planned to . . ." She stopped in mid-sentence and fell silent for the remainder of their trip to Clearwater.

Fine, then he would leave a message and hope to get on Krevins' schedule one day next week. If he dangled the right bait, maybe Victor would agree to see him. He'd have to build an enticing story to trap Krevins.

* * *

The receptionist told him Doctor Sherman was between patients. Dan had her announce him and Tom told her to send him in.

"Have a minute, Tom? I get the impression you're a busy man."

"Hi, Dan. Still hectic around here since we lost Barry. We've been *up to our ears in busy.* It's a good thing Pete's here to help out."

"Pete? Oh, the doctoral candidate. Krevins' protégé."

"With Marge gone, too, he's the only link I have to Barry's patients. What can I do for you, Dan?"

"I won't take but a moment. Just like to get your okay to look for something in Barry's office."

"Fine with me. Do you have the password for his computer?"

"Sure thing." Dan went in and closed the door behind him to guard against prying eyes.

Now if he could perform the sequence of keystrokes Jud had written down for him, he may have more important data to report back to his pal. Tom had left the machine off even though they had assured him there was no danger in letting it run. Dan pulled out his cheat sheet, fired up the computer and carefully followed the steps on the paper.

Jud was right again. There in the saved email was the Secret Treasures message with its mind twisting attachments. In addition, Barry had kept an exchange with Jason in which they had expressed concern to each other about their suspicions regarding Victor Krevins. The exchange had taken place only days before Barry's plunge from the bridge. Dan copied the files to a diskette. He knew the hidden video attachment was too large to copy without a long CD write process, but he did capture the audio file. Now they could establish that Marge's killer could have been in Barry's office on Saturday with his computer turned on to erase files. But how did he miss these? Had Marge's arrival interrupt him?

* * *

Ellen and Susan were laughing as the sun set and they turned up the driveway in Safety Harbor. It was good to see Susan finally brighten. Even when they were cruising around the streets of New Orleans it was as if she was with them in body only and was going through the motions. This was the first time Ellen had heard Susan laugh since before that terrible morning when they clung to each other and mourned the loss of Barry. They were beginning to slowly make progress in getting her to move on and live.

"Stop by for awhile, Ellen. Dan could be some time getting home. We can put our feet up and unwind."

They walked to the front door and found it unlocked. They saw no lights in the house except for a dim glow from the den office. Even that faded before she turned the doorknob.

"That's odd. Why would they be sitting in the dark?"

Ellen stepped inside and Susan followed, reaching for the wall switch. A blurred image flashed by Ellen and shoved her to the floor. There was the sound of scuffling above her. The hall light momentarily flickered on then went out. In the darkness Ellen couldn't make out what was happening. She heard a loud thump and Susan moaned and dropped beside her.

Now Ellen was panic stricken. Someone was viciously attacking them. She had to find a way to mount a defense. Got her feet planted and lunged toward the dark figure in front of her. Her momentum propelled the attacker against the wall plate. An overhead light sprang to life. Ellen was still woozy from her fall but she could make out the bleary form of a man struggling to reach the front door. She locked her arms tightly around his legs. Her shoulder hurt from the force of their impact. He tugged to shake her loose. Ellen caught a silvery glint then a soft blue glow; some indistinct parts of the fleeing form. That was her last conscious thought. A sudden burst of pain sent her spiraling into darkness.

* * *

Ellen slowly returned to her senses. Her head hurt and she still wasn't seeing clearly even in the stark brightness of the foyer. She reached out toward the figure lying next to her.

"Sue. Are you hurt? Talk to me, Sue."

Susan wasn't moving and she didn't answer. Ellen's eyes began to focus. She was confronted with a horrifying sight. Susan lay with her head against the foot of the hall table resting in a pool of blood. When the intruder struck her she must have fallen heavily. Could have hit the table's corner and suffered a serious wound.

"Honey, wake up. Speak to me. Oh, God, please speak to me!"

Ellen already knew the awful truth. Susan couldn't answer—now or ever. She felt for a pulse and found none. Her first impulse was to hold Susan in her arms and cry uncontrollably but she was aware this called for action and not to giving in to emotions.

She found her purse and fumbled through it for the cell phone. Punching in 9-1-1, she forced herself to a sitting position and formed the words.

"310 Palm Drive. Safety Harbor."

She heard a voice ask, "What is the nature of your problem?"

"Mugged. Hurry."

"Are you injured?" the dispatcher asked.

"She's hurt! My friend is hurt!"

Ellen dropped the phone and cradled Susan closer to her. She felt a warm haze descend around her and slowly slid into the void, one arm holding her motionless friend with Susan's bloody head on her lap.

* * *

Dan's taxi rolled up to the Trinity neighborhood gate. He had been in such a hurry to take a look at Barry's computer that it hadn't entered his mind the gate would be secured by this time of night. His opener was in the car with Ellen. He told the driver to scroll to the name Cooper on the gate call box. Ellen would activate the gate for them to enter. But there was no answer. Probably still gabbing at Sue's house. Dan dug in his wallet and came up with a card he had written the entry code on weeks ago. Handed it to the driver to punch in the numbers.

He wondered what could be keeping Ellen so long. She had told him how fatigued she was after their whirlwind trip. Said she just wanted to get home and relax after a trying week. He walked into the dark house and went directly to the kitchen phone.

Susan's mother answered.

"This is Dan Cooper. Is my wife still there?"

Her voice filled with panic as she answered, "Oh, Dan, finally!"

"What's wrong?" He could hear her crying. She tried to continue.

"Sue and Ellen . . ." His first thought was that there had been an auto accident. *Please let them be all right* he silently pled.

"Where are they?"

"Ellen's in Meadows Hospital. Sue is . . . is . . ." He was afraid he knew the rest.

"I'm on my way."

He raced to find Ellen's spare keys and kicked her car into action. As he sped down the highway toward the hospital, all sorts of chilling thoughts hounded him. What was he facing when he reached Ellen's side? Was his darling lying there only clinging to life? Why hadn't he been with them instead of on a side trip that could have waited for another day? Damn, damn, damn.

* * *

Susan was awake but groggy when he rushed into her hospital room. She managed a weak smile for him and he bent to kiss her. The nurse stood nearby with a somber look of concern.

"Honey, I should have been with you. I'm sorry."

"Not your fault," she said and it came out barely above a whisper. "Sue's hurt."

The tears welled up in her eyes and the nurse urged him from the bedside while she checked her IV drip. Ellen was working hard to stay awake but her eyes kept closing. The doctor appeared and took Dan aside.

"She's had a rough time of it. Took a nasty blow to the head so the nurse is trying to keep her awake. The best thing for her right now is for you to talk to her and keep her aware of her surroundings until the shock subsides."

"You couldn't tear me away with an army, Doctor. I'm here to stay. Tell me what happened."

"There'll be plenty of time for that later. Just keep her company now and I'll be by later to fill you in. You need to know she still hasn't accepted the fact that her friend is dead."

Dan pulled up a chair beside her bed and took Ellen's hand in his. He had been so caught up in chasing a mad doctor and his partners in crime that he had lost track of what really mattered to him. Lying here fighting a mortal battle was the centerpiece of his life. He couldn't let her be taken this way. He wouldn't let it happen. Every time her eyes fluttered closed he picked up the volume and talked to her faster.

"El, honey, I need you to keep me sane in this world turned on end. You give everything purpose. Hang tough, baby, for both of us."

He couldn't tell whether she heard him but he'd keep on talking non-stop if that was what it took. Maybe if he gave her happy memories to hold onto she'd fight harder. Dan prattled on about everything that came to mind. Occasionally there seemed to be the hint of a smile on her lips. She closed her eyes periodically, a gesture that renewed his determination to keep flooding her with good thoughts to keep her awake.

Sometime during the night he felt the touch of a hand on his shoulder and bolted into a rigid sitting position, his hand pressing Ellen's and his words spilling out.

"You remember the time we went up to the cabin in the mountains . . ." It was as if he had only stopped to catch his breath before continuing.

"Guess she finally wore you out, Mr. Cooper. She appears to be resting comfortably now. You kept her alert until the initial danger was past. Now we can let her have some sleep." The doctor was standing over him.

"Can you tell me what's going on here, doctor? I've dreamed up all kinds of bad scenes in my mind."

"The way I understand the sequence of events, she and her friend returned to what they must have thought was an empty house just after dark. The grandparents had taken the two teens out for dinner and didn't return until shortly after the EMT team arrived on the scene."

"But they took a beating," Dan interrupted.

"Police believe a prowler was in the house and attacked both of them in the foyer as they entered," Doctor Lake continued. "Mrs. Cooper sustained a blunt object blow to the head and must have lost consciousness at least temporarily. She revived long enough to call 911for help but was unconscious when the emergency team reached the house. The good news is I believe she's past the crisis now and it's a waiting game for us. We have to help her heal gradually."

"And what about Susan Millwood?"

"Mrs. Millwood had two wounds. She had head trauma from a blunt object. Then she apparently fell and struck a table with her temple. Either impact could have been fatal. She likely died almost instantly. Your wife was holding her in her arms and covered with her blood when the police responded."

Dan pictured the grief his wife must have felt with her best friend lying there bleeding when there was nothing she could do for her. Now they both had experienced that painful moment of realizing the loss of someone so close they were hard to replace in your life. He could think of only one person who was closer to them than their dear friends—Danielle.

Of course, Danielle! What had he been thinking? She needed to know her mother was hurt. Maybe now he could tell her that Mom was out of danger but she eventually had to hear the whole shocking story.

"I suggest you go home and try to sleep," the doctor was telling him when he snapped back to full awareness. "You can come back in tomorrow and stay as long as you like. She should be more alert by then."

Dan acknowledged his words and bent to kiss Ellen. "Rest easy, sweetie. I'll be back in a few hours. I love you."

He was aware this was an unusual hour to be calling Danielle. She would be immediately concerned when she heard his voice well past midnight. But it had to be done. There was so much of her mother in Danielle that he could trust her to hold it together in the face of the terrible news. Despite the doctor's encouraging report, he felt she should be here for Ellen.

"Danielle, it's Dad. Honey, we have a problem here. Mom needs you."

* * *

Before he went home, he had to put his mind to rest about one more matter. He dialed the Millwood house and a sleepy Grandpa answered.

"Mister Jergens, this is Dan Cooper. I know it's terribly late, but I have to come by the house if that's possible. I think it could be important for both Susan and Barry and help me find their killers."

"It's been a long night, Dan, but if you think it's necessary, come on over. I can't sleep, anyway. I'll put on the coffee pot."

Jergens stood in the doorway by the time Dan turned off his car lights. He stepped out onto the stoop and said, "Let's try to avoid waking anybody else. They're all cried out and exhausted. I can't believe the horrible things that have happened to this family."

They walked quietly to the den office and closed the door. It was time Sue's father was aware of the real nature of the misfortunes his daughter and son-in-law had suffered. Grandpa was hurting and once again Dan's mind turned to his precious Danielle and how devastated he would be to lose her. That was an ugly vision he couldn't bear to dwell on.

"Please keep this between us, but I have reason to believe Barry was driven to leap from the bridge and we know Sue was killed. There are at least two other deaths I can tie to circumstances similar to Barry's. If I confirm my suspicion by scanning this computer, I'll know tonight was a part of the same plan."

He pulled the sheet of paper with Jud's prompts from his pocket and brought the computer up. Then he remembered to take a necessary precaution.

"Don't look at the screen until I tell you. I'll explain why later." Jergens crossed to the easy chair and sat patiently.

Maybe he was beginning to get a feel for computers. With the proper instruction from Jud he may yet rise above the rank of klutz where these mysterious machines were concerned. He methodically searched and found, or more correctly didn't find, what he was looking for.

"Now you can watch." Jergens came and stood at his shoulder. "Don't know how computer literate you may be, so let me explain. Do you know what a daemon is?"

"Assume I know nothing about those things and you'll be close to right."

"A daemon is a file that can be put onto a computer that will cause recurring things to happen—acknowledge authority to access Internet sites, prompt routine operations to be performed. In this particular case, two daemons were placed on Barry's computer without his knowledge. Every time he turned the machine on, the daemons brought up two hidden files and played a sequence of visual images and a low level audio over and over."

"I think I follow so far. What do those files do?"

"We believe they drove him subconsciously to go to the Skyway Bridge and jump to his death without knowing what he was doing. Barry wasn't a suicide, he was purposefully and brutally murdered as surely as if someone had stood over him and pushed him off that bridge. Two other victims in Washington and New Orleans were murdered in the same fashion."

Grandpa emitted a soft whistle. "It's mind boggling, isn't it?"

"Exactly. Mind-boggling is precisely what the criminals behind this plot are doing. The victims never had a clue what was happening to them. It was all in their subconscious. If it's the last thing I ever do, I intend to nail the people that did this."

"But what does that have to do with Sue being attacked?"

"I asked you to not look at the computer screen because I assumed the daemons that we found on this machine earlier were still there. We kept it turned off so they couldn't be erased. No one has had access to the computer until tonight. The intruder broke in to get physical access to the machine and deleted those files. An exchange of emails the trespasser didn't know we had found is also missing. Whoever killed Barry is also responsible for Sue's death and I'm bound and determined to catch them. I know it won't bring either of them back but at least they'll be revenged."

Dan was weary and his nerves were ragged as he drove home and flopped atop his bed. He desperately needed a few hours of rest before returning to Ellen's side. A nagging notion kept rolling around in his head and he couldn't get hold of it. He was about to nod off when it finally came together.

He sat up in bed and wrinkled his brow. "It couldn't be Victor. He's out of town."

CHAPTER 21

Dan set out for the hospital for his daily vigil. Yesterday he had spent every waking hour by Ellen's bed. He didn't want her to need anything and find he wasn't there. She did appear to be coming around and acknowledging most of what he was saying to her, but the doctor had cautioned her to save her voice.

He had so many questions to ask Ellen, not the least of which involved whether she could identify her attacker. But one of the side effects of the blow to her head was difficulty in forming words and speaking clearly so he listened to the doctor's advice and didn't push her.

"Yes, I'm concerned that she's not speaking yet, Dan," the doctor agreed. "What's even more worrisome is that she appears to have only limited motor ability. There's no paralysis but her limbs don't seem to be responding to her mind's commands. We'll have to start physical therapy if that continues. The best case is that her coordination begins to return on its own."

"Do whatever's necessary. I need her whole and happy again. What could cause what she's going through?"

"I have lab tests working to determine that. We see no skeletal damage or obvious trauma from the blow she took so it's subtler than that. We'll pin it down. Keep thinking good thoughts for her sake."

Dan thrust out his hand and thanked him for his efforts. He turned and went into the room to stand by the bed. Ellen opened her eyes and smiled weakly at him. He took her small, delicate hand in his as he spoke.

"Just let me do the talking, sweetheart. Your job is to follow the doctor's orders and regain your strength. Danielle is making sure everything is taken care of at the house and she'll be in to see you later."

She tried so hard to speak but he placed a finger softly to her lips and moved his head slowly side to side.

"You know by now that Sue wasn't as fortunate as you. Mercifully, it was over quickly for her. You did everything you could to help her."

His wife struggled to form an answer and a single tear rolled down her cheek. He cautioned her once again.

"Relax, honey. Doc will get you back on your feet and we can talk then."

God, it hurt to see her lying there. Unable to make her body do what her mind wanted; her frustration mounting with each failure. Such a vibrant woman. He envied her energy level. When she set her mind to do something, she did it. Had to run to keep pace with her.

This was getting out of hand. He was caught in a maelstrom. The whole world was spinning madly. Barry was gone. Susan was brutally killed. Now Ellen. If she didn't make it, his sanity would be gone with her. Might as well take him away, too.

She was trying to draw his attention to something. It was clearly a struggle for her.

"Slow down. Take it easy, Ellen," he cautioned.

He felt so small and helpless. Paced around the room and his ragged nerves took over. Danielle was doing her best to keep his mind off the horrible events. But he felt surrounded, smothered. Wanted to lash out and fight back, but at what or who?

Dan heard the rustle of the bed sheets. There was a guttural sound like a grunt.

"Honey, don't exert yourself," he chided and drew close to her.

With great effort she moved one hand in a slow circular motion. Dan was trying to interpret her movement, overjoyed that she was finding it possible to move her limb. Then he realized her fingers were formed as if she were holding a writing instrument.

"You want to write something?" She made enough of a head movement to answer him and her eyes sparkled.

He remembered the doctor's hope that she would find a way to effect movement on her own. His adrenaline was surging. Dan reached for his ballpoint and searched for a way for her to write. Lifted the patient chart from the foot of her bed and placed the metal board under her hand for support. A get well card from Johnny and Carol Millwood was lying on the night stand. He turned the card over to the blank side and slid it under her fingers. She worked to hold the pen.

"Slowly, now. Take your time."

The effort involved was a severe test of will power. He had often told her that for such a small woman she packed a mighty load of determination. In this case it could more appropriately be termed sheer stubbornness. She was bound to give him her message. Her jaw was set and her eyelids squeezed tightly shut until tears trickled down her cheeks. Slowly, the pen moved in a scrawl across the card. He steadied her hand to aid her grip. The letters were shaky but readable.

"I see, baby. M . . . A. Your attacker was a man?"

She opened her moist eyes and curled up the corners of her mouth. This may work. How far could he let her go before she exhausted herself? *Come on, Dan. You know she'll stop when she's good and ready. She's hell bent on telling you something.*

The small hand tensed and managed to move the pen in a wavy upward line, then added a curved line atop it that resembled a jagged downward grimace. Dan thought hard then grabbed at the first thing that came to mind.

"Up? High? A *tall* man." He felt like he was playing charades but they were getting somewhere.

An almost imperceptible head nod seemed to confirm he had guessed right.

Her fingers worked to keep the pen from slipping. She forced it to form another set of scrawled markings. Then her grip failed and the pen fell.

"B . . . L . . . U. What is this last letter? E? Blue?" With a feeble smile playing at her lips, her eyes faded and she closed her lids. He would have to be content to hold her hand and talk to her while she enjoyed a well-earned rest. It was a small victory but he was heartened to see that Ellen was fighting to come back to him.

Much later he felt a presence in the room and turned to find Danielle.

"Hi, Daddy. How's Mom?"

"She communicated with me today—sort of." His daughter perked up at that news.

"Her voice is returning?"

"Not yet. But she managed to scribble some words and nodded for me. Her movement is slowly coming back."

"What did her notes say?"

"I now know that it was a tall man who attacked her and Susan. There was something about him that made her remember the color blue. It's a start."

"Maybe blue eyes? A blue shirt?"

"Don't know. I can see the wall slowly breaking down. Mom is clawing her way back to us. In my heart I know she's going to be okay." Dan thought how desperately he needed to believe that.

"You go and eat dinner, Daddy. Let me look after her and you get some sleep."

What was there about a color that was so important to Ellen? The gangly Victor Krevins certainly filled the bill as a 'tall man.' Dan was happy for what she had been able to give him. Now he would have to wait until she came around and was able to tell him more.

Then a sobering thought returned and smacked him hard. Victor couldn't have been at the Millwood house. He was still in Kansas City. Or at least he was supposed to be there. That was something Dan couldn't confirm until the school offices reopened on Monday.

If not Krevins, then who? It could be that the sudden attack was a random act with no connection to what he and Jud were investigating. A burglar? If so, then why was the computer turned on when Dan knew it had been sitting silent at his request? An even more frightening possibility was that there was another person involved in Victor's scheme. That may or may not be the computer whiz they were trying to track down. Maybe the odds were increasing. How many bad guys were they pitted against?

He was going to stay on this like an angry pit bull until someone paid and paid dearly. There would be total and final reprisal for Barry, Marge and Susan. He had a special fate planned for whoever had dared to harm his darling Ellen. His plan had something to do with separating limbs from torso.

CHAPTER 22

What a crappy day this had been. Paula couldn't wait to escape from Crash and Burn and lay some hurts on her poker partners. Sam had agreed to meet her around the corner from Connie's place before the game started so she could discuss something with him. She was certain she could count on his cooperation in a little experiment.

At the moment, one of the youngsters at work was having trouble with his assigned section of code on a new program. Although he didn't know it, Paula already had the code written. She had only given him this task to see if he had any talent or was just another of those pimple-faced ciphers that rotated through this piss ant company.

"Can't put my finger on it, Miss Taylor. Just can't run down what's wrong here. Maybe it'll be obvious to you."

It was obvious. The little toad wasn't even in the ballpark. Just as she thought—another loser. Why did her day have to be populated with jerks; immature lunks who addressed her as 'Miss Taylor' and didn't know their ass from second base?

Her alter ego Athena would have had a forceful answer for him. Athena would have hoisted him on a verbal lance so sharp he would have thought long and hard about coming whimpering to her again. However, Paula knew she had to bite her cheek and make nice.

"Try this," she said with honey in her voice and the neophyte programmer felt anointed. He went away mumbling his thanks and missed her whispered dismissal.

"Pitifully dumb."

Soon she could turn her back on this boring routine and occupy herself with more challenging work. Tonight would be her first foray into an exciting new world.

* * *

Paula stood beside the car on a back street in Ocala, the night air rippling through her hair. Her hacker friend approached on foot and crooned his greeting.

"Hi, doll."

"Thanks for meeting me early, Sam. I wanted to set up a little ruse with you before we join the others. Should be fun to watch their reactions."

"Anything for you, sweets. What do you have in mind, Athe . . . . I mean Paula."

"Damnit, Sam! You've *gotta* be more careful than that. Our other lives don't exist on poker night. I'm just plain old Paula here."

"You should never use plain and Paula in the same sentence, chicky." He flashed a big grin.

"No sale, Sam. Pay attention now. I want to lay a story on the group and see if any of them bite. My real target is Fred so help out when I give you an opening."

"Is that it? Wanta tell me more?"

"Let's keep it a surprise to everybody. It'll be more fun."

He shrugged and they moved on to Connie's house.

Four men and two women for a long night of serious poker. Connie and Paula added some female beauty to the gathering. Sam, Fred and two other male regulars completed the table. Paula tossed the bag with the pork skins to Fred. She winked as he checked to see they were his customary card night ambrosia.

"Hope you brought lots of green stuff, guys. I feel lucky tonight," Paula taunted.

"Thanks for the goodies," Fred said and lit his cigar.

"Do you have to smoke that disgusting thing?" Connie asked him.

"Hell, I was thinking about having one myself," Paula chided. Fred fished another cigar out of his shirt pocket and tossed it to her.

"That's what I like about you, Paula. You're just one of the guys. Sometimes I wonder if you're really a Paul or a Bill under those slacks."

"Speculate all you want, buster. But if I catch your arm on my side of the table, I'll break it off at the socket."

Sam looked around, first at her then at the others, and smiled. "In case any of you think she can't do it, I'll cover all bets."

There was a moment of nervous silence before Fred choked on his cigar, coughed and expelled a loud guffaw.

"Get it up, folks. Feed the kitty," Connie prompted. She tossed in her ante and dealt the cards.

They were well into their session and Paula was actually up a few dollars when she tested the waters. Her remarks were issued to the group in general but she was waiting to hear how Fred in particular would respond. It was a poorly kept secret that he had connections with a rather questionable crowd. Paula suspected he knew his way around on the dark side of the law.

Paula said, "Friend of mine hit me up with an unusual concept the other day. You know, one of those software types at Crash and Burn. Wonder if it sounds as queer to you guys as it did to me."

She took a pull on her filter Kool and a large swallow of Coors. The cigar Fred had provided was long since discarded after the group shock effect wore off.

Sam came in right on cue as if they had actually rehearsed.

"Most of that crowd is a little queer to begin with. What was it?"

"Hey, some of us bitheads resemble that remark," Paula shrieked and threw a peanut at him.

"Come on, kiddies," Connie admonished. "This is serious poker here. Your move, Paula."

Paula called the bet and continued. "Anyway, it was a really wild idea. My friend wondered what kind of client list she could build for a scheme she's developed. It would guarantee hands-off, remote control assassinations over the Internet."

"What the f . . . ," Fred stammered. "That's the weirdest thing I ever heard. How can you whack a guy by remote control?"

All right. She had Fred's attention. Now it was time to go for the kill.

"Here's how it works. A client would pick a target individual and hire her to make the hit. She'd prompt the target electronically to take a specific action that leads to his death. Wouldn't have to come within miles of him. Swears it's entirely doable. The client pays only after the target is confirmed dead. Sounds like a nice clean, risk free way to remove nuisances."

"Wow! Long-distance contracting," Sam interjected. "A new era in arranging a hit."

"Exactly. This method leaves no way to tie back to either the client or the contractor. The target appears to have an accident or commit suicide—say jump off the side of a mountain, walk into deep water and drown, maybe step out onto a busy Interstate Highway."

Sam picked up the baton to keep the conversation going. He winked at Paula and she figured he was warming up to toying with their minds. It was okay if Sam thought she really was playing a game. Whatever kept Fred's interest would be fine with her.

"How does the Internet play in this thing, Paula? Does it send him an electrical shock or something?" Sam chuckled.

"Not exactly. Have any of you ever read about the scare back in the fifties over something called subliminal persuasion? It was the hot topic for awhile I'm told. People were afraid they were being prodded in movie houses to buy Coke, eat Twinkies, drive a Ford, whatever an advertiser wanted them to do. The whole idea was that an instantaneous message could be added to a film track that would flicker repeatedly on and off the screen. This all happened so quickly that the unconscious part of the mind saw the message but it never registered in people's conscious eyesight."

"Sounds like when my wife slips something past me and I don't know it for days," one of the players quipped. A ripple of laughter around the table.

"Not exactly. Point is you remember this; you just don't know why. This gal claims she knows how to use an improved version of SP. It would cause a target to take a single preprogrammed fatal action that would serve the same purpose as a face-to-face hired hit. Far out, huh?"

"But why would this friend of yours talk to anybody about her plans?" Fred asked. "Hell, this ain't legal, baby."

"No shit, Fred. She's a little weird. Probably thought I'd figure she was pulling my leg but I believe she's dead serious. It's too far fetched to be made up."

Fred looked at her as if he wanted to say something but Connie interrupted him.

She set down a new round of suds and said, "When you're finished with your shaggy dog story, Paula, can we get back to serious poker? I'm playing catch up."

The seed was planted. Paula could see that Fred was digesting her words. Best for her to move on for now.

"There's no punch line. Just amused me that someone would hatch such a wild scheme. I wondered what you guys would think."

One of the players mumbled, "I think it sucks. Deal."

Not until the game broke up much later was Paula sure she had gotten her point across fully to her target Fred. He approached her as they headed for their cars.

"Say I knew somebody who was interested in that SM thing. How would he go about contacting your friend?" The fish had swallowed the worm.

"SP," she corrected. "Let me give you a telephone number. I understand my friend is at the number every evening."

What she wrote down was actually a covert telephone arrangement she kept for special purposes. Any calls placed to that number would go to a cutout location and be automatically relayed through to the telephone at her apartment in Gainesville. Hopefully, she had just gone into business for herself.

"My friend answers to the name Minerva," she said and turned away, a broad smile lighting up her face.

CHAPTER 23

A call to Doctor Krevins' campus office on Monday morning verified that Victor had, indeed, returned from his trip just this morning. Dan introduced himself to the doctor as a local writer named Dan Polk. He said he was interested in publicizing the doctor's revolutionary research to the general public. The response from Krevins was rapid and enthusiastic.

"I'd be happy to meet with you if you're flexible as to time. My schedule is rather full."

"I appreciate that, doctor. You name the time. I have several medical publications in mind that would love to spread the word about this exciting work."

Dan enjoyed reeling in the egotistical genius. Fact was, he had no intention of submitting the results of his interview to *any* magazine, let alone *several* of them. If he was correct about the doctor's moonlight activities, Krevins' own words would be used to tighten a noose around his scrawny neck. By the time Krevins learned he'd been taken for a one-way ride, it would be too late for him to retaliate.

"The next four days will be extremely busy for me, but I could meet with you, let's see . . . Thursday late in the afternoon. Say five o'clock?" Victor offered. "I live near the campus. We could talk in a more relaxed atmosphere at my home."

That would be interesting, Dan thought. Talk about returning to the scene of the crime. He wondered what that townhouse actually looked like in the light of day.

"You don't know how much I appreciate your carving out time for me, Doctor. I understand you have a story to tell about some startling advances in brain research."

Dan was careful to ask for precise directions to the doctor's house and inquire what type of home he was looking for. He wanted it to appear he was completely unfamiliar with that section of town. Krevins painstakingly directed him from Clearwater across the bay to his neighborhood.

"Thank you, sir. I'll be there promptly at five o'clock as you ask. I'm honored to have this opportunity."

* * *

Dan made his daily visit to the hospital to see how Ellen was progressing. He admitted to himself that his visits were as much for his own benefit as to lift her spirits. Without her to warm his day it wasn't much worth getting out of bed. During those first days after the attack he was frightened he would lose her, but the situation was slowly improving. Danielle reluctantly agreed to get back to her husband and her job. Daddy would take up the full time watch. It was only a matter of time for Mom's healing to occur at its own pace.

Ellen was looking better and she was regaining control of her muscles. The highlight of his visit was when she urged him closer and unexpectedly curled her arms around him for an enthusiastic but slightly unsteady hug. An after effect of her injury and the liquids she was receiving had been a slight swelling of her glands. The doctor had strictly forbidden her to speak until the swelling subsided. But, oh, how wonderful those slender arms felt around his neck.

"Doc says I shouldn't press you for answers, El. We'll have time for that when your throat is back to normal."

She patted his hand and he lightly touched her lips with his. She formed the words *love you.* Dan was content to wait for as long as it took for her to speak to him. Those were the only two words that mattered, anyway.

* * *

When he drew up in front of the row of townhouses on Thursday, Dan scanned the neatly manicured neighborhood that shouted affluence. An assortment of Jaguars and Mercedes sat in the driveways. No children in sight anywhere. He catalogued this as a locale handy to midtown for professionals and well-heeled retirees. On his first visit his most lasting impressions had been a row of high rear fences, a heavy flop in the bushes and a hurried search. The interruption occasioned by Victor's return that night hadn't left time for more than a frantic exit and a sprint to safety.

Krevins answered the door, his lanky frame a bit stooped. But his piercing eyes were as probing as the last time Dan saw him.

"Mr. Polk? Victor Krevins. Come in, please." Dan saw a flicker of something in his gaze, perhaps a hint of recognition? The doctor quickly recovered and showed him to his office.

Dan opened with, "As I told you, I contribute to a number of magazines including some of the medical publications. Your research has come to my attention and I believe the public needs to hear about your pioneering work with the brain."

"Which of the periodicals do you have in mind?"

This was probably a probe for credibility but Dan had prepared a response. He rattled off the names of three of the medically oriented pubs he had seen in Barry's waiting room. Dan professed to be known by their editors. That seemed to satisfy Victor that he was on the up and up.

"Just where would you like to begin," Krevins asked. The tall man straightened and struck an imposing stance behind his desk.

Dan's mind flashed back to the recent night when Jud had sat in that high backed chair and coaxed Victor's deepest secrets from the machine on the doctor's credenza. Dan had no indication yet that the tall, intense man facing him was aware how totally he had been violated. The information they gathered that night had exposed Victor Krevins to their intense scrutiny and suspicion. That knowledge would be Dan's advantage in the conversation to follow. Krevins only thought he knew the reason for the interview. Dan would be evaluating everything Victor said on two very different levels—his actual words and their implications regarding his possible guilt as a multiple murderer.

"Why don't you give me an overview of your clinical work, Doctor. Tell me about your goals and where you are in reaching them."

Victor drew himself up to his full stature and said in his most officious tone, "I'll try to keep this at the layman's level. My work is very complex."

Conceited ass, Dan thought, and gave him a mental one-finger salute.

"Oh, I'll stop you if you get too deep for me. I do have a biological sciences background and I'm also an engineer. Don't hold back too severely. I would like to record you, though."

That may have been an invitation to overload but let him talk. Dan never intended to use the material, anyway, except to hang the spooky bastard. Let him rave on and Dan would make the most of it.

Victor took his statement as an open license to mount his soapbox. He spun off into areas that were so foreign to Dan he could scarcely connect them with his original question about overview and goals. He merely nodded agreement at what seemed to be the appropriate points in Victor's diatribe. Dan tried to look interested to the point of fascination. He wrote furiously on his pad, taking down nearly every word Krevins spoke, even though the recorder was running. At the expense of looking somewhat uninitiated at times on the subject of the brain, Dan even threw in relatively safe requests for clarification. Victor continued his flight of self-aggrandizement and his indictment of associates for not recognizing his genius.

"Do any of your tests in the laboratory involve human subjects?" Dan inquired.

Krevins seemed to carefully consider his answer before he replied.

"I've lobbied for permission to extend the testing to volunteers. There are many shortsighted people in my profession. They're too squeamish to push the envelope. Without their sanction I must avoid my instincts to enlist human subjects. This significantly slows the pace of my progress."

Yeah, I hear you Crazy Vic, the little voice inside Dan mocked. *What about the volunteers you bribed off the back streets and pumped who knows what into in the name of science? How many of them never returned to the streets or anywhere else as breathing, functioning human beings?*

On and on the doctor droned about the importance of his astounding discoveries hampered only by the ill-conceived conservatism of the psychology community. The more vocal he became, the more animated Dan was in encouraging his outrage. By the time Krevins finally began to wind down, his face was livid. His delivery had increased several decibels above reasoned discussion. Victor was a man on a crusade, the Don Quixote of psychology misunderstood and taken for granted by fellow practitioners of the art.

Krevins struck the desk with his fist time and again and his eyes were transformed to white-hot reservoirs of contempt. Dan's worst fears had been verified. He was dealing with a man so focused on his quest that he teetered on the verge of insanity. Barry had certainly been square on when his jotted note had labeled him Crazy Vic.

"Are you sure we haven't met earlier?" Krevins asked.

Dan was stunned by how quickly Victor had interrupted his soliloquy to ask the question. No point in denying that Victor might have seen him. Otherwise, the doctor may remember later why he recognized him and become unnecessarily suspicious.

"I did attend one of your presentations. It was at a symposium over at USF. That's what piqued my interest in your fascinating work. We never spoke, though, until I called you two days ago."

The doctor heard him but didn't register a reaction. Dan surmised he had dodged that bullet. Victor simply picked up where he had left off and began a new verbal onslaught.

At one juncture, Dan heard electrical signals mentioned in the context of encoded instructions simulated by computer input. This was the opening he'd been waiting for.

"Let me ask you about that, Doctor Krevins. As an electrical engineer I'm keenly interested in how that may be accomplished. Do you have computer experts working with you?"

For several seconds, Victor stared at him and a spark of uncertainty hovered between them. Dan's question had struck a nerve. Regaining his composure, Krevins answered.

"We have a fine EE department at USF. I have talented faculty and students available to advise me. We're making real progress in what I have named cerebellar inspiration or CI. That's my term for transmitting these structured signals to the cerebellum to achieve precise results."

"Do you think I may be able to talk to some of those engineers to add another angle to my story?"

"That would be a bit premature, I think." Victor had opened the door for Dan then summarily dismissed his attempt to probe deeper. This wouldn't be the last time Dan would float the question if he was given half a chance. He wanted some clue as to how Krevins had hit on the right format for signaling the brain and who had programmed the complicated inputs for him.

When he paused to exercise his cramped writing hand, Dan glanced down at his watch. Had it really been that long? Victor had been at it nearly non-stop for close to two hours. The tape recorder and his note pad contained much more than Dan ever cared to know about the brain, the cerebellum and the wonders of clinical research and testing.

At last he noted a distinct pause in the dissertation and remarked, "I think I have enough information to get started. May I call you in a few days for an appointment to show you my article and refine it with you?"

"That will be fine, Mr. Polk. I thank you for your interest and your attention. Often the laboratory is a lonely place when others don't appreciate your work."

When he left the townhouse, Dan felt sullied, contaminated by association. After his close encounter with that warped brain he just wanted to get home. He needed to stand under the shower until the grime of that vengeful, evil mind was washed from his skin.

* * *

True to his promise, Jud had returned to Tampa. He was sitting poolside waiting to hear Dan's report. Dan sorely needed to have a conversation with someone who was on the safe side of reason. As he often told his buddy, that described Jud Black. Well, most of the time.

"He must have put you through the full wash cycle, fellow. You look like you've been left on spin too long."

"You're not gonna believe what I've been through for the past couple of hours. The mad doctor really is as far out of orbit as we suspected. He's no doubt a super intelligent scientist but he's turned that brilliance inward until he's a danger to himself and to society. Thinks everybody has it in for him because he's smarter than they are. Webster should put his picture beside the definition of egotist—maybe wierdo."

"Any clues we can use?"

"Won't open up about using human subjects. Claims he's adhering to the ethics imposed by his colleagues, most of whom he considers to be straight laced, backward prudes."

"What about the computer side of this mind game, Dan? Any hints there?"

"I tried but he clammed up. All he would say is that engineering students and faculty were cooperating with him. I sensed that he was very nervous about that."

"So what's next for you and Doctor Krevinstein?" Jud took a pull on his Murphy's and pointed to another cool one on the patio table.

"I'll have another shot at him when I take him a draft of my fictitious magazine piece. Maybe I can crowbar more information out of him then."

"I haven't exactly been idle myself," Jud said. "Did a little info surfing." He picked up a handwritten sheet and began to read.

"Paula Ann Taylor. Born St. Paul, Minnesota. Thirty-one years old. Degree in EE and computer science from a small Minnesota college. Highest honors. Worked up there till three years ago then relocated to Gainesville, Florida with Craft and Brown, a software house. Found an electronic resume and her evaluations—shall we say on file? She's considered an exceptional talent and a fast burner. Holds a technical manager position. Saw a couple of hints in her evals, though, that she tends to be very independent to the point of being a revolutionary. Sounds like she's a bit much for a small, conservative company. I saw a picture in her files and I gotta say, *she don't look like no geek to me, pilgrim.*"

"So do we need to check her out up close, Jud? How do you propose to do that?"

"I'm already working on it with a friend of mine in Ocala. Going up there tomorrow."

Dan popped the top on the waiting longneck and said, "One caution, Jud. If you do meet her, don't mention COB. That would connect you with me. Don't want to do that until you decide whose side she's on."

"Which brings me to the kicker, Dan."

"What does that mean?"

"Paula's a continuing fan of psychology. Took courses at two colleges. Can you imagine a bithead hung up on psych?"

"So?" Dan took a long pull on his ale.

"Guess what long, tall movie look alike taught both the courses she audited in Minnesota and the ones she's been taking at USF?"

"You gotta be shittin' me. Victor Krevins?"

"You got it, babe. Wonder what's up with that?"

Dan flopped back into his chair and said, "Well, I'll be damned. Victor and Paula. Now I understood why I thought Krevins had singled me out of the audience at the symposium. *Victor was looking at Paula.* Probably saw me in his peripheral vision. That's why he thought we had met earlier. Wonder if those two have something going? That would be beauty and the creep. Surely not!"

CHAPTER 24

"Beginning to think you were avoiding me, Jud." Sam was sipping a brew and chewing on popcorn when Jud found him at the bar in Gainesville.

"Sorry 'bout that, pal. Got caught up down in Tampa. Ran out of time last trip down here. Like my enote told you, I had to hurry back and finish a job at home."

"Thought you'd graduated to wealthy playboy, Jud. Why would you get in a hurry about anything?"

"Wanted to put the finishing touches on a new security program I wrote. You'd like this one, Sam. Makes home security measures now on the market look pretty puny."

"Still like to scoop everybody with radical new software, don't you?"

"One of the great joys in life, Sam. Where is this heavenly body I'm supposed to meet?"

"Relax and have a brew. She'll be along."

Jud ordered a draft and they fell into easy chatter.

Minutes later an absolute vision appeared and headed across the floor in their direction. The photo in her personnel file hadn't done her justice. She didn't just move; it was more like a glide. Golden curls flowed to her shoulders and she had the most dazzling blue eyes Jud had ever seen.

"Pinch me, Sam. I think I'm smitten."

Jud stubbed out his cigarette and turned his full attention to the lovely woman.

Sam broke out in a broad grin. He stood and motioned to her. She wasn't just an illusion after all. Jud hadn't felt this way since he was a horny teenager. Maybe he would get through the introduction without sounding like a tongue-tied schoolboy but he wouldn't take any bets on that.

Sam said something that came across faintly like, "Paula Taylor, my buddy from Virginia, Jud Black." But it could just as easily have been, "*Raving beauty, this is my friend, a slobbering idiot*" and Jud wouldn't have known the difference. She was a knockout. His own response must have been something intelligible because she didn't laugh in his face.

The conversation was pretty tame at first with no hint that any of them were into out of the ordinary activities. Jud had recovered enough to make idle chatter and she made the conversation light and natural. They finished a round sitting at the bar then found a corner table.

"Sam didn't say what you do back in Virginia, Jud."

"Oh, I'm sort of a free agent. Write some software and I'm in the music business as an independent." Jud had no reason to believe Sam had alerted her to his hacking abilities.

"Unusual combination." She looked at him with genuine interest. "Most of the coder whimps I work with can't carry a tune."

"You a code slinger, too?" Jud was beginning to make a real connection with Paula on something more than a purely physical level.

"Den mother for a bunch of bitheads over at Craft and Brown. No real challenge but it's a living."

The conversation took a new turn. Computer related language seeped into their exchanges almost as if they were probing each other's knowledge of the field. Jud for one was duly impressed. Paula was no phony. She knew her way around. Up to speed on the most current developments.

Paula loosened up. She had a natural ability to take on the persona of one of the fellows with her hard drinking, rough talking ways. Body of a goddess, mouth of a sailor. Regardless, anybody that would dare refer to Paula as a fellow needed his mouth scrubbed down.

Finally, Sam stuck a toe in the water. He broached the unspoken bond they shared.

"Paula, this guy's one of the slickest wizards you'll meet. Hacker maestro. May even be able to show you and me a trick or two."

She scanned Jud up and down and he felt like her eyes were x-raying him. Gave him a warm feeling all over.

Paula didn't make an outward show of it, but Jud could tell she still had reservations about Sam broaching the subject of her interest in hacking.

Well, if she needed reassuring, Jud was certainly willing to make the first move.

"Sam and I were part of a tight little group when he lived up my way. We spent many a day shaking off raster burn but we located a lot of very interesting trap doors. Even did a few gigs as sneakers."

In a few words he had conveyed to her some markers about his hacking activities. If she was genuine, and he suspected she was, she would know he had really said, "*We were part of a hacker group that spent so much time in front of our computer screens we suffered from eyestrain. Our interest was in finding holes in computer systems that allowed us to access them. We were good enough to be hired by network owners to break into their systems then help them correct their flaws.*"

She chewed on his words. He'd soon know if she would welcome him as a fellow devotee of the fine art of hacking. Maybe she'd just shut down completely to avoid disclosing her own love of the chase.

"How about taking a lady for a trip around the dance floor, Jud?" *Nothing bashful about her*, he thought.

They joined the bodies on the small dance floor. She was a skilled, energetic dancer. Then the music slowed and he held her close to him. He could get used to this with no trouble at all. Dan had told him she was a pretty dazzling woman but that was an understatement. When they rejoined Sam, both of them were flushed and laughing. Jud couldn't be sure whether the warmth he felt was from the exertion or something else altogether. There was a glow about this girl and he felt strongly attracted to her.

She picked up a pack of smokes and Jud lit one for her.

"Finds his way around out there pretty well, Sam. Wonder if he surfs the networks equally well."

"He really is okay, Paula. We were long time atomic. He knows the rules and I'd trust him with my life—as well as my identity. Hell, considering some of the bar fights we've been in, I guess I already trusted him to save my hide more than once."

That was as glowing a recommendation as he could have given her. The two men had been so close they were atomic or, in computing terms, they couldn't be split up. His words were his guarantee that she had no reason to fear loss of her hacker anonymity because of Jud. She could safely remain, interchangeably, Paula and Athena as she wished.

"If you vouch for him, I can take a chance," she relented. Her long fingers touched Jud's forearm and it was like an electric charge.

"So, It looks like we have contact," Sam announced. "How do you two feel about a session at my place?"

Hell, right now Jud would have followed her anywhere. He was lost somewhere in those blue eyes.

"Always up for that," Paula replied. "Had a mighty boring day and my brain's craving a challenge. But my place is a lot closer."

They stocked up on a supply of six packs at the corner store to fuel their evening and headed off for Paula's apartment. Jud was a bit bewildered by what he saw when they arrived. She appeared to live a rather Spartan life in a nondescript neighborhood. Her apartment building seemed to be populated by blue-collar types and a smattering of university students. The college kids would have been looking for a place close to the University of Florida campus with cheap rent. Okay, he could understand that, but what was she doing in this building? His probe into various computer records for data on Paula had included her current salary. She could definitely afford better than this.

Her two-bedroom apartment was furnished in early warehouse, a real abomination of non-styles in a collage of clashing colors from mildew to watermelon. Then he saw the spare bedroom. What she had done with that hacker's retreat was a visual feast for a computer jock. Two complete state of the art computer configurations and a server. Jud concluded she didn't spend enough time in the rest of the apartment to care what it looked like. This was her private world. She was connected and he guessed she may even provide server space to others. If she wasn't a guru then she had spent one hell of a lot of money on toys some hackers would kill for.

Jud noticed an unusual addition to each of the workstations. He was reasonably sure he knew the answer to his next question, but he asked her, anyway.

"What kind of rigging is this, Paula?"

"A lady can never be too careful. These machines contain some confidential data it wouldn't do for others to see. I can set those nasty little thermal charges for a precise time delay and *poof!* goes the hardware. Makes big melted lumps in minutes."

She was in a playful mood tonight. She broke into computer networks and tied them in knots. Paula was wreaking havoc and enjoying every second of it. Jud detested what she was doing but she was, without a doubt, a computer wizard. She had deteriorated into what his fellow hackers disdainfully called a cracker.

Sam whistled. "You're in the zone tonight, Athena." Jud catalogued her hacker name. Could come in handy later.

The next order of business was to bug another member of their hacker cell and see if he picked up on who was harassing him.

"Let's send Jerry a wav file that'll knock his hat off and screw him over by anonymizing. See if he goes bats trying to figure out who broke one off in him or gets back to us with some obnoxious rebound."

She was warming up slowly. Jud guessed she didn't want to tip any of her real techniques until he had showed his hand first. Well, he would just watch and see where this little game went.

She arranged a sound file in wav format that would produce an annoying sound somewhere between a Bronx cheer and flatulence on the recipient's computer. Then she followed with a message to the same destination and routed both of them through an intermediate point to mask their point of origin. For good measure, she put them through her anonymizer program before sending them. Even if her target made it back through the relay server he would play hell finding her on this end. The anonymizer was designed to make it look like the sender was someone else at a different location. And her target would know it could be any of his many dispersed hacker friends.

Paula laughed and said, "If ol' Jerry doesn't find a solution for the maze I'm putting him through and 'rebound' with a smart ass answer, it's points for me. Pure test of wits. Even if he identifies me, he has to explain exactly how he did it. No guesses allowed."

At this level her actions were mischievous but non-destructive. Jud wondered what would happen when she really got rolling.

Her text message stated tersely:

Check your .wav files, Boarshead. Clock's running.

Guess Who

"Let's give old Jerry some time to run that through his filters." Paula took a long swallow from the beer Jud handed her and reveled in her gotcha on her hacker buddy.

"Clever, Paula," Sam told her. "I like the way you masked that one."

She may have unwittingly told Jud more than she suspected by opening this harmless little game. The routing for that cutout server she was using to relay the messages to Jerry was very familiar. Jud had a special affinity for strings of numbers and symbols and tended to remember many of them in snapshot fashion. He closed his eyes and played back that endless CD in his brain and there it was! Secret Treasures had been somewhere beyond the other end of that routing.

Try as he might Jud had been unable to get back to the origin. He'd tried packet sniffers on that intermediate server to divert any identically addressed incoming packets to his machine. However, there had been no more Secret Treasures messages through the cutout since the one that was fatal to Barry. Now he knew that even if he had located packets, the sender probably had anonymized them and he would have been sent to a dead end. He was dealing with people who knew their stuff.

"By the way, mystery boy, what's with nodding off while I'm cruising?" Paula taunted.

Jud snapped out of his intense concentration. "Just putting something through my data banks, gorgeous. I already saw what was going on well before you finished."

"Sure Sam and I aren't keeping you up? Or maybe us two-fisted drinkers are too much for you. Not a wuss, are you, tall and strange?" Something about her tone told Jud she enjoyed entirely too much putting people down.

"If you get to be too much for me, I'll let you know. Don't hold your breath."

Her eyes lit up at his testy comeback. This was a woman who thrived on challenge and Jud had laid down the gauntlet. The hacker in her was rapidly rising to the surface and she seemed bent on proving her superiority.

"Okay, super Jud, let's see what you've got. Show me some radical pings that'll get my attention."

If that's what she wants, watch out, he chuckled to himself. *Let's see if she's ever seen this little beauty of a routine.*

The battle was on. They jockeyed back and forth for advantage in the 'gee whiz' category while Sam sat by in a state of awe and amusement. Two titans locked in combat and Sam just wanted to avoid getting trampled so he let them go at it.

After long hours of electronic combat and a rising level of annoyance, Paula slumped back in her chair and looked stymied.

"I gotta admit you're one talented guy, Jud. Feel like I've been in a sauna. I need a break."

He noted with a great deal of satisfaction that she was pale with the strain he had put her through. Her brow was more than a little moist. Sauna, huh. Boy, did that evoke interesting images.

Jud had to give her credit. She had put his brain in overdrive and made him work until he was really smoking on that machine. Considering the bias that lingered in the community against female hackers, this enticing miss was a strong argument for equal rights among the brotherhood regardless of gender. Wow! Beauty, wit and intelligence; she had it all. She was a fantastic bundle. But overbearing.

They were enjoying a respite from their computer war and Sam was working the keyboard. He stopped and called out. "We have incoming here. Want me to check it out, Paula?"

"Give it a shot," she answered, too wasted on the big sagging couch to move.

"Looks like Jerry made the catch," he said.

"Damn," she spat and rose from the sofa. She and Jud headed back to the screen to see Jerry's answer. The meat of the comeback was short and nasty.

Gotcha, Athena. Checkmate. My points. ESAD.

Boarshead

The text then gave a precise explanation of how he had traced her message and identified Athena as the probable sender. She appeared to doubt his sleuthing was legitimate but it certainly made sense to Jud. This Jerry was more than your pedestrian grade hacker. Jud wondered how many other talented people she knew.

A sound file had showed up and when Sam opened it, there was a loud wolf whistle. Jerry was really rubbing it in. Paula was visibly perplexed. She saluted her machine with a single finger and turned away to find another brew. One tie and one loss tonight weren't improving her disposition. The tag line must have really hurt. ESAD is an expression usually reserved as a genuine putdown. But 'Eat Shit And Die' could also be a playful, if upsetting, taunt between close hacker friends.

Paula returned with a frown holding a half empty long neck in her hand

"He's going to have some more explaining to do at our next get together. Wonder what the little SOB really used to track me down. He doesn't get any points in my book yet."

Hmmm, she's a sore loser, too.

"Must be on his game tonight," Sam said. Paula looked at him and sneered.

By now Jud had concluded that Paula Taylor was a good candidate to be the elusive partner Victor Krevins may be using to carry out his scheme. Using, however, was certainly a misnomer in anything having to do with Paula. What had Sam said when he first mentioned her name over the air phone? She was a master ball buster. He could picture her with leather boots and a cat-o-nine-tails. May be fun to see how far she went to try dominating him before he burst her bubble.

She did have staying power, though. Paula wanted to weave magic all night; but they all finally crashed sometime around three AM and decided to continue after daylight. Jud knew she had come to the bar from a full workday and he assumed Sam had done the same. Hard to tell in Sam's case, since he had been close hold about what it was he'd moved to Florida to do for a living. That was his business and Jud wasn't about to pry.

"I have to take care of something in Ocala, guys." Sam was tired but determined to get back home tonight. "Since this is Saturday, how about we restart around noon and go as long as you want."

That sounded good to Jud. He'd actually be able to get in at least six or seven hours sleep and be ready to go head to head with the surprising Paula/Athena by noon.

"Maybe you want to stay over, Jud, so we can get an earlier start," Paula offered.

Whoa! He had to run that through his somewhat foggy brain. Was that an innocent invitation to the lumpy couch and a blanket or perhaps something more? The weekend was only beginning and he wasn't about to continue this relationship, if it was one, on *her* terms. *He* would make the moves if and when the time came.

"No. I'll ride back with Sam and keep him from falling asleep and killing himself. We'll see you by noon. In fact, I'll bring lunch for three."

When they left, she hung close to Jud. Her hand lingered on his arm. Those impossibly blue eyes seemed to be pleading, pulling him closer. But the timing wasn't right. He drew on his small reserve of strength and bid her goodbye.

What an unexpected evening it had been. His brain and his hormones told him Paula Taylor stimulated him more than any woman ever had. He'd known lots of women, some of them very well indeed, but she was a new level of delight. Jud was spinning but there were those annoying alarms going off in his head saying *caution, caution*. So many small indicators. She was devious and dangerous. And what about her possible connection to Krevins and the multiple remote killings? Careful, Black, you have miles to go and there could be quicksand ahead.

CHAPTER 25

Dan was encouraged by Ellen's rosy look today. He sat by her bed and felt the glow of her energy returning. More than a week had passed since that first frightful morning after the attack. On that day he had feared she would never recover to her full vitality. Now her progress, although it seemed painstakingly slow, was steady. With her throat back to near normal, she was beginning to carefully exercise it.

"You and Jud okay batching?" She swallowed tentatively but the words were coming more easily.

"It's not like eating your cooking. Danielle did her best to spoil me, too. But we manage."

"Not bar food?"

"Haven't been out a night this week. In fact, Jud's up in Ocala today and tomorrow, so I'll whip something together. You know, like gourmet frankfurters and baked legumes."

"Beanie weenies, huh?" She spoke slowly but the scolding tone came through.

"Just yanking your cord, sugar. The neighbors have dropped off a couple of casseroles and we're doing all right. Don't worry that pretty little noggin about me. Your job is to get back up to full speed."

"Doc says I can talk. Questions?" She actually seemed anxious to exercise her newfound voice.

"Only if you'll be sure to not overdo. I know it was a tall man who attacked the two of you. But you said something about the color blue. I don't understand what you meant."

"Saw a silver glint and a blue glow." She began to cough. Dan decided she had been too optimistic about her throat. That was about all the talking she could handle for now.

"I'll work with that. Just shake your head yes or no and rest your voice now." She understood.

"Did you see the man's face?" No was her nodded reply.

"Where was the silver glint?"

He touched his leg. No, she indicated. His waist. Again, no. His head. Another no. She seemed to be growing impatient. Then he touched his forearm.

She began to vigorously move her head up and down. So her last impression of the hazy figure standing over her was of a shiny glint somewhere around the tall man's forearm and a blue glow. Even this time of year it was too warm for a long-sleeved blue shirt in the Bay area and the silver part had him stumped.

Ellen was tired so he'd back off for now. He would go away and roll the bits of information through his head; bounce them off Jud later.

Her response had been at once both encouraging and worrisome. Had she just not seen any more in those brief moments before she was struck or was she still unable to remember what else she'd seen? Perhaps he was being a worrywart, as his mother would have said. But that blow to the head may be causing a loss of memory. The word memory brought him back to his recent acquaintance, the cerebellum. If his research had done one thing, it had made him sensitive to how delicate an organ the brain can be when it's injured.

Please don't let her have permanent effects from this terrible trauma.

The doctor stopped in on his rounds and Dan took him aside to ask, "Does she have a serious memory loss, doctor?"

Ellen wasn't quite asleep. The doctor steered Dan into the hall.

"How do you know about that, Dan? What did she tell you? I told her to save her voice."

Dan filled him in on the episode with the picture games and their short conversation today.

"It's too early to be sure, but there does seem to be a lapse. We do gentle probes regularly and we've determined that her memory of events for the past two weeks or so is all but erased. She doesn't recall being in New Orleans, apparently has forgotten almost the entire day the attack took place, doesn't at this stage even know that her friend Susan is dead. She asked if Sue had come by to see her."

"She mentioned the colors silver and blue, doc. That seems to be all she captured from the scene at the Millwoods' house."

"For some odd reason she's held onto that scrap of information," the doctor replied. "She said those same words to us but had nothing more to add."

"I know I'm being extremely impatient for her to recover, but she's so important to me. I can't bear to see her like this."

"You're her life preserver now, Dan. Keep telling yourself she's going to be all right, because I firmly believe she will be. But, above all, don't let her read any uncertainty in your eyes. She needs all the encouragement you can provide, not doubts."

"But why the memory lapse?" Dan wouldn't let go; there was something amiss here.

"It's not the norm given the circumstances of her injury. We're doing all we can with monitors and blood tests to determine the reason. There could be a chemical imbalance or some other cause for her difficulty in remembering. We'll know soon."

*　　*　　*

"Dan, it's Jud. Just have a few minutes to talk. I'm heading back to Sam's with a gourmet lunch. Do you believe that for Ocala?"

"When did you get to be a gourmet? I thought you were part of the Whopper and fries crowd."

"Listen up. Met Paula Taylor last night and spent most of the night at her place in Gainesville."

"Oh, Studley. Not again."

"No. Hold on. Let me restate that. Sam and I were at her place until three this morning. She's a hacker and I mean first class. Unfortunately, she's turned that talent toward cracking systems and trying to screw up people's data. We're headed back up there today to continue our session. She could be the wizard we're looking for. I mean she could be Vic's accomplice."

"Good work. What can I do to help?"

"Not a thing. Sit tight and let me scope this out. I'll be back to your place before the weekend is over.

How's Ellen today? I know you've been there by now."

"I'm in the hospital parking lot now on my cell. Just keep using that number. I'm here more than at home. If I'm inside where I can't use the phone I'll call you back."

"And Ellen?"

"She's making some progress but it's a slow pull, buddy. She can't remember anything for the past couple weeks except a silver glint and something blue associated with her attacker. Managed to tell me the colors were somewhere near his arm."

"How about a silver watch band?" Jud asked.

"Could be. Why not? But the blue glow baffles me."

"Ever seen one of those fluorescent watches with a blue face? Maybe it was a blue faced watch with a silver band."

"Of course. Did it again, didn't you? Now all we have to do is find that watch among how many hundreds of thousands of locals and tourists?"

"It's a start, Cooper. Don't look a gift pony in the chops and all that, you know."

"See you. I'm anxious to hear about your exploits up there."

CHAPTER 26

Paula was ready to get down to some power hacking on Saturday. Jud wondered if their encounter last night had so whetted her appetite to excel that she had been practicing before they arrived. She did look fresh and energized.

This woman fully turned on and at her peak was about the limit of what he could take. She really had knocked him for a loop with both her mind and her body. He kept saying to himself that she may be the enemy and he shouldn't get sucked in by her charm. It wasn't an easy sell to think about her negatively given all the strong positive convincers she possessed.

"You're a walking, talking contradiction, Jud. I must say I wasn't expecting such an elegant lunch today."

"Can't get on a guy's case for showing a little class now and then. Besides, now I can kick your booty on the net while you're all warm and contented."

"Yeah, in your dreams. I'm ready to get down to business in this round. Stand back and hang on."

He could tell from the outset that this wasn't going to be pretty. She dove directly into some heavy grade cracking. There was pure beauty in the way she was manipulating systems and networks and tying them in knots. She was also operating totally outside his sphere. It wasn't that he was incapable of doing the same things or worse; he just had no desire to be destructive.

"Holy hard drives, Batwoman," Sam marveled. "You're on a roll."

Jud was, and always would be, a hacker in the best sense of the word. He would probe and learn, even white hat to let people know when they had serious systems flaws he had discovered. He wanted to know as much as possible about the vast electronic world out there. But he wouldn't use that knowledge maliciously as Paula was doing to create problems for the civilians that lacked defenses. He didn't try to create disasters for the systems administrators and security people who did their best to keep the networks running and in sound order day to day.

After an hour of watching her punch holes indiscriminately and glory in her exploits, Jud stood and walked away from her machine.

"What's the problem, boy wonder? Give up so soon?"

He couldn't blow his cover now so he urged her up out of the seat and took over. "Watch me closely and you may learn."

His fingers were a blur on the keyboard. Networks began to unfold before their eyes and yield their innermost treasures. Codes were no obstacle and passwords offered little resistance to his manipulations. Paula should surely appreciate the back doors he was creating for later access, the Trojan horses he was installing to give systems administrators large headaches at predetermined future times. Jud could see by her expression that she was beginning to appreciate the depth of his talents.

"Impressive," she said and bent nearer to the monitor to absorb what he was doing. She slid one hand across his shoulders and Jud found it difficult to concentrate.

"Routine," Jud taunted. "Just playing around."

What she didn't know was that he was cataloging every one of his moves for reversal. They would all be negated and the systems would be returned to normal as soon as he returned to Dan's house. If she tried to exploit anything he had done in this session, she would find walls thrown up to prevent her malicious actions. If she checked back she would assume that some sharp system administrators had found and corrected the problems when in fact they never even knew what Jud had done to them. It was harmless and all for show but she would swear by now that he was a first grade cracker.

"Pure wizardry," Sam said. Paula didn't see the puzzled expression he sent toward Jud. There would be time to explain to Sam later why he was play-acting as a cracker.

The smooth elegance of what Jud had demonstrated seemed to fire her up to a fever pitch. She dove in with new purpose and wreaked havoc on two randomly selected systems that would never be the same after her onslaught. Jud winced when he thought of the extreme agony her actions would put scores of users through. And all the while she was positively glowing with the flush of her victories.

He turned to leave the room in disgust.

"What's the matter, wonder boy? Give up so soon?"

"No, but I do have some self-imposed limits. You're enjoying this too much. It's destructive. You're blowing holes in systems and cracking for the sheer pleasure of doing damage."

"Oh, I see, you're one of those do-gooders. The whole point is to trump the also-rans and find new territory to conquer. Better than sex, man."

"I doubt that. But I yield to your art, lady. No contest here."

"You and Sam. He's a bleeding heart, too. I say if the system protectors can't secure what's on their networks then it's fair game. This is the real challenge that keeps my adrenaline pumping."

"Paula, you have special talents from what I can see. You're purposely destroying valuable data. Causing problems it could take weeks, maybe months to fix. Why not play white hat and help these people close their security gaps rather than exploiting them?"

"No challenge there, faint heart, unless maybe I dinged them double," she said. "Could take their money for fixing firewall faults while I'm installing new trap doors only I would know about. That would be a rush."

Jud noted the look of distaste on Sam's face. He was just as put off by this kind of mentality. Beautiful Paula Taylor who looked too good to be true was beginning to prove she was exactly that—way too good to be true. Black had seen this tendency before and it could become a sickness.

One of the fellows in their group back home went beyond the pale before they froze him out. No room for crackers in their midst. A particularly talented wizard could grow to be so fascinated by his or her abilities that the only game in town was 'me against the world'. Each new hacking victory only set the bar higher and the next breakthrough had to be bigger and more damaging than the last. A hacker became a full-fledged cracker and no one was safe from destructive attack.

"I'm not going to lecture you," Jud said. "Do your own thing. I'm just telling you that's not my scene and I don't have a lot of patience with a cracker."

"After what you showed me tonight?" she shot back.

"Just settling a couple of old scores," Jud lied. "Not my normal behavior."

He lit a smoke and fixed her with a cold stare. "Like I said, crackers like you turn me off."

"HACKER!" she shouted. Even those that crossed the line detested being placed in that other category. They fancied themselves the best of the best and saw others as too weak or too unsure to practice their art to the limit.

After this confrontation, she rapidly lost interest in continuing their activities. Her whole disposition change shouted that neither Sam nor Jud was worthy of her time. Not if they were going to draw lines in the sand. They did test some harmless techniques on each other but Jud was on guard to give away nothing of value to this queen of computer deceit. She had grabbed his attention completely at the outset but he now felt only disappointment and a degree of apprehension after she had exposed her true nature.

"What makes you so high and mighty, anyway?" Paula hurled at him. "What's your claim to fame?"

He wasn't about to tell her anything she could end up using against him later. Until he knew whether she was tied up in Victor's nasty scheme, she only needed to know that he was a hacker named Jud from Virginia. He hadn't used his real hacker moniker as they battled, keying in MadDog instead. Jud also remembered that Dan had met this charmer and told her that he was one of the principals of COB Software. The last thing Jud wanted now was for her to connect him and Dan in any way.

"Not looking for fame. Just plugging along freelancing software. I know which side of the line I come down on using any talents I may have. That's not about to change."

The lady was beyond annoyed. She was in a rage. He couldn't tell whether it was frustration at not being able to get the upper hand or something else. Maybe he had hit a nerve and tweaked a residual spark of ethics. He had slammed her hard when he reminded her she was misusing her considerable expertise to hurt others.

"Too bad you're such a prude. We could have been a dynamite pair," she sighed.

By late afternoon the spark was gone out of their session and Sam was ready to leave. "Well, I have things to do yet today. Better shove off. I'll see you at the next poker game, doll."

"I'll bet you're one hell of a poker player," Jud told her. "Wouldn't want to try to bluff you."

Both men had driven their cars to Gainesville so Jud could head back directly to Tampa this afternoon. When he rose and searched for his own keys, Paula stopped him.

"Stick around awhile. We'll shut down and just talk. You know, get to know each other better. Hard headed as you are, Jud Black, you're also a challenge. Get a brew and I'll be right back."

He'd give it a chance. May even pick up some tidbits of information that would be useful in his investigation. The big question was where, if anywhere, this disconcerting woman fit into the Victor Krevins plan. He had come to Gainesville to answer that question. So far it was still very much open. And who could say what extra bennies may come his way.

She was gone for at least fifteen minutes and he was beginning to wonder why he had stayed. Then she returned with a sly little smile playing on her lips

"Paula Taylor, you are an enigma. I don't know what side of you to believe."

"That's part of my charm, hacker boy. Like to keep 'em guessing."

"Have to admit you caught my eye immediately. You have a lot going for you but there's an undertow here that worries me."

She leaned closer and whispered in his ear. "Don't like aggressive women, huh, long and cranky?" He supposed that move and her fingers at the nape of his neck were designed to melt him down.

"Can't say I do. If you're looking for a boy toy to dominate, you've got the wrong guy. I'm used to sharing the play calling."

"Maybe you need a little help to loosen you up."

She produced a small bag of white powder. Now he understood why she had been gone for so long. When he looked into her eyes they verified his suspicion. Paula had already had her hit and she was offering to share her coke stash with him.

"Wrong again, Paula. I don't touch that stuff. I'm shocked that you do. How can someone with your level of intelligence not understand what that crap does to your brain?"

Jud had long ago written off the escapist world of drugs. He'd made two false starts as a user. Both of them had ended in rotten experiences. Marijuana was the experiment the first time; then someone had goaded him into trying speed. On both occasions his system had reacted and he became violently ill. Black's body clearly didn't tolerate drugs and his brain certainly didn't need the shock.

"Where do you get off preaching to me?" she demanded. "I could make this very interesting for you."

Paula bored a hole through him with her eyes. But her eyelids were already starting to droop as the fix took control of her.

"Sorry. Not my business. It just galls me to see you destroying the phenomenal brainpower you have. And your timing stinks."

"You're turning me down? You're rejecting Athena, the goddess of wisdom? I despise you chauvinistic pigs."

"Maybe I should just get out and let you enjoy your hazy world," Jud threw back. "Sorry it turned out this way, Paula."

"The snort only helps me fly but Athena's already above mere mortals. Everyone will know that when she snares them in Minerva's net."

She was floating now and he wondered when she would lose touch with reality. Her speech was slurring. She was swaying. But Paula had given him an opening he dared not pass up.

"What does that mean, Minerva's net?" She didn't answer. The garbage she had put into her system was in total control now.

"Whooee, this is grand. Give it a try. Take a ticket and ride. This could be your lucky day."

She dropped the bag on the floor and reached down to retrieve it. Her legs gave way and she settled heavily onto the floor with a giggle.

"No, thanks. I much prefer you when you're conscious. What or who is this Minerva?" Paula was really out of it now.

"Minerva lives not far away. Call for service any day." She sang it like a jingle and threw an arm around his leg and tried to pull him down.

Paula was somewhere in the clouds. Jud flashed back to a scrap of paper lying beside one of her computers. It had contained two sets of numbers. One was the telephone number he had called before they came back to Gainesville today to taunt Paula about continuing their electronic duel. The other was an entirely different area code he didn't recognize. He had memorized both sequences and then written them down while they were fresh. Jud had long ago become a compulsive gatherer of data with his photographic memory. Could the other number have something to do with this Minerva?

Jud marveled at the stupidity of this beautiful genius gone sour. He tossed an afghan over her. She mumbled something incoherent as he quietly left.

Finally Jud had time to think after twenty-four hours of totally mind bending intensity. Paula drove herself relentlessly; it was no wonder she needed a complete letdown now and then. But coke was a terrible choice. Of more immediate interest was the alter ego Athena she had shown him today. When she unleashed that marauding cracker personality the results were downright petrifying. How much damage had she inflicted on the systems of unsuspecting individuals and institutions? Few secrets would be safe from her prying eyes once she went after them.

Still, for all the potential danger she may present, she could be mesmerizing.

He had to know more about her. She was wigged out for this day. But he was already putting together a scheme for delving into her secrets. It just might tell him if she was a killer or only a victim of his ingrained suspicious nature. She had so much going for her. He wasn't anxious to be a reformer, but if his suspicions were unfounded, he may yet have a chance to bring her around. At the very least it would be one hell of an interesting undertaking.

CHAPTER 27

"Hello?"

"Is this Minerva?"

"That depends. Who's calling?"

"Friend of a friend named Fred. I'm told you can provide a service I may be interested in buying."

"Then Minerva's listening. What is it you want?"

"Well, there's this little problem I need a cure for. Let's call it runaway lips. Anyway, somebody close to me has it and I fear it may be terminal."

"And you'd like a prompt, sure cure for this affliction? One that can be applied without the need for first hand contact with the patient?"

"That's about it. How long and how much, Minerva?"

"We'll get around to that part. First I need to know if you can supply me with the information I need to effect the cure. Got a pencil?"

"Got it. Shoot."

"I'll need the patient's name, a good computer email address, preferably both at work and at home, for the patient, and the name of the town or city where he lives. Also—and this is important—give me whatever information you have on his most intense interest or passion, what attracts and holds his interest. Send the information over your computer and I'll answer you there. Is that clear?"

"Sounds easy enough to me. Computer addresses and hometown of the, ah, patient and his biggest hobby in a message from my computer. Can't we do this by telephone?"

"It's essential that you follow my instructions to the letter if you want the service performed. Otherwise, this conversation is over."

"Okay, I understand."

She hadn't even asked him for a down payment. Didn't need to. All her efforts would cost her was a little time and imagination. As soon as she had the client's email address, his identity and location were easy to find. If he balked on full payment down the road, she would have numerous ways to apply direct pressure. If all else failed, the client would himself become the target of an electronic file that would make him terminally regret being tardy paying his bill.

"Now one final item." She told him. "My message to you will specify where payment is to be delivered as soon as I render the cure. Seventy five large in old paper."

"That's pretty steep."

"Depends on how much the patient is suffering and how deep your concern for a remedy. Don't waste my time if you can't handle the ante."

There was a delay and a nervous cough. "Agreed. I'll be in touch. When can I expect results?"

"You worry about getting me that data and I'll apply the cure in a matter of days. My email address is *Minerva@downstream.net.* The quicker I hear from you the quicker the patient gets the cure."

So that quickly the first real test case was set in motion. This one was for big bucks and the word would get around. There was no stopping her when the news spread that there was a foolproof method to eliminate nuisances without the messy business of a hired assassin. It was a win-win situation for everybody except the professional hit men. They were about to lose a considerable share of their commerce. They'd never figure out what hit them.

Ernie thought he had her under control but he was sucking wind. She was light years ahead of him and soon she wouldn't even need his annoying presence. Minerva had downloaded everything she needed from his twisted brain and she was branching out.

Yes, Minerva was set for the big time.

CHAPTER 28

Dan was running to keep up with the pace of events around him. Ellen's long term recovery was still in doubt and had him worried sick. His visit with Krevins had confirmed that the doctor was a real head case who could explode at any instant. Jud would be bringing back a report from his trip to Gainesville.

Something was gnawing at Dan that he could only define as a new sense of urgency. He'd been very late getting home from the hospital last night and found Jud conked out in the guest room. They had a lot of ground to cover today.

He was absorbed in the morning newspaper when Jud stole up behind and goosed him. It was a shock that nearly separated him from his chair.

"Yo! Sure know how to make an entrance, don't you?"

Jud flashed a mischievous smile. "Just getting your heart started, my man."

"So what's the tale from Gainesville? Meet any interesting people you want to tell me about?"

Jud poured himself a cup of coffee, stretched and yawned. He sat down and looked disapprovingly at the cereal and fruit Dan was munching.

"What?" Dan asked, sounding a bit annoyed.

"That dog kibble's gonna gum up your works, man. We gotta get that sweet little gal back home to cook some regular food for you. How's she doing, Dan?"

"Every day I hope I'll show up and find her back to normal but it's not happening. If I was sure that crazy Krevins was behind this, I'd turn him inside out by his tonsils."

"We're getting there, pal. Be cool. Anything new on Krevins?"

"I don't think he suspects I'm tuned in to what he's been doing. May take another crack at him under the guise of checking my draft magazine article. Told him I'd get back with a draft in a few days. What did you find out about Paula Taylor?"

Jud slid down in his seat and shook his head. "In your weirdest moment you couldn't dream up a more dumfounding woman than Paula. She's so beautiful it blows me away. And brilliant? Ought to have a law against one woman having a monopoly on smarts *and* looks."

"Sounds like you've found your dream girl."

"Hardly, Dan. She strikes me as someone who would be willing to do just about anything if it suited her fancy. That woman has a nasty streak all the way to her core. She scares the shit out of me."

"So what do you think; could she be the computer wizard that's putting Victor's plan in motion?"

"Absolutely, Dan. No question she has the potential to pull something like that together. Her computer skills are pure magic. I don't doubt she has the smarts to follow through."

"Okay, what's our next step?"

Jud smiled and said, "I have a plan. Believe I can get the evidence on our miss nibs. If things work out like I suspect they will, we'll know Paula and Victor are a pair. Then it'll be takedown time. Have to get back to my own equipment at home to carry this off, though."

Dan's curiosity was definitely aroused but he knew better than to question Jud further about his plan. He was, however, more than a little anxious to hear more about the intriguing Miss Taylor.

"So why does she alarm you?"

Jud hesitated, then took a deep breath and frowned.

"That woman is a control freak. She wants to dominate every man she meets. I'm here to tell you, Jud Black doesn't take that from anybody, including Athena."

"Thought her name was Paula?" Dan looked perplexed.

"She's a hacker, Dan. More correctly, Paula's what we call a cracker. A talented hacker that goes in for creating serious problems for computer systems for fun or profit. She uses the hacker moniker Athena."

"Let me see," Dan pondered. "If I remember my Greek mythology, Athena was the goddess of wisdom. Sounds like our friend Paula may have a super size ego."

"Exactly my point. Paula's convinced she's something really special. Entitled to do whatever turns her on. Doesn't hesitate to screw up computer networks at random. I watched her sabotage systems and build in problems that could take weeks and big money to fix. She's so self-centered it's a mania with her."

"You'd better be careful how you mess with her dream world, Jud. She could turn on you."

"Don't I know it! I can only imagine the trail she's left behind her; guys she's strung along and stepped on.

Somebody has to stop her. Whether she's Victor's partner or not, she has to be taken off the internet one way or another. She's out of control. We can't afford to have fanatics like her running around."

Dan sat staring at Jud, trying to figure out what had his pal so riled up and confused. Sounded as if Jud knew what had to be done but wished there were an alternative. Paula Taylor must have made a big impact on him and it wasn't all negative.

* * *

Ellen looked improved today. Both her sunny smile and the absence of the feeding line were encouraging.

"I see they're finally giving you some solid food, beautiful," Dan said and kissed her. "Your color is coming back. You look so much better."

"I'm not up to steak and fried chicken yet but we're getting there. You fellows eating okay?"

Jud came along side her bed and nodded toward Dan.

"This guy may teach me to eat health food yet. You know you've totally corrupted him since you kidnapped him to Florida. The way he's behaving, he may live forever."

"That's the idea," she said. "We're just now hitting our stride. Watch out. I may get you matched up and living a clean life, too."

"Dan already tried that."

"And?"

Jud shrugged.

Dan reflected that Ellen wouldn't believe how that turned out. She wouldn't think a contradiction like Paula existed. He had never steered Jud wrong before but this one sure had fooled him. From Jud's description she was a brilliant blonde temptress on the outside and rotten to her center.

"Dani sends her love, Ellen. Talked to her yesterday. She and Rick are fine," he told her.

"Well, I certainly feel a lot better. Just can't seem to remember things yet."

That was a continuing source of worry. There didn't seem to be an organic reason for her memory loss. Nevertheless, Ellen was still struggling to recall what had happened to her. It was a sobering thought for Dan that she may never fully regain the past few days in any coherent way.

"What's the last thing you remember before this happened, El?"

"You and I were just back from shopping at the mall. I was looking for some new slacks and tops. After that it's all a blur."

She had a look of helplessness that told Dan he shouldn't pursue this further. The doctor would draw her out in time. Patience was a burden he was beginning to live with reluctantly.

"Don't worry, honey. Give it time."

She wasn't quite ready to let go yet. "I do remember the silver glint and blue glow then a sharp pain just before I blacked out. The doctor has told me I was at Sue's house when that happened. He also told me she died. I'm trying to deal with that."

Her lip trembled and she set her jaw as if determined to continue. "Everything before the shopping trip is clear. It's only since then that I can't recall—except for that one instant and those colors."

"No need to hurry things, baby. You're coming along fine. I can see the twinkle is back in your eyes." He had to get her away from dwelling on her problem.

The three of them talked for a long while until Dan was sure Ellen had settled down. They joked and laughed, recalled pleasant memories of times together back in Virginia. Ellen had her first chance since Jud had come to Florida to catch up with what he was doing. Dan could see that she was coming around if only they could beat this bewildering memory loss.

"Tell me what's going on in your life, Jud. How's the music career?" She really did seem more talkative and that warmed Dan's heart.

"Just cut a new release, Ellen. Think it may do well."

"Still an independent?"

"You bet. Can't tolerate the big houses trying to tell me how to handle my music. No spoon-feeding for me or my fans. They know what they like and I give it to them unadulterated, just like Zappa did."

"I love to hear you talk about your music," Ellen said. "You light up all over. Everybody has to have something they're passionate about."

Dan heard Doctor Lake making his rounds. Ellen appeared to be tiring and talked out, so he and Jud made their exit. Dan sought a word with the doctor in the hallway.

"Mr. Cooper, I think Ellen is making great progress. She's come a long way in ten days."

"I agree, doctor, but the memory blackout scares me numb. She's drawing a complete blank recalling anything for almost two weeks. All she remembers are those flashes of color when she was attacked."

"We've run repeated tests for clues and come up dry. I've ordered more extensive blood work done. We should have the results within the next two days. Think positive."

As he and Jud drove toward home, Dan pondered what the doctor had said. In so many words he had admitted that he was as stumped by Ellen's condition as everyone else was. What Dan feared was that the outcome of a prolonged absence of recollection could be serious. It may be a roadblock to Ellen's ever returning to full capacity.

A thought rolled around in his head and nagged at him. It had to do with something he had read recently—but what was it? Short-term memory. Cerebellum. Test subjects.

Of course!

"Jud, I think I may have a line on what's wrong with Ellen. Some of the papers in Victor's filing cabinet made references to using natural, herbal drug preparations. He aimed the drugs at the cerebellum to observe memory changes. Victor implied he could affect how the brain controls memory. I need to go back to the hospital now."

He found the duty nurse and inquired of her, "Do you know Doctor Victor Krevins?"

"Yes, I do. He's a psychologist. The doctor makes occasional visits to patients here. In fact, I believe he was on our floor at least twice during the past week."

Dan winced when he heard that. "I don't know the exact procedure for this, nurse. I want to leave strict instructions that Krevins is not to go near my wife's room. I'll talk to whoever can make that happen, sign whatever you require. He is *not* to be anywhere around Ellen. If he gains access to her room, I *will* sue the hospital."

The nurse summoned the senior administrator on duty. Dan repeated his insistence on barring Krevins from coming in contact with Ellen. The administrator balked but Dan wouldn't take no for an answer. He signed a written statement to that effect before leaving the hospital. His next step would be to again ask the police department to provide a 24-hour guard for insurance.

Dan and Jud drove home to Trinity. Dan said, "You know I'm not by nature a violent man. But I swear if I find Krevins has slipped some drug to Ellen, they're going to have a hard time finding enough of him to bury."

Jud cast a long look at Dan as if viewing him in a whole new light.

CHAPTER 29

Dan tossed and turned trying to put the day's worries behind him. Jud would be leaving for home tomorrow and it wasn't yet clear how they would go about pressing their pursuit of Victor Krevins. The mugger had robbed Ellen of two precious weeks of her life. Dan couldn't be sure there weren't more long-term implications to her health.

Maybe the doctor would learn more about her condition from these new tests. Think positive the doctor had said. But that was a little harder every day Ellen spent in that hospital.

He and Jud had to find a way to fit the puzzle pieces together. He wrestled with the sheets and touched the empty half of the bed where Ellen should be lying. If he could only feel her beside him now he could drift off to peaceful sleep. But the torment of the uncertainties facing him made rest impossible.

Hours later he was still agonizing and sleep was no nearer. He threw back the covers and plodded to the family room. Maybe there was something on the tube to distract him. Damn, the cable system was off again; seemed to be a recurring problem these days.

"Screw it," he mumbled. "Nothing works for me tonight. Maybe I'll drink myself to sleep."

He sat and stared at the snowy screen and conjured up images that would only prolong his sleeplessness. Dan couldn't even muster the energy to head for the liquor cabinet.

What if Ellen never returned to normal and they had to make a permanent adjustment in their lives? There was no question he would make whatever sacrifice was necessary to protect and cherish her. But at what cost to the future they had dreamed of together? Life had given them everything they wanted and things were as near perfect as either of them could ever wish. Then his best friend was taken away, Ellen's closest friend was brutally murdered, Ellen was almost lost. How much more could they endure?

What had he done to deserve his whole world going to pieces?

A sleepy-eyed Jud Black emerged from the guest room. He took one look at Dan and walked between him and the TV set. Jud waved one hand back and forth in front of the screen.

"Do not be alarmed. We have taken control of your television set."

Even then it was a few seconds before Dan reacted and snapped out of his trance. He shook the cobwebs from his brain and looked at Jud.

"Dude, you were gone. I mean you were completely zonked out. Do you know what time it is, Dan?"

"Late, I'd imagine," Dan replied.

"More like early. It's after two. What's going on?"

"Need to sort things out. This has been a frustrating week. Now that you're up, can we recap what we know and maybe plot our course from here?"

"Whatever it takes to bring you around, pal. The way you looked when I walked in here was downright scary."

They sat down at the morning room table and Dan grabbed a pencil to jot down notes. The clincher had to be locked away in their heads somewhere. It just wasn't clear yet. Dan's engineer's mind told him they could begin to clear the fog by listing the facts and diagramming where they'd come so far. Then they could arrive at the necessary actions to nail those responsible for all those deaths and who knows what damage to Ellen.

Jud leaned forward and said, "Okay, we know there were hidden video and audio files on the machines of two of the victims, Millwood and Wainwright. They tie back to email messages I haven't been able to track to their source. We know the videos directly relate to the actions three men took that led to their deaths."

Dan interjected, "We believe Victor Krevins is a prime candidate for bad guy in all cases. He's been severely put down by his peers for his far-out theories and dangerous practices. Barry and Myron knew him well enough to realize the danger of what he may be doing. They even tried to warn him to clean up his act."

"Right," Jud said. "For all the good it did them. He's a nasty, vindictive man who could be on the verge of flipping out completely. But what about Gernsbach? Where's the connection to him other than his criticism of Victor's lecture?"

"Too bad I couldn't get to Jason's computer in New Orleans. By now, if there were hidden files, the sender has probably deleted them. We do know that he and Barry had discussed Victor by email. They were worried about the work he was doing."

Dan was scribbling on a pad as they talked. Suddenly a thought hit him so hard he broke the pencil lead and tossed the pencil across the room.

"Well, I'll be damned! Ellen isn't the only one with a temporary memory loss."

"I can see the gears cranking. What is it?" Jud coaxed.

"There is a direct connection to Gernsbach. Paula was with me when we had lunch at the symposium. She knew Jason's passion was building model ships. In fact, he even told her he was working on whittling a model of a paddle wheeler. For her, finding out his net addresses at home and at work would have been no obstacle. I'd even wager I know why Jason stopped to empty his pockets before he stepped into the water on Toulouse Wharf."

Jud urged him on. "You're on a roll. Give me a dump."

"There was a paddle wheeler sitting tied up exactly where he went into the river. One of those tour boats that takes visitors up the Mississippi. The video on his machine, and I'm convinced there was one, steered him to that wharf. He must have homed in on the paddle wheel. Thought he was looking at one of his models. He emptied his pockets and found his pocketknife, then headed for that big wheel to start working on it. He was still clutching his open knife when they found him."

"Now let's talk about the night Ellen and Susan were attacked," Jud said. "Somebody was in that house because they needed hard access to Millwood's computer. Had to turn it back on and delete the incriminating daemons for the video and audio files. The intruder, or perhaps Paula, knew about the email exchange between Millwood and Krevins because those files were also deleted."

That evoked Dan's painful memory of the scene at Tom's office after Marge had been brutally murdered.

"Just like the assassin at the office got access to Barry's computer and erased the hidden files. He did do us the favor of missing those saved emails, though."

Dan was writing furiously.

"But it wasn't Victor at the house because he was out of town," Jud said. "Whoever it was could have been wearing a watch with a silver band and a luminous blue face. But who was it? Wasn't Paula unless she packs a man sized wallop."

"I'll work on that. Let's try for a few hours sleep. Have to get you to the airport early for your flight home."

The information overload was finally under control. Dan knew they were on the right track. He could, at least for now, rest with full confidence they were going to unravel this mess.

* * *

Jud was chatting away when they broke out of the early morning fog on the back roads to the airport.

"We'll know very soon whether Victor and Paula are in cahoots. I wouldn't tell this to another living soul but I'm hacking her computer as soon as I get home. Whatever she has on that baby will soon be mine. We'll know what she's been up to recently. I'll be in touch and I plan to fly back in about a week—maybe sooner if things heat up."

No answer. "Hey, Dan. You with me, fellow?"

Dan jerked his head around. "Sorry, Jud. What's that?"

"Said I'm going to hack Paula's computer from my place and explore all her dirty little secrets. Be back here in a week or so."

"Okay. And I'll visit the mad doctor one more time," Dan told him. "I'll take along my article, rough as it is, and see if I can get him to make a slip somewhere." Dan stared intently ahead and plotted as they neared the airport.

"Watch your back," Jud told him. "I'm going to try to reach somebody named Minerva, too. Got a possible phone number. There's a link between her and Paula that I need to learn more about."

"Minerva?"

"Yeah. The name Minerva came up when Paula took a cocaine hit and got loose lips. Then she tried to talk me into sharing her stash. You know me and my aversion to drugs. Sang me a ditty and said something about Minerva's net. Didn't understand that."

They parted at curbside and Jud scooted off to catch his flight. Dan drove away with his pal's last comment chewing at him in an irritating manner. Why did the name Minerva strike a chord? Then he connected the dots. He picked up his cell phone and punched in Jud's number.

"Hey, you're getting too attached, man. I just saw you a few minutes ago." Jud chided.

"Listen up, smart ass. Minerva was the Roman goddess of wisdom."

"Okay. So?"

"Minerva and Athena are parallel figures in Roman and Greek mythology. They both represent wisdom and intelligence. Don't you see? . . . superwoman Paula may have *two* alter egos. She could have more than a link with Minerva—Paula could actually *be* Minerva. Be careful and realize who you could be talking to before you call."

Dan had done a decent job of putting together a draft magazine article on Krevins' dramatic approach to brain research. He had completed most of the work while sitting with Ellen. When they ran out of something to talk about, she would watch TV or read while he wrote. That was the best of all worlds for him. He could be near her and still move along with his plan to snare Victor. Now it was time to corner the mad doctor and put the squeeze on him

* * *

The follow-up interview with Krevins turned out to be easy to arrange. Before he reached the hospital Dan called Victor's school office. The doctor was preparing for his week in class and the lab.

"Dan Polk, Doctor Krevins. I'm ready for you to take a look at our proposed magazine article. Can we arrange a time to meet this week?"

"Ah, yes. Mister Polk. I'm anxious to see what you've written. Hope it does justice to the far-reaching implications of my work."

What a flaming asshole Dan thought to himself. But he was careful to keep a civil tone.

"There are a few points I need to revisit with you to be sure I have them correct. When may I come by?"

"It will have to be here at the office, Mr. Polk. I could give you an hour tomorrow starting promptly at eleven AM. Can you make that schedule?"

"You're the doctor. I'll be there." He thought about how inane his last statement sounded. But it was much better than what he wanted to say—*You're the crazy bastard I'm going to put away.*

Krevins was a man on a crusade. It was obvious he couldn't wait to show up his myopic associates and bask in the glory of publicity for his bold achievements. The catch was made and now it was time for Dan to pull him in. He wanted to extract all the incriminating information he could from that sick brain.

* * *

Tuesday morning Dan sat quietly while Victor carefully concentrated on each word of his draft. He felt like a schoolboy watching a teacher critique his essay. And from the number of tick marks and scribbles the doctor had made he anticipated a lengthy discussion of how to improve the article. When Krevins at length stared over his glasses with those cold, dark eyes, Dan was ready to be dispatched for a rewrite.

"Surprisingly good and largely accurate, Mr. Polk. I think you've caught the spirit of what I'm attempting to do in the face of heavy odds and too many nay sayers."

Dan was shocked by Victor's acceptance of what he had written. However, he was fully prepared for the diatribe that would surely follow. Let Krevins rant. There would have to be openings for questions. He'd trap the doctor in statements that would come back to haunt him.

"I'm ready to listen. Perhaps the notes you've made will answer most of my questions."

Victor seemed more than pleased with the way this conversation was going.

Get on your soapbox, Crazy Vic, Dan thought. *Give me something I can hang you with.* If he knew what Dan was thinking now, he'd go airborne.

Just then there was a rap at the office door. A gaunt young man walked tentatively into the room. Dan saw who it was and reacted immediately. He turned toward the bookshelves and bent down to fumble with his papers. Hoped the intruder hadn't had time to recognize who was sitting with the doctor.

Peter Drake was asking Krevins for the lab test schedule for the week.

"I'm very busy, Pete. Take your lunch break early and be back in the lab by noon. I'll finish up the schedule and discuss it with you then."

Drake left the room and Dan exhaled. He had held his breath so long his face should be crimson by now. Apparently his hasty cover up went unnoticed by the focused man behind the desk.

At this point Dan had totally lost his own concentration. The near encounter with Peter Drake had shocked him so that it had taken him off target. Why hadn't he at least considered the possibility of running into the young man here? Dan knew Peter was closely tied to Krevins as his school laboratory assistant. If Peter as much as remarked to Victor that he also had met Dan Cooper, the whole game could be exposed. Dan wouldn't even know his identity had been compromised until he was blindsided. Oh, well, may as well hope for the best and gamble that he hadn't been recognized. He was in too deep to back down now.

Krevins showed no sign at the moment that he suspected he was being scammed.

"Let's talk about this part first, Mr. Polk. I'd like to suggest some modifications to your description here."

They talked on and Dan took Victor's suggestions, lavishing him with praise whenever possible. He would take anything Krevins offered. He wanted one opening and a reaction to a single planned question. That opening would come sooner or later or Dan would manufacture an opportunity.

"We have much work to do on perfecting my cerebellar inspiration techniques. However, I remain convinced that our breakthrough is just around the bend."

Okay, here goes. It's now or never.

"My understanding is, Doctor Krevins, that will involve extraordinary talent in electrical engineering and computer programming. You mentioned receiving help from the engineering department. Is there something we can add to the story now?"

"I think not. That's not important."

"I have an admission to make, Doctor. I've been doing some background on campus for the story. Happened across someone who mentioned a particularly brilliant psychology student of yours. That student also happens to be a gifted computer expert. Didn't know if you were aware of it."

"Oh, and who might that be?" He asked the question after hesitating and there was a note of suspicion rising in his voice.

"Her name is Paula Taylor I believe."

Victor went pale which was quite a stretch for the swarthy doctor. But his eyes never lost their penetrating intensity. He bore down on Dan and cut him with his stare. Maybe he'd pushed Krevins too far this time.

"Pau—oh. Yes, I remember her now. She's a lovely girl and a good student. But she's not a part of my project."

He fidgeted with his pencil and tried to redirect his attention to Dan's draft. Victor had delivered his answer in an unconvincing fashion. Dan felt extreme nervousness in the doctor's actions and his tone. The question had caught him completely off guard. It had also exposed Dan to instant suspicion that was obvious in the way Krevins was now regarding him. Time would be running out on both sides of this contest very soon. He was certain he had prompted Victor to search for every scrap of information he could find on 'Dan Polk'. That would inevitably lead to his true identity given Paula Taylor's resource for information harvesting.

Dan still held the edge for the time being. Unless Victor and Paula acted quickly, they would be safely tucked away before any harm could come to him. He was now certain beyond the slightest doubt that he knew his adversaries by name and they *would* fall.

CHAPTER 30

Time to see what secrets the delectable Miss Taylor is hiding on her computer. If she had any idea what he was about to do to her machine she'd be drumming a tattoo on Jud's head. Probably do it with a heavy sledge. Crackers consider everybody else fair game. It would be demeaning to her if she realized she was being violated in the same way she assaulted everyone else. Well, she'd brought it on herself.

Jud Black sat in his darkened basement with his black dog, Downbeat. He started his hack of Paula Taylor's computer. She would never be aware of what had transpired since he was covering his actions. Any files he opened would continue to show the last access date prior to his intrusion. Even if she routinely checked for queries from outside, he had taken the precaution to mask the true source of his probes. So she would logically interpret it as a hit by another cracker. And with her freewheeling habit of attacking others, it should come as no surprise that someone may return the insult.

"Okay, I'm in, Downbeat. Now let's start by scanning her stored files. That should give me some nasty little tidbits about what our Miss Taylor's been up to recently."

By now the big dog should be used to Jud addressing him as if he were human. They had spent long hours together isolated from the world in this dark basement. Downbeat laid his head against his master's leg.

Jud called up Paula's menu and found some prime candidates for further inspection.

"Hmmm. Some interesting files listed here. Let's see what the folder BM Treasures contains."

At last he had positively located the source of the video and audio files sent to Barry Millwood. No doubt if he opened the email there would be a sent message with these two files as attachments from Secret Treasures to the *milldoc* address. The digitized video daemon would be a very large file. Jud fished for the stack of disks he had preformatted for recording and popped one into his CD-ROM drive.

No surprise there. MW Dressage was a folder with two file attachments to send to Myron Wainwright. Now he had to link the files to the emails that had gone to the two victims. He worked his way into her saved email. There were the outgoing messages to Wainwright and Millwood. He began the process of downloading them with their large digitized video attachments to discs. Jud hoped Paula was at work and wouldn't try to access her home computer while he was probing.

"Well, look what I found, boy!" Downbeat growled in response.

It was bonus time. He'd located a message to Jason Gernsbach with attachments. It was sent from BoatCarvers and transmitted both a video and an audio as part of the attachments. The routing went back through that same server address he'd seen Paula use at her apartment. Now he was sure he could tie Paula's vicious little email game to Jason Gernsbach's final swim in the Mississippi. That video would be interesting to see later, he thought, as he continued recording.

"Got you on three counts now, you conniving witch," he proclaimed so loudly that Downbeat leaped to his feet and howled. "And you almost blinded me with beauty and intellect. Now I know the real vixen behind those blue, blue eyes."

As he prepared to return to Paula's master menu, he stopped short. Better spot check her incoming stored messages. There was one that read:

Subj: quick cure
Date: 03/11 17:22:41 PM Eastern Standard Time
From: *pvjack@trail.com*
To: *minerva@downstream.net*

Cure is for Samuel B. Trotter. Address home *airnut@calnet.com,* work *sbt@regency.com.* Hobby interest private pilot, owns Cessna 180. Action needed soonest. No contact, no trail. Advise location for payment 75 old after cure.

The message was addressed to *Minerva@downstream.net.*

Jud blurted out, "Gotcha!" This confirmed the suspicion raised by Dan that Paula was, in fact, also Minerva. But it added a new dimension to the sorry war she was waging by Internet. Until now Jud and Dan had assumed that the electronic attacks on the three psychologists were all about revenge and protection for Victor Krevins.

Jud had little doubt about the real meaning of the word cure. A thinly veiled acronym for contract murder of one Sam Trotter. Sam would no doubt receive an email related to his flying interest with hidden attachments prompting him to crash in his Cessna or something equally disastrous. If he hadn't already received that message, perhaps Jud could warn him. The proviso of no contact certainly fit the hands off mode of the previous killings with no trail back to either the assassin or the client.

But what was this about payment? He took 75 old to mean a payment of 75 thousand dollars in old money. Did Minerva have her own scam going—murder for profit? His fantasies about the intriguing Miss Taylor were rapidly being transformed into a gruesome, vivid picture. The vision involved Jud being at the mercy of a sadistic woman set on destroying his manhood slowly and painfully.

"Just proves you can't trust any of them, Downbeat. Remember that the next time you meet some sexy little four pawed bitch."

He found no outgoing message to the proposed victim in Paula's stored file so there may still be time. Jud fired off an email to the address provided. The message warned Sam Trotter in the strongest way possible to open no further messages from unknown sources. Jud included his own cell phone number with an urgent request for Sam to call and speak with him.

* * *

There was another important call to be made. Jud unfolded the scrap of paper in his billfold and read Minerva's contact number. He dialed through a cutout relay that would redial and conceal the true starting point of this conversation. Then he switched on the tone modifier to alter his voice. Paula was too sharp for him to chance her recognizing his voice.

"Minerva?"

"Who's calling?"

"Someone in need of help. I'm told you can provide a valuable service."

"So? You made the call. Talk to me."

She's hard as steel when she feels in control, Jud thought. *Turns the charm on and off like tapping a maple tree. I could get verbal frostbite from listening to her.*

"I need a troubling situation cleared up, Minerva. Friend of mine needs immediate help to solve a sizable problem. You come highly recommended as a reliable source in these matters. He's not to know where the help comes from so there can be no direct contact."

"You say immediate. Do you understand the solution may take from a few days to a couple weeks? That will depend on how receptive your friend is to my help."

"That's okay by me. Just start your work right away," Jud answered.

"Take down my instructions and follow them to the letter. I want a message from your computer giving me the friend's name and email addresses at home and at work. Provide the name of the friend's hometown. I need to know his favorite pastime or hobby, something I can use to attract his attention. I'll answer you with an email confirming our agreement. After that any communication between us will be by Internet. Payment is 90 large in used paper payable where I specify when the service is completed."

"No problem," Jud said. "I have all the information you want and I can give it to you now."

"Do exactly as I've told you. I don't need suggestions, just compliance. Send the information by email."

"Understood. You'll have it today."

Nice little business she has going here, Jud mused. *And there's already price creep. My quote is higher than the last guy is paying. She's a bit overconfident, though. Didn't even make an attempt to disguise her voice. It was clearly Paula Taylor.*

She needed his email address to track him in case he balked on paying up. Didn't even ask for a down payment. Hell, she's sure her plan will work. If the client balks on paying, she'll just work up a clever way to dispose of him as well. It's all in a day's play.

Good luck, Paula. This will lead you to a machine in Lanham, Maryland that automatically redials my computer and forwards your message to me. Some poor SOB in Maryland is going to be confounded when you demand ninety thousand dollars for services rendered. Well, here goes.

Jud's message directed Minerva's wrath on Bill Lawson, *willieboy@cfd.net* home, *wklawson@jasco.com* work, Las Vegas, Nevada. Bill's passion was advertised to her as hiking and mountain climbing. That should provide her with an assortment of ways to get her jollies. Should be plenty of available stock photos of local spots on the Net for her to choose one to adapt to her own purposes. She could have Bill hurl himself off Hoover Dam or step out of a helicopter over the Grand Canyon. Maybe she'd prompt him to walk into the desert or try to climb some mountain and not come back. That is, if there really *was* a Bill Lawson. Whatever she chose, Jud would have a first-hand audit trail through a recorded telephone conversation and exchange of emails that proved her murderous enterprise.

The trap was baited and set.

"Well, old boy," Jud said, sitting back and rubbing Downbeat's neck, "sometimes we have to make hard choices. Damn, I wish it didn't have to be this way. But she asked for it."

CHAPTER 31

"Jud, I'm calling you from outside the hospital." Dan Cooper stood in the evening breeze after his third trip to see Ellen today. The fresh air helped but he was weary from spending nearly every waking moment standing vigil over her bedside.

"What is it? Is Ellen okay?"

"Actually, there hasn't been much change. She's slowly regaining her strength but she can't remember anything that happened the past two weeks. It's all one big blank to her since then. Today she seems a bit groggier than usual."

"What about your audience with King Victor? What's the story on that?"

"He's operating somewhere out in lotus land, Jud. This yahoo has to be one of the weirdest human beings I've ever met. We have to act fast. When his mainspring snaps this character's going to be one unpredictable maniac."

"Wound that tight, huh?"

"You bet. And there could be another complication. While I was in his office, his assistant, the one Barry was training, walked in on our conversation. Think I managed to hide my face from him but I can't be sure. How soon can you be back here so we can put a full press on Victor and Paula?"

"I'm booked on a flight tomorrow. Planned to call you today. Should be at your place by mid-evening tomorrow night. I'm picking up a car at the airport."

"Oh, one other bit you need to have. I asked Victor if he knew one of his students is also a computer expert. When I mentioned Paula's name he damn near lost it. Tried to dismiss my question like he wasn't interested but it was obvious I stunned him. Now I'm more convinced than ever that they're a team."

"Wait till you hear the story I've put together with some selective snooping, Dan. We've got her positively tied to all three dead docs with files I've copied from her machine. There's some other foul business going on that I'll tell you about face to face. Hang in."

"Hold on, Jud. You also need to be aware that I left a standing order barring Crazy Vic from going near Ellen. I suspect he's done something to complicate her memory loss."

"Can you get the police to assign a guard outside her room?"

"Tried but they say they can't do that without stronger proof that she's in immediate danger. Somehow it's not enough that she could possible identify Susan's killer. I can't spill my guts to them about Victor until we have him all packaged for delivery."

"I'd be on the plane tonight if I could. You and I could alternate shifts watching over Ellen," Jud told him.

"No sweat, pal. I don't intend to budge from Ellen's side without someone friendly hovering over her. I'm not about to take as much as a coffee break unless a nurse I trust can spell me by her bed. Doc Lake is with her now. Have to get back up there."

"Give her my love, Dan. I'll fill you in when I get there but my trap for Paula worked famously. She sent me a hidden video today and I have her locked as Minerva. See you tomorrow."

* * *

"How's my best gal doing?" Dan was by Ellen's side as soon as the doctor left.

She smiled. "Better be your only girl, buster. Is this your first trip here today?" Ellen asked without making a direct reply to his question.

"No, I was up here for awhile earlier."

The fact was he had been in and out of her room three times since this morning. That last trip he'd spent more than two hours with her and he'd only been gone for a short time to make his call.

"Can you find these magazines for me?"

She reached out and struggled to retrieve a list that contained the same titles he had brought her yesterday when she first requested them. Those magazines were neatly stacked in the night table but he didn't want to confuse her at this stage. He would place them on top of her table when she took her next nap.

"I'll look in the gift shop for them," he told her.

"Wish I could get up out of here and go home. I need to do some shopping for spring clothes. Need new tops and slacks." Even as she said the words, Dan sensed the real resolve just wasn't there.

"I thought the ones you bought week before last were really nice," he said before thinking.

"What do you mean? I haven't had any new clothes since the ones you bought me for Christmas."

This was beginning to frighten him. What was that insane Krevins doing to her and how had he managed to get in here? How much more was she going to forget? Well, that ugly doc would play hell coming near her again without Dan using him for a dust mop. Victor's playtime was coming to a screeching halt as of now.

"Remind me, Ellen. You said you saw a silver glint and . . . was it a blue glow just before you blacked out?"

"When did I tell you that? Oh, Dan, what's happening to me?" She fidgeted with her hands and frowned weakly.

He went to her and held her close while she shivered violently. Good old Dan Fumble had opened his big mouth again. He punched the call button and the nurse responded.

"I think she could use something to settle her down, nurse."

Dan was sure he had upset her with his stupidity. Her sudden inability to remember events only days or hours old had sent a bone-chilling tremor through him. He'd overreacted and been too anxious to probe the depth of her memory lapse. Something had to happen, and fast, or he was going to lose a part of the dearest person in the world. Maybe he should just look up Victor Krevins and pound on him for awhile. Dan wanted to hear Victor admit his crimes. Even more urgently, he wanted to know how to bring

Ellen out of her growing stupor. The sheer pleasure he'd derive from trashing the morbid doctor's butt while solving Ellen's dilemma would be doubly satisfying.

"Doctor Lake is nearby. I'll call him in and see what he wants to do." The nurse hurried away to retrieve him.

After he had attended to Ellen, the doctor motioned for Dan to follow him outside the room. He spoke barely above a whisper but with a marked tone of concern.

"I have to ask you a ticklish question, Mr. Cooper. It's about the results of our latest set of blood tests on your wife. We detected a substantial presence of a substance quite similar to MDMA in her bloodstream."

"I don't understand. What is MDMA?"

"You may have heard of it by its more common name—Ecstasy. This substance seems to be chemically similar to Ecstasy but it's apparently slightly different. There's something else in there we can't isolate."

"Hold up, doc. I know what you're going to ask me and the answer is HELL, NO. She wouldn't touch drugs of any kind. There has to be a mistake somewhere."

"This is critically important, Dan. Research shows that repeated use of drugs like Ecstasy can cause temporary short-term memory loss. That could explain Ellen's continuing problem. We aren't certain how long the effects last or how much memory they blank out."

"Doctor Lake, I've never been more certain about anything in my entire life. Ellen wouldn't be in the same room with illegal drugs much less use them. She's beginning to blank out things that occurred less than a day ago. But until she entered the hospital, she'd always had a crystal clear recollection of things I'd forgotten. If you found foreign substances in her system, someone put them there after she came to the hospital."

"That's a pretty serious indictment, Dan. We have excellent security here."

"You know about the restraint I placed on Doctor Krevins coming near her. I have my own reasons for making that request.

Are you sure he didn't get in here somehow? Or maybe other medical personnel slipped those chemicals into her IV or in a routine shot a nurse gave her."

"Don't make accusations unless you have good reason, Mister Cooper." Doc Lake was going on the defense.

"The only reason I need is lying right over there fighting to get herself back to normal. I'm telling you that stuff had to get into her system after she was admitted. And her ability to remember is getting worse. She can't even recall now what she told me about the colors she saw before she passed out."

Doctor Lake walked away shaking his head. Dan wondered if Lake thought he'd been talking to a man who refused to believe his wife had a drug problem. Maybe the doctor was as baffled as everyone else. Either way, Dan would be suspicious of everyone and question everything they did for or near Ellen for as long as she remained here.

The pattern was becoming clear to Dan. Krevins sends someone to wipe clean any evidence from Barry's computers. Marge walks in on him—or her—and panics the intruder into hitting her so hard she dies. Susan is accidentally killed as someone, maybe the same person, tries to flee from the Millwood house and Ellen is seriously injured. Victor is afraid Ellen can identify her attacker and that the killer will implicate him. He walks boldly onto the hospital floor and no one takes note since he is accredited to Meadows Hospital as a visiting doctor. Then he stalks directly into Ellen's room and administers a dose, or maybe repeated doses, of one of the concoctions he's been using on his test subjects. The effects ensure she won't recall the events of that night at the Millwoods' while he buys time to decide how to squirm out of his predicament.

The good news, if there really was any, was that Dan could hope the effects would eventually wear off. He had to prevent any new doses from getting into her bloodstream. And he could guarantee that wouldn't happen because they'd have to go through him to get to her. Strange personnel and unusual treatments would be reason for Dan to take action immediately. If they wanted to see a grade A horse's ass, he could be one, but no one was hurting Ellen ever again.

* * *

Dan informed the nurse he wanted some quiet time and the door would be closed. He established his post by Ellen's side and took her hand in his. The long hours were exacting a toll. He knew sleep was coming on no matter how adamantly he fought against nodding off. No one, least of all Victor Krevins, was getting near Ellen tonight Dan vowed as he slipped toward an exhausted slumber.

A strange feeling had returned, a dizzy sensation in his head. For the past two days he seemed to lose his concentration again and again. It was oddly similar to how he had felt after first scanning Barry's computer with the hidden files installed. He had been on his own computer briefly during his short trips home from the hospital to check some data on the brain's inner workings.

That was after his visit to Krevins' office and the chance encounter with Peter Drake. Was he only creating ghosts in his mind or could there be a connection? He hadn't opened any emails except those from sources he recognized.

Wait a minute. He opened that long explanation from his Internet Service Provider about new services they were offering. Posing as his ISP to transfer a hidden file to him would be no challenge to someone of Paula's ability. Dan Cooper was the dunce of the year! Drake had somehow tipped off Victor about who Dan actually was and the doctor was hot on his trail.

He was furious that the chase had swung in favor of the bad guys. In fact, maybe his assumption they were dealing with only Victor and Paula was no longer correct. There could be a whole team of assassins aligned against Jud and him.

Dan resolved to pull the plug on his machine until Jud could do a thorough check. Even as he speculated about what fate they had conjured up for him by remote control, sleep finally won out.

CHAPTER 32

A sound, a feeling, something amiss brought Dan around. There was a sense that Ellen was in danger. Rising onto his elbows, he tried to focus in the direction of Ellen's bed. Someone was standing over her. A dark figure in a doctor's coat. Victor Krevins!

Dan cleared his head. Mustered his will to close the distance between himself and the unwelcome visitor. He vaulted toward Krevins and yanked him bodily to the floor. Ellen stirred and moaned softly. His worst fears were realized and Victor was going to pay. The men struggled and rolled on the floor. Dan heard a commotion outside. Startled voices seeped into his half-awakened brain.

Krevins was stronger than he had expected. Maybe Dan's fatigue was also working against him. He fought to maintain his hold on Victor. The room whirled around him. Then he saw Krevins' arm extend high into the air, He was holding something that was no more than a blur to Dan's clouded eyes.

Instinctively, Dan reached up and grasped the arm. He looked past Victor long enough to see that the object in his hand was a hypodermic syringe. A white hot fury surged through Dan. That needle was for Ellen. How much had Krevins already given her?

"You slimy dirtbag! Here's a sample of your own medicine."

Adrenaline replaced his exhaustion. He bent Victor's elbow inward. Watched the sheer fright in the doctor's eyes and shoved the needle into Krevins' gut. Pushed hard with his palm to empty its contents into his adversary. Hate registered in those cold eyes and Victor's eyelids fluttered. Then an audible gasp. Dan withdrew the needle and held it tightly in his hand. Then he felt himself collapsing backward, striking his head on the tile floor, the world closing in. Ellen cried out for help and Dan's world spun down into blackness.

By now the nurse on duty was in the room spluttering questions to the two prone men. An orderly was close behind her.

"Doctor! Mr. Cooper! What are you doing?" she stammered. The orderly reached down and helped Krevins to his feet.

"He attacked me," Victor stammered out. "I don't know what got into him. I'll be all right, just control him."

Krevins staggered to his feet holding his stomach. Dan still lay motionless where his head had met the hard tile. Victor dusted himself off, assumed his professional posture and simply walked away.

By the time Dan finally recovered enough to speak, the room was packed with medical staff and security personnel. He touched the back of his skull and found he was bleeding from what must be a sizable lump. His head throbbed but his real concern was how Ellen was taking all this frantic activity. He looked in the direction of her bed and her face floated somewhere in the distance.

"Hi, angel. Is my noggin lopsided?" he asked sheepishly. Tried to laugh but it hurt too much.

She smiled and the pain became incidental. They had both survived Victor's bold attack. That's what really mattered. But what about Victor?

"Where's Krevins? I still want a piece of him." Dan rose too quickly and found that the effects of the head blow were more than he expected. He stumbled on unsteady legs.

The orderly grabbed Dan and helped him to a seat. The security man asked, "What started this fight?"

"It wasn't so much a fight as my trying to defend us against a madman. Where is Krevins?" he asked again.

"The doctor left. He said you attacked him."

Dan grimaced with pain and blurted out, "Get after him. He was giving Ellen drugs and I interrupted him. God only knows what he's done to her."

He opened the fist he had clenched tightly around the hypodermic needle. Showed the guard what he was holding. A small amount of liquid remained inside.

Dan handed the syringe to the nurse. "Give this to Doctor Lake to analyze. I think he'll find it contains something very much like Ecstasy. Doctor Krevins was injecting Ellen with it. But he's carrying some of the dose in his own sorry hide now."

"That's a serious charge, mister."

"It's meant to be. Get the police in here so I can make a statement. This is exactly why I asked that Krevins be barred from her room."

The nurse sensed potential trouble for herself and muttered, "I didn't let him in here."

"I know he was just another white coat among many but that's why I left my instructions about keeping him away. This is exactly what I was afraid would happen."

Ellen's doctor surged into the room and breathlessly asked, "How is my patient?"

She's okay, Doctor Lake," Dan replied. "But I'm not so sure about Doctor Krevins. He's carrying around a dose of something in his system. I think we'll find he was giving Ellen mind-bending drugs." He nodded toward the syringe the nurse held.

Dan sat, head in hands, feeling like he was going to throw up at any second. Finally the police arrived. They had apparently been dispatched to take Dan into custody. The erratic husband of a patient needed a night to cool off in the slammer. But he had an earful for them, too.

"I tried to warn your police captain that my wife was in dire danger after she was mugged and her friend was killed. Somebody's worried she can identify the killer. Krevins is tied up in this mess somehow. He's been giving her doses of drugs to cloud her memory. Now they've let him get away."

Ellen related to her doctor what she had seen. "I heard a terrible ruckus and saw two men wrestling on the floor. I kept pushing my call button to get the nurse's attention. Then I realized one of the men was Dan and heard him groan and roll over. I screamed as loudly as I could for help." She was getting herself worked up again and that vague weakness was returning to her eyes.

"Lie back and calm yourself, Ellen. Dan's going to be fine. It's all over now." The doctor spoke in a measured, soft tone of reassurance. "I'll take him down the hall and get his head checked. He appears perfectly normal, just a bit groggy."

Lake turned and took Dan by the arm to lead him away. The policeman followed.

"I don't think you need to watch him, officer. He won't cause any trouble. I believe his story that he was defending his wife. Seems to me you should be looking for the real cause of this fracas. Find Doctor Krevins."

Dan added, "And until you have him locked up, I want an around-the-clock surveillance on my wife's room. I think by now it should be apparent that my fears were justified."

"There'll be someone here as soon as possible. I'm convinced," the officer replied.

"I'll get an analysis started on the residue," Doctor Lake said and held up the syringe. "As soon as we know exactly what it is, we can start treating Ellen to counteract its effects. Too bad our solution to her memory loss had to come this way."

"Doc, right now there isn't time and I'm too whacked out, but I have a long sad tale that will interest you. Has to do with some amazing discoveries in controlling the cerebellum. Afraid Ellen has been one of Victor's guinea pigs. Some of his other subjects didn't survive."

Doctor Lake's eyes widened. "That sounds a little over the edge, Dan. I hope you understand what you're accusing him of."

"Not only do I understand, doc. I have *proof*."

"Looks like you badly need some rest, Dan. But I can't let you go to sleep until we're sure about the bump on your head. I'll have someone walk with you and keep you on your feet for awhile."

"Do what you need, Doctor Lake, but don't take too long. I'm tapped out. As soon as the guard arrives, I'm going to crash in that other bed for awhile. You still don't believe what I'm saying about Krevins, do you?"

"Later, Dan. Just keep walking and stay alert."

"I'm not hallucinating, doc. My friend and I have the proof. I know from talking to Barry's partner, Tom Sherman, the implications of what Krevins has unlocked. He's a threat."

"Okay, Dan, we'll talk later. But our priority is Ellen. Let go of it for now and trust me to get her past the crisis."

As soon as they gave him the go ahead and the guard was on duty, Dan piled headlong onto the bed. As he began to fight his way to a fitful sleep, he thought about what a terrible waste Victor and Paula had made of their unique talents. If only they had possessed the moral fiber to put their astounding successes in mind prompting and behavior control to work for the good of humanity. Doctor Sherman had told him the potential such findings could offer to victims of epilepsy, Alzheimer's, multiple sclerosis and brain injury. But Victor and his partner had been too busy using the knowledge to punish his associates and to make money for her with 'Minerva's net'.

Such a shame. No justice. Cold world. Twisted genius. Have to sleep . . . .

CHAPTER 33

A policeman stood guard at Ellen's hospital room. Dan had filed assault charges and the search was on for Victor Krevins. He let his fatigue take over. Sprawled on the empty bed in Ellen's room. By the time his tortured mind had to face a new day, there should be some good news for a change. The analysis of the syringe's contents was being rushed so Ellen's corrective treatment could get underway. And if the police had acted quickly enough, Krevins could soon be in custody. Finally feeling some of the weight lifting, Dan slept soundly.

"Mr. Cooper. Please wake up." The nurse tugged at him. He bolted upright.

"Wha . . . nurse? Is it Ellen?"

He turned to look at his wife's bed. Empty! The nurse shied back when he fixed her with a thoroughly riveting stare.

"She's being looked after. Doctor Lake is with her."

"Where is she, nurse?"

"Down in IC."

"Intensive Care? What the hell is going on?" By now he was shouting.

Dan was on his feet, his head spinning and his eyes darting in all directions. Someone had a lot of explaining to do about what had happened while he was asleep. The nurse tried to calm him down.

"She's getting the attention she needs. They have the results of the chemical analysis from that needle. He's started giving her counteracting medications."

"Then what's she doing in intensive care? What are you not telling me?"

"The effects of chemicals in her system had built to a near overdose. They moved her to ICU as a precaution so she could have constant surveillance. Doctor Lake believes they've started the reversal in time."

"I want to go to her now!"

"An orderly will take you down there. You can wait for Doctor Lake. He'll give you an update."

* * *

"She has an iron will, Dan," Doctor Lake reassured him as they sat near the doors into the ICU.

"Give it to me straight out, doc. How serious is it?"

Lake leaned in very close and confided, "A little while ago, I wasn't sure we had done enough in time. Doctor Krevins has apparently been sneaking in here and injecting her with something. She was nearly in overdose shock when you stopped him tonight. But she's coming around. If we hadn't acted quickly, well . . ."

"So what does that mean in terms I can deal with?" Dan was apprehensive. The doctor was avoiding any solid commitment about Ellen's condition.

"She's out of danger, Dan. We want to keep a close eye on her, but she should begin a noticeable recovery within the next few hours."

Dan experienced an incredible wave of relief. For the first time since she was attacked, he genuinely felt Ellen could be winning her battle. He wanted to know everything.

"What did your tests show? Was it Ecstasy?"

"A clever liquid created to produce effects similar to MDMA. Seems it wiped out her near-term memory. An overdose could have killed her. It also had other components the lab was able to isolate. Whoever did this to her is a good chemist with uncommon knowledge of natural substances."

"And I'm sure I know who that is," Dan said with a sneer.

"Maybe. But making designer drugs isn't all that difficult any more for someone with knowledge of chemistry and access to the components. There are sites on the Internet that describe the step by step mixing and distillation to manufacture drugs like MDMA. Exactly what our drug crazy culture needs."

Dan snarled, "Sounds like Victor Krevins was using Ellen as an experimental subject. Or wanted to kill her slowly. Either way, his luck has run out. Sooner or later he's mine." It wasn't a threat but a statement of fact that Dan firmly believed.

"Let the authorities handle this, Dan. I don't need two Coopers to worry about. I'm going to let you see her briefly. Then I think you'd better go home and rest. We'll call you as soon as Ellen is able to talk."

"No way. I'm staying right here. She may ask for me."

"Believe me, she'll be all right now. But it may be hours before she's up to a visit. You'd best do what I ask. You've pushed yourself to the limit. Want to look your best for your gal, don't you?"

"Okay, I'll go. But I want a call if there's any change. And I want to see her now if only for a minute."

They proceeded into the unit and Dan took Ellen's hand. She smiled up at him weakly and he knew. It was there in those big, brown eyes. She was back.

"You're the most beautiful sight in the world. Welcome back, sweetheart." He kissed her softly.

She was mumbling something. He leaned closer and made out most of her words.

"Going home soon. Bring my new green top and beige slacks. Don't forget my magazines in the night stand."

"Yes, Ellen. I hear you, honey." He gripped her hand and wiped at his wet cheeks.

"Dan . . . find the man with the blue watch."

Her eyes fluttered and closed as a smile lit her face.

She was on the mend and her memory was flooding back. Dan's feet scarcely touched the floor when he slipped away, beaming.

* * *

Dan rushed out and dialed a number in Virginia.

"Danielle, honey, it's me again. Can you come back down?"

"Oh, Daddy, what's wrong?"

"Mom's fine now but it was touch and go for awhile. I'll explain when you get here. Just think you should be with her if you can manage it. She should be ready to see us by tomorrow morning. I'll keep her company until you arrive."

"I'll be there as soon as I can get a flight. And you're sure she's recovering?"

"She had a couple of rough weeks but the crisis is behind us now. I just know what a comfort it would be to both of us if you were here. If you can possibly arrange a few days off, I think you'll see Mom much improved."

"I'll be there. Tell her I love her."

Before he left for home, Dan wanted to make one last check with the guard on duty.

"Any news about Krevins yet?" Dan asked the uniformed policeman stationed at the entrance to the intensive care unit.

"They're keeping me updated. I don't think he'll show his face around here again. But then that's why I'm here, to make sure he can't do any more harm."

"But they haven't caught him yet?"

"We sent people to his house and his office at the school. Appears he took off in a hurry after you two tussled. Unfortunately, it looks like he also made a quick visit to his townhouse and torched it. It was beyond saving when the firemen arrived, totally gutted."

Dan had a strong idea where Victor had gone. He wasn't likely to wander away from there with everyone looking for him. Victor would be reasonably sure his connection to Paula Taylor was unknown to others. He would hole up in Gainesville with her for as long as possible. That was perfect as far as Dan was concerned.

The old boy and his beautifully wicked partner owed Dan this one. He was going to enjoy ruining their plans.

Jud Black was due in tonight and together they'd rope those two. Right now, Dan wouldn't lay bets that Krevins would survive the take down. He itched to pound him.

* * *

Dan pulled into his garage. His short nap at the hospital had helped but he needed another rendezvous with a soft pillow. He just wanted to find the bedroom and sprawl headlong onto that big bed. Jud knew the gate code and he could find his way in.

From the instant he stepped from the garage into the dark kitchen Dan could feel tension in the air. There was definitely something out of sync. The house was deathly quiet but his head told him he wasn't alone. He took one backward step just in time.

A tall, shadowy figure charged out of the dark. Already in retreat, Dan dodged a punch and stepped forward to deliver one of his own. His attacker expelled a rasping breath and doubled over. Dan rushed him and drove him backward into the kitchen, jamming him against the island. Pummeled him with both fists. Found himself hoping it was Victor Krevins because this felt good.

The intruder cowered and clawed, raking fingernails down Dan's check. That only served to enrage him more and spur him on. Cooper was like a madman.

His unwanted visitor, taken by surprise at the fierce attack, lay helpless and tried to cover up. Then he raised one arm to shield his face and Dan saw a silver glint and a glowing blue watch face. Ellen's mugger! It drove Dan blind with a new fury.

A helpless whimper. "Don't kill me."

The voice didn't sound like Krevins. Who had he walked in on? Dan held off long enough to flick on the wall switch and look down at the huddled figure. Victor's student, Peter Drake!

"You have a lot of explaining to do. I may just tell the police I killed you in self defense."

Peter cringed at his feet.

"No! Victor Krevins sent me."

"That's good for starters. Spill it." Dan cocked one bloodied fist for another assault.

"Said I was to erase your files."

"You recognized me in Victor's office, didn't you?"

"Yes. Told him you were Millwood's friend. He went berserk."

Dan grabbed him by the collar, dragged him toward the cabinets.

He retrieved an extension cord from a drawer and tied Peter's hands behind his back. Then he lifted him to a standing position.

"Keep talking. This better be good or I'll kill you with my bare hands."

"They accessed your computer. Sent you files. That can't be good for you."

Yes, Dan could imagine what was in those files. No more than he had used his machine in the past few days, he could feel their effects. He knew he was being prompted to make some move that would prove fatal to him. Wasn't about to look at the screen again until Jud fixed it.

"Keep going."

He tightened his fingers around Peter's throat and the fear deepened in Drake's eyes. Then he relaxed his hold to let him continue.

"They were afraid of the evidence you may have. Wanted your machine on to get rid of files."

"And who are 'they'?"

He slammed Peter hard against the counter.

"Victor Krevins and Paula Taylor. She does the computer work."

"Don't stop now," Dan threatened, tightening his hold.

Peter's voice cracked. "They learned how to program the brain." He choked on his words. "They can control people like robots. It's frightening."

"And what do you get out of this?"

"I had no choice. He trapped me before I knew how insane he is."

"Meaning what?"

"He's using human subjects. Three of them died."

"And he involved you?"

"Said he'd see I shared the blame for the deaths."

Peter was scared out of his skull and his tongue was loose at both ends. No time to let up, Dan decided.

"Now something very personal to me. You were at Millwood's house two weeks ago. Caused the death of my best friend's wife and nearly killed my wife. I should even the score with you before I call the cops."

"No, please. You need me. I'll testify," he whined.

"So? About the night at the Millwoods'?"

"I don't know about that." His look gave away his desperate lie.

"Don't smoke me. My wife identified you as her attacker."

Dan once again tightened his fingers around Peter's throat. He spluttered and pled with his eyes. When the pressure was released Peter coughed and continued.

"Millwood had emails that would lead back to them. I was to turn on his computer for Paula so she could access it. Then I would leave."

"But you attacked two innocent women, you coward."

"They showed up before I could get out. Never meant to hurt them. Your wife fought like a wildcat to keep me from leaving the house."

Dan took a long look at him. Peter's promising career was gone and he could spend a big part of his life in jail. Then Dan saw the extent of the injuries he had inflicted and wondered about his own capacity for rage.

God help me, I never want to have that devil inside me released again, he mumbled.

Still, it was all he could do to restrain his anger when a final revelation struck him.

"You son of a bitch, you killed Marge, too, didn't you? Tom and Krevins both call you Pete. That's what I heard when Marge dropped the phone and I thought she cried out 'Please. No'. She was blurting out your name and pleading 'Pete. No' just before you bludgeoned her."

"I'm sorry . . . so sorry," Pete wailed, slid back to the floor and sobbed like a child.

By thc time the police arrived, Dan had securely tied and bundled him to be released into their custody. Peter was already babbling about cooperating to help them convict the 'real' guilty parties.

"You do understand your rights as I've stated them to you?" one of the policemen asked. "Maybe you should zip it, fellow."

"But I'm a victim, too," Pete wailed.

Dan gave the police the facts about Pete's involvement in at least two deaths. He lodged a complaint against Drake for assault and trespassing. That would hold him until Dan could make a statement to support a formal charge of murder and conspiracy to commit murder. Couldn't make it to the station or anywhere else in his present condition. For now, he'd have to settle for some precious rest. Then he'd concentrate on Victor and Paula.

Dan wiped at Peter's claw marks with a handkerchief. He was bleeding from both face and knuckles but there was a peaceful glow that followed his intense rage. They were about to close in on Victor Krevins and Paula Taylor; the whole matter could be over within hours. Then he just wanted to bring Ellen home and get on with their life together.

Jud Black walked in as the police were completing their work. He cast a puzzled look at an exhausted Dan.

"Looks like I missed the main event here, Dano."

CHAPTER 34

Jud Black was back and ready to move on the pair in Gainesville. Dan was sure that was where Victor ran when he set the police on him.

"Glad I saw the other guy first, Dan. You look like the winner by a fourteenth round TKO."

"Yeah, guess I do look a little ragged. I'm out on my feet. This is my second bout tonight. Got these the first time around." Dan touched the bandage on his head, winced, and held out a set of bloody knuckles.

Jud smiled. "*Two* fights? See what happens when I'm not here to keep an eye on you?"

"Haven't slept for two days except for cat naps at the hospital. I'm really wasted, Jud. Right now Ellen's doing a lot better than I am." Dan plopped down on the sofa and rubbed his eyes.

"Then I guess an explanation for all this will have to wait." Jud was already on his way toward the refrigerator.

"Give me time for a cold shower. There's a lot to be done yet tonight and I don't have time to rest."

When Dan returned, feeling like he could function again, Jud was on his second cold Murphy's Ale.

"Jud, how do you swing those marathon sessions when you program for forty-eight hours running? After that long I felt like I'd been julienned. Made sure my arms were spread out wide so I didn't slip down the shower drain."

"Yeah, but I recognize you now. What have I missed here, hoss? Fill me in."

"Krevins tried to sneak into Ellen's room this afternoon and give her a dose of drugs. I caught him off guard and wrestled him to the floor. Took the needle he brought for her and shoved it in his gut. Turns out it was something like Ecstasy. Apparently he'd been slipping her shots that were causing her memory loss. With that mixture in him I imagine he'll spend a long night somewhere."

"And what about Ellen? You said she's doing better."

"Doctor Lake was able to counteract the effects of the drugs once he knew what he was dealing with. Her memory should be returning. She already looks better."

"So the police know about Victor?"

"They're searching but they won't find him. I suspect he ran to Paula's place. Don't know where else he would go unless there was enough in that needle to kill him. Policeman said Victor's townhouse burned down. Sounds like he's left Tampa for good."

"When we drop the hammer we want both of them at once, Dan. I have a sure way of finding out if Krevins is with Paula."

"How?"

"By calling Sam up in Ocala. I owe him a heads up that he's playing with fire hanging around Paula. She's so unpredictable she'd do him in without a second thought."

"But what if he tips her off that we're looking for Victor?"

"Sit tight and let me handle it. I can count on Sam." Jud picked up the phone and pulled out his address book.

"Sam, it's me. I'm back in Tampa." He punched the speakerphone button and motioned for Dan to listen in.

"When will I see you, Jud?"

"Soon. Very soon. But first I have to warn you about Paula. She's extremely dangerous."

"Hey, I know she's dangerous . . . for my blood pressure. What else do I need to know?"

"Listen up, Sam. This is dead serious. She's a killer and I mean that in the literal sense. She's already caused three deaths and she's involved in at least two others. Man, she's a blowtorch and I don't want you singed."

A long silence followed and Jud asked, "Are you still there, Sam?"

Finally they heard Sam clear his throat nervously.

"I can only say this once, Jud. I came down here to help the FBI fight computer crimes and she's one of my assignments. We suspect she's into some wormy stuff including tampering with government systems. Can't say any more right now."

Now it was Jud who went mute. He looked at the phone, stunned.

Jud finally recovered his voice and said, "With what I have on her she's nailed but good, Sam. Dan and I want to come up there tonight if you confirm what I suspect about a visitor at her place. Can you get an indication whether she's alone then let me know? I believe her partner in crime, Doctor Victor Krevins, is at her apartment. Time is critical since they could bolt at any minute."

"Can do, Jud. I'll leave for Gainesville now and get back to you soon as I can. You can meet me down the street from her apartment if it's a go. Sure you can trust this Dan?"

"He's my former business partner and he has a personal stake in reining in Paula and Victor. Sam, I can truly say I trust him with my life."

"That's good enough for me. What does this Krevins look like?"

"He's very tall, skinny as a cadaver and has chin whiskers. If you see him, there'll be no doubt who it is."

"You'd better catch all the winks you can while we wait to hear from Sam," Jud said. Dan grunted, sank onto the couch, and went out like a candle.

* * *

Ten o'clock in Gainesville and Paula was bored out of her gourd. She could hardly wait for Sam to drop by in the morning to start their hacking session. Her mind was running open. She needed a challenge.

The doorbell rang. Who could be here at this time of night? One glance through the peep hole and she called out, "Go away, Ernie."

"But, darling, I have nowhere else to turn. I need a place to stay and I'm hurting."

Victor stood in the dark, suitcase in hand, looking like a confused foundling seeking shelter.

Paula cracked the door and looked at him disdainfully. She felt nothing but revulsion.

"Come in before you create a scene. I do have neighbors. Gad, you look awful, stick man."

He had been a tool, an instrument of achieving the goal she was now on the verge of attaining, mind manipulation for profit and fun. The novelty of casting Minerva's Net over targets for big money would eventually wear off. Then she would market their barrier breaking achievement in electronic control of the human cerebellum for more cash than she would need in a lifetime. Victor was expendable. She just hadn't made up her mind how he would disappear.

He shuffled in and stood just inside her door, trembling. She smiled her superior smirk and showed him the couch, throwing him a blanket.

"Man, you look terrible Ernie. Shaking like a dog shitting peach pits. We'll talk later. Keep it quiet in here."

He curled up on the couch and prepared to endure a journey of the mind gone terribly wrong.

"Why do you belittle me, Paula, when you know how I adore you?"

"Because you're a little man, Ernie. A pitiful little man who is nothing without me to drive him. You have theories, I have solutions. You wonder and speculate, I act. You're a twit, Ernie."

"If you could understand what I've been through tonight, you'd treat me better, Paula."

"Wrong again. It's Athena you're talking to, toad, and she has no time for you."

"But I'm hurting. You can't imagine. Hold me. Let me be close to you."

"What makes you think I'd let you anywhere near me in your condition?"

"We've shared such wonderful times together, Paula. All I ask is some comforting. I hurt so much."

"Oh, you got lucky a couple times, Victor. Both times I was flying high on smack. Hell, I could have entertained half the bums in Ybor City in that condition. Just wanted it quick and over."

She took a closer look at his eyes growing unnaturally dim and hazy. He could barely keep his words sorted out. He was drooping and gagging, rolling around on the lumpy couch.

"Well, howdy, here. I think Doctor Egghead got himself some bad stuff. Didn't realize you flew freestyle. Have to be careful where you buy your tickets to float, Ernie."

"This may be an overdose, Paula. I went to Ellen Cooper's room to silence her and fought with her husband. He turned the needle on me. It's a large amount of natural MDMA. Help me."

"Like you helped those poor slobs you put through the wringer with your experiments? Drake blubbered to me about how you'd involved him. Or maybe like you helped the three doctors that tried to warn you before you turned on them? Get real, Ernie. Tough it out on your own."

"But, Paula, dearest . . . oh, God, how it hurts."

"Your problem, Ernie. Work it off. No concern of mine."

She retreated to her bedroom, leaving him to feel what others had suffered at his hands.

CHAPTER 35

Dan tossed and switched around on the couch, his mind a jumble. He felt like hell but they were so close to ending this whole mess. If only he could muster enough reserve energy to bring it off.

Ellen's improvement had him skimming along on top of the world. Then he walked into the kitchen and ran into Peter Drake. The outcome of that bout felt good but only briefly. He was confused and battered; on the edge of exhaustion, his sore head pounding. Things had to improve.

Danielle would be here soon. She'd booked a morning flight to Tampa. Dan told her to go directly to the hospital while he took care of some last minute business. Her being here would do wonders for her Mom's spirits.

The cold shower helped but this had been a draining day. Needed to hold himself together for a little while longer. Soon the whole sordid mess could be over. Soon as Sam called back he expected to be on the way to a rendezvous in Gainesville.

His eyes snapped open and he scanned the room. Jud was sitting near the phone with a book in his hand, nursing another Murphy's.

"Howzit, Dan? Snooze help?"

"Don't know yet. I need a pick up."

Jud held his bottle out and tapped it with a finger.

"No. Something to clear the fog. Strong coffee."

Dan made it to his feet in stages and stumbled to the kitchen to brew a pot of extra strong coffee. Handed Jud a cup and gulped down two cups to keep his eyes open.

"What's that you're reading?" Dan asked.

"Oh, some light stuff to keep my mind honed. Working my way through a few of the classics." He held up a copy of The Prince by Machiavelli.

"You're scary, pal. Just when I think I've got you pegged I find you have a whole new dimension."

Jud gave him one of his gotcha grins. "Ones and zeroes aren't my only world."

"While we're waiting, Jud, why don't we see what they put on my machine?" He steered Jud into the office to check out the hidden files Peter had admitted were on his computer. Jud made short work of isolating the video and slowing it down for viewing.

"Good thing you recognized that eerie feeling before you spent too much time on here, Dan. Watch the message across the middle of the screen. It's repeating the words 'HOWARD BEACH, and 'REACH THE LIGHT'. Alternates with a night-time shot of a light in the distance."

"Looks like the lighthouse near Anclote Key, Jud. Sits in the water beyond Howard Beach."

"If you'd been fed those messages and the low pitch hum enough times, we'd be fishing your drowned body out of the Gulf."

In his current condition, Dan couldn't even react. Jud made a CD copy and erased the files from the computer. They returned to the family room and Dan dozed off sitting on the sofa.

The phone rang. Dan dimly heard Jud's voice across the room.

"All right. That's a winner!"

A short silence followed.

"You bet. We're leaving soon as I slap Dan awake. Thanks."

Dan turned to him and said, "No sweat, I'm already awake. Was it Sam?" He stood and wobbled a bit.

"Right. Guess who showed up at Paula's place?"

"Let's roll." Dan was up and charging.

* * *

They made the trip to Gainesville hopeful that their ordeal was nearly over. As Jud pointed the rental car up Interstate 75, they reviewed the bidding and laid their plans for the remainder of this critical weekend.

"As you heard earlier, Sam is working for the FBI as a computer consultant, Dan. I had no idea."

"What does that do to this trip to Gainesville? Is the place going to be crawling with agents?"

"It really doesn't change anything. I needed Sam's help to feel out the situation with Paula. And I was obligated to warn him about her. Turns out he's already up to speed on her. In fact, she's one of his targets."

"We don't need the government preempting us, Jud. I want first crack at Krevins."

"Sam's an old friend. Owes me a favor. Let me work this with him. Already told him the first shot at Krevins is ours. I'll ask to have the bureau come in behind us after we've collared this pair."

They whizzed along in silence for a long while. Both of them were in deep thought about what lay ahead of them. Dan was totally immersed in imagining the events about to unfold. He found himself mesmerized by the passing lights and tree lines. He nodded off without warning then snapped back to a drowsy consciousness. A quick look at his driver verified that Jud, too, was dangerously close to driving with his eyes closed.

"We are two punchy cusses, Jud. How about pulling off at the next exit. Let's find some wakeup coffee before we go sailing off into those pines."

"Driver can't hear you. He's snoozing," Jud retorted, laughed, then agreed. "Sure, I could use a caffeine kick."

Jud normally walked around with his worn no-spill coffee mug in one hand and sweet snacks in the other to keep him charged. Dan had often pulled his string about having the mug surgically attached to his wrist to free his fingers for marathon key pounding sessions. When Jud was focused, he may go around the clock driven by little more than caffeine and sugar jolts.

Reenergized by the hot coffee, they brought each other fully up to date on the events of the past few days.

Then Jud asked, "What was that deal back at the house? You never did tell me exactly what caused you to beat the crap out of that dude. Even his bumps had lumps when they took him away."

"Started to tell you earlier, Jud. Peter Drake was involved in helping Krevins with his dirty deeds. Found him in my house and damn near pounded him into the floor. He'd been on my computer and doing a search of my office. It was Peter who broke into the Millwoods' house and killed Susan. He's also responsible for Marge's death. Drake's lucky he's still alive after waylaying me in my own house."

"So what will the cops do with him?"

"He's safe in jail. I signed a complaint against him for trespassing and assault. But they also have the story on his knowledge of the deaths of Victor's human test subjects and his own guilt in the deaths of both Marge and Susan. So he'll stay tucked away in a cell."

"If he was on your machine that means Paula knew your password. Any idea why they took a chance by sending him to your home?"

"He admitted there were hidden files sent to me. They attached them to a message I opened believing it was from my Internet Service Provider. You saw what they had planned for me. I leave my computer turned off most of the time. Paula needed the machine on long enough to remotely scan my files for any evidence I may have against them. He said they wanted him to do a complete search of the office, too, for any written evidence against them. I was their next victim. They didn't need any trails left in my office."

"Stand in line, pal. Paula's victim list is long enough to hold a reunion. I talked to Minerva and found out she actually is Paula as you suspected. I ordered a hit and sent her the info she needed to target a Bill Lawson in Las Vegas. The files she sent actually came to me in a roundabout way." Jud raised an eyebrow. "Would have prompted the fictitious Bill to take a header off an upper floor balcony inside the Luxor Hotel. She contracted to target a guy in

Los Angeles, too. I warned him by email. Urged him to call me but he didn't, so she succeeded in filling her contract.

"How do you know that?"

"I read the newspaper account today of an accident in Los Angeles. A Sam Trotter walked into an aircraft propeller blade. Hacked to death. Wish he'd made that return call to me. She pulled this one off in four days time. Who knows how many people she's getting ready to whack in her game of emailing for dollars?"

"Let's hope we bring all that to an end for her tonight, Jud."

CHAPTER 36

Dan and Jud cruised along Paula's street in Gainesville. They spotted Sam's car down the block at an alley entrance. They circled around to park on the next street and returned on foot.

Jud sneaked up to Sam's car and barked, "Boo." Sam whirled in his seat and pointed a small caliber gun at him.

"Whoa, pal! It's the friendlies," Jud choked out. "Man, you're spring loaded."

"Jud, you crazy code mangler, you damn near got yourself shot."

"Sorry, Sam. Just couldn't help myself. Never knew you to carry heat."

"Strictly for emergencies. This seemed like a good time to be prepared. Could be a couple of pretty desperate people in that apartment house."

"Put it away and forget you have it, Sam. Best way to get yourself shot. Leave the gunplay to the professionals."

Dan asked, "What can you tell us, Sam? Seen any movement down the street?"

"A man went in after ten. Tall, ugly dude. That was almost three hours ago. I can see Paula's apartment windows clearly from here. Lights went out not long after her visitor showed up. No signs of activity since. She's on the first floor at the far end. Count two windows to the right from the last entryway. You remember her place. That's his Mercedes sitting out front and hers is the white SUV. Neither one has moved."

Jud looked where he was pointing and asked, "This man . . . you're sure it was Krevins?"

"Hey, I'd hate to think there were two creeps like the guy you described. It was the doctor, all right. After they doused the lights

I was getting bored so I checked my messages at home. Paula had called me to call off our morning hacking session. Said a girlfriend had dropped in unexpectedly and we'd have to cancel out on fun and games for this weekend."

"Sure. I see her girlfriend now," Dan chuckled. "Six-four, hollow cheeks and a goatee. If there's one thing Victor isn't, it's a girl."

Jud broke in. "Looks all quiet for now. Sam, you sly devil, tell me about this deal with the Feds."

"You remember I was out of touch for awhile when I first left our group in Virginia." Sam kept glancing at the dark apartment window as he spoke. "Actually I was at Quantico getting my indoctrination before relocating. Signed on for a long-term stint helping the FBI crack some troublesome computer crimes in Florida."

"Give me time to get used to this, Sam. A fed, no less." Jud shook his head and looked dumfounded.

"Not exactly. I was too old to go through the training and become an agent so I don't carry a badge. I'm just a contractor, but they've been great to me. Even arranged a day job with the company in Ocala where I keep my hand in writing software."

"So you went legit on me."

"Hey, it's honest work, Jud. I still get to hack for fun as long as I keep the boys in Washington clued in to reverse any upsets I cause. Have to play the part to look credible to people like Paula. You know, like the act you put on for her the other night. She's real poison, Jud. Up to her neck in diddling with government systems but I can't get any documented proof."

"Well, ditch the weapon anyway, buddy. Don't need to outshoot them, just outthink them."

Sam deposited the gun in his glove compartment. "Suits me. I'm a peace loving guy."

Before they launched, Dan reasoned that Sam should be aware how royally they had the hacker girl glued to the wall with their evidence.

"Tell him what *we* have on his friend Paula, Jud."

"We've got the goods on her for conspiracy to commit murder. She played a major part in four—no, counting Trotter it was five—

remote killings by the cleverest scheme you ever could imagine over the Internet. Two more people have died and Dan's wife was hurt as the result of sending Peter Drake out to do cover-ups. She also sent both Dan and me files that were intended to make us do foolish things and die."

"Unfortunately, I know exactly what you're talking about. She couldn't resist flaunting her scheme at a poker game. We all thought she was kidding about her friend that had this wild plan for remote killings."

"She's deadly, Sam. We have to stop her."

"It's time I called in the heavy artillery, guys. Not only can the bureau get Paula out of circulation; they can lock her up pending trial for murder." Sam reached for his cell phone but Jud stopped him from dialing.

"Wait. I'm sure Paula's computer will yield some interesting data on her other activities. We'll give you everything we've collected, Sam. But we owe it to Dan to have his shot at Victor and Paula for what they did to his wife and friends. All I ask is that you delay the feds' arrival and give us first crack at them."

"I've already alerted the local contact we could take down Paula. Said we could catch her in the act of hacking a Government system. He has a team standing by. Didn't give them the address yet. Don't know if I can hold them off without raising suspicion about the delay."

"Look. Sam," Jud told him, "I'm asking you for a big favor. We can play it like Dan and I slipped in without your knowledge and made our own collar. I'll make it sound like we jumped the gun."

"Okay," Sam said reluctantly. "As soon as you go in, I'll call and say it's time to bust her. I'll tell them you had a score to settle with her and wouldn't wait like I asked. That way they'll be alerted to avoid catching you in crossfire. The team should be here within minutes. Make it quick once you're inside."

"That's all I ask. I want my hands on Victor one more time," Dan told him.

This was all enlightening for Sam but Dan was itching to get on with springing the trap on Victor and his sexy accomplice. His already scraped knuckles throbbed but he looked forward to using them on Krevins.

"You two have been in there," Dan said. "Describe what we're dealing with here. What's the layout? How do we corner these rats?"

Sam rolled that over in his mind one more time. "Stairwell goes all the way through to the back. Her apartment opens onto a patio in the rear. There's parking behind the building. We pick up the car, park in back and come in that way. Should be easy to beat the lock on the patio doors."

"Agreed," Jud answered. I'll try to keep Dan from killing the son of a bitch. I've seen what he can do when somebody really pisses him off. Dan, these two still have a date to keep in court so leave them intact for us."

"I promise," Dan said impatiently. "Now let's get on with it."

* * *

Victor unfolded from his fetal position on the couch. He looked like he had struggled through the gates of hell and back and was much the worse for wear. In the throes of battle with his accidental drug overdose, he had virtually collapsed on the couch. Nearly two AM. He'd been out for almost four hours. Paula sat silently in the dark and watched him turn toward her bedroom door, unaware she was viewing his every move. Then she clicked on the lamp on the table beside her chair. He whirled in her direction.

"It's about time, Ernie. I wasn't sure whether you'd come around or just give it up on that old sofa. Bony carcass the size of yours would be a problem to drag out of here on my own." She taunted him with the total indifference in her words and laughed that she had startled him.

Paula sat in the lumpy overstuffed chair, her long limbs carelessly tossed. One silk clad leg draped over the chair arm, the other was tucked beneath her. A sticky warm front had passed by Gainesville and left the air outside calm and stifling. Her silk pajama top lay casually open and fluttering in the cooling breeze of the overhead fan.

Victor drank in her essence and started toward her.

"Paula, please. Tonight has been bad enough. My head feels like someone is pounding it with a hammer. Do you have to make it worse?"

"Seems like justice served to me. Now you know how those unfortunates felt when you pumped that crap into their veins in the name of experimental science. How many of them didn't bother to wake up?"

"I just want you to give me a sign you care for me. You know how much you mean to me." He drew near and she motioned for him to halt.

"Stop. Don't even come near me. You smell like a sewer, Ernie. Go clean up your act."

"Please don't call me Ernie." He tried to come closer but she raised one foot and nudged him away.

Victor reluctantly obeyed, picked up his suitcase and retreated to the bathroom. When he returned later and found her in that same old chair chewing on toast and sipping coffee, relief was written across his face. Paula thought he looked reassured that he would live through his hellish experience after all. That made the challenge more delicious for her while she pondered ways to dash his hopes.

"Honey, we have important things to discuss." She scowled when he addressed her that way.

What important things could they possibly have to say to each other? And what was this 'honey' bullshit? The wimp actually thought she had feelings for him. Talk about delusions. His real usefulness to her was nearly at an end and she could soon shake him off. She smiled and squirmed down deeper into her seat. *But she'd play along and see what he had to say.*

"We're on your token, skinny man. Make your pitch."

She knew he hated it when she assumed this superior attitude and put him through his paces. The pain of her repeated rejections must be unbearable for a man who perceived himself as a genius among his peers. Paula tormented him by jiggling about, her pajama top opening and closing with every movement, leading Victor on with the hint of forbidden delights. She followed his penetrating gaze downward and spun around to face him directly.

He dropped to his knees in front of her and pled.

"Dearest Paula, you know how I adore you. Let me take you away from here. I have the resources for a comfortable life for us wherever you desire."

"What makes you think I'd agree to that?"

"Together we are an unbeatable team. With my knowledge and your skills we can change the world. We're so close to the final solution to the control of human behavior. People will do what we want when we command it."

"Small successes. I have much bigger plans for our work," she mocked.

"Tell me and let me help you make it come true, goddess of wisdom."

"Don't slobber, Ernie. Just listen to me. Your profession has shut you out and you'll never gain their acceptance."

She stood and he followed her to the table.

"We can prove that cerebellar inspiration works," he said. "We have three cases in point, demonstrations with resounding success that confirm our methods. The major work is done and now we can set to refining our techniques."

"You silly ass, don't you realize that doesn't prove a thing? What we did with those three men can never be used to convince anyone without convicting us of multiple murders. And any more hits on acquaintances of yours would be foolhardy. We've covered our tracks so far but the results will be suspiciously beyond coincidence by now to the authorities. I can capitalize on what we've accomplished. Who cares that they doubted the sheer genius of our work? We know what we've accomplished. I have a better idea."

"Then what is it you have in mind?" he asked.

"My grand plan is already in motion. I'll use the same methods of Internet persuasion—CI, if you insist—to perform remote control jobs for fees. Clients are contacting me now to have me rid them of nuisances. I can prompt targets to carry out actions beneficial to the client—like jump off a building or walk into a spinning propeller. This will be a continuing enterprise of untraceable, clean and swift eliminations for substantial fees."

"But I have money, Paula. It's the recognition I want. We deserve to be known for the genius of CI. We'll go somewhere and assume totally new identities. Then we can cautiously introduce CI when the time is right and bask in the recognition we deserve."

"You're right about one thing, Victor. The money isn't what's important—only the game. The rush of imposing my will and making the robots dance is the rush. Fees for services are the door openers. They attract flies to the honey. I just want to enjoy this while I can."

"Don't you see, we can be world renowned once we shed our names and our past. We can go to Switzerland or Brazil, wherever you want, and build new backgrounds."

"Humor me, Victor. I want to enjoy this now. We can play the rest by ear."

"Whatever you say is fine with me. Just tell me I can be with you, Paula. For now we have to disappear. You pick the place and we can pull up roots immediately. I've anticipated trouble building and placed my funds in places they can't be located and frozen. All I need is your consent and we can begin anew."

"I can't leave my equipment and the jobs I have underway."

"Name what you need and a whole new equipment setup is yours. I want you and I want to be away from danger. I told you Dan Cooper was onto something posing as a writer to get near me. Now there's reason to believe that Cooper and maybe even the police have tied us to the deaths of my associates. There's also the matter of Drake's attacks on the women. If he talks, questions about dead test subjects will surface. We need to leave as soon as possible."

"Dan Cooper has his own problems. I did as you asked and sent him some nasty little files. Peter did his job. Turned on Cooper's computer last night. It was on long enough for me to check for other mail files. He's opened my message from his Internet service.

Mister Cooper could be taking a long, deep bath very soon. And Peter is your problem to silence."

"Take my offer, Paula. Let's get away now."

"I'm thinking, Ernie."

"I've been in your bed more than once. We share something special."

"Hey, Ernie, I told you that was random because you were handy at the time. Don't get a big head about it. I still own you with or without playtime and you know it."

He tried to dismiss the insult and move on but the pain showed.

"While we're debating, the police may be making the connection between you and me, Paula. They could be here at any moment. We can't delay."

She shrugged.

There was an endless supply of business waiting out there once the word got around about Minerva's efficiency in solving problems. She could hold off Victor's advances until she got her hands on all his money then remove him from the scene by more direct methods. Had the important data on her computers replicated on ROM disks. She'd torch her equipment to prevent anyone else from using the information it contained. Why not go along with him?

"Give me a few minutes to throw my things together and we can shove off."

She went first to her computers and set the timers on the thermal charges.

Victor beamed. Paula was enjoying this. *He thought sure he had finally won the lady of his dreams. He didn't know his days were numbered.*

"You've chosen wisely, darling. I'll place the world at your feet."

"Yeah, sure, Ernie."

CHAPTER 37

The plan of attack was set. Sam had to remain above the fray. He didn't want to have too much to explain after the fact to his FBI friends. He agreed to sit tight in the alley and alert his local bureau contact as Jud and Dan entered the apartment building. That would give them time to make a quick assault and finish their business with Victor and Paula before the authorities descended. Sam's role then was to ensure that neither of their quarry escaped out the front entrance.

They were nearly ready to leave Sam's car when the lights came on in the apartment.

"Oh, shit," Jud barked. "Looks like we need a Plan B. Somebody's up."

"The lights were doused for a long time," Sam said. "Maybe Victor's playing Lucky Pierre tonight."

"Ugh," was all Dan could manage. "Don't make me gag. We've all seen that dreamy bombshell. What a totally disgusting mismatch."

"Yeah, but think about it. Old Victor could be waking up now minus body parts," Jud said. "Listen for blood curdling screams."

"Oh, no! Disassembling Krevins is a privilege I've reserved for myself, Studley," Dan replied. "Just pull me off him in time, because I'm giving no quarter this go around."

"Gentle Dan. Can't picture you opening up a can of whoop ass on anybody."

"Not until he hurt Ellen. Now all bets are off."

"Okay, here's the drill." Jud was in his zone, improvising on the fly. "We park in the rear and you cover the patio exit of Paula's apartment. I take the dumb ass approach, walk right up and knock on her door. The shock of my showing up at her front door this late should send Victor your way." He turned to Sam and instructed, "Don't let anyone out on the street side."

Dan took up his position at the rear corner of the stairwell and watched Jud casually stroll toward Paula's entrance. He was careful to remain concealed but could both see and hear Black's bold move.

"Howdy, Ma'am. Wanta buy some hot software programs?"

"Jud! What in hell are *you* doing here this time of night?"

Dan didn't hear Jud's reply because there were sounds of someone scrambling toward the rear of the apartment. He spun around and riveted his attention on the patio doors as they slid open. Victor Krevins was in full flight and Dan was instantly energized. He took two long steps in Victor's direction. Left his feet, sailing through the air. The two men fell heavily across the patio furniture and sent chairs in all directions. This was the moment Dan had dreamed would be granted to him. There was no stopping him now.

"Gotcha! No way out this time." Dan ignored how much his bloodied hands hurt and set about pummeling Victor.

He was all over the startled Krevins, pounding him with both fists. Dan flailed at the prone figure and flung insults at him that Dan himself couldn't translate. He only knew that his words had something to do with paying Victor back for several people, most of all Ellen. He grasped the doctor's large head and smashed it against the concrete patio floor as if he were trying to open a coconut. The devil had once again escaped from his enraged brain but this time he didn't care. A blind rage took over and enveloped him. Victor was struggling to elude his grip but Dan was a man on a mission.

"You win, you win. Please," Victor pled helplessly.

Victor's wail broke Dan's fury. A measure of reason gradually returned.

Don't kill Krevins. He should spend a long time in a jail cell thinking about what he's done.

Dan rolled off and grasped one of Victor's arms. He dragged the limp heap back through the sliding door into the apartment.

The beaten man lay motionless at his feet and stared up at him with fading eyes.

Jud came puffing up behind Dan shoving Paula ahead of him. "Did I make it in time or did you snuff the old boy?" Dan couldn't decide whether that question was asked with fear or hope.

"No, he still has most of his skin," Dan answered. "It was a close call but my better side won out." Dan took a step back and stared at Jud. "What got hold of you?"

"She did. Fought like a pen full of wildcats. Scratched me good. But I'll heal. *She* has to stand trial for murder."

Jud stood there bleeding from a nasty looking red gash in his cheek. Paula was glaring at Dan. Her hate hung in the air. She twisted around to examine Jud with those blue eyes turned cold as glacier ice in the instant she heard his words.

"Murder? She spat. "You're dreaming."

"Do the names Millwood, Wainwright and Gernsbach resonate in that confused mind of yours? You're busted. And I know about your other game, too, Minerva."

She visibly slumped in his grasp. "I should have known. Where was my head? Let two lousy men set me up."

As she spoke, a series of sharp cracks almost like pistol shots sounded from behind them. Jud glared at her and she confirmed his suspicions with a triumphant smile.

"Poof go the goodies. No more evidence on little Athena. What you gonna do now, smart ass?"

Jud said, "Her computers were rigged for destruction, Dan. The spare bedroom will be a blazing inferno before we can do anything about it. We've got to get out of here before the whole place goes up."

"Check, faint heart," Paula sang out. "Where's your case now?"

"No problem," Jud answered. "Got my own copies right off your computer. Sorry 'bout that. Checkmate, Paula."

"It was all Victor's idea. He devised the whole scheme and blackmailed me into helping. I'll testify to that."

As she spoke, Paula snaked out her free hand and reached for something on the dresser. Dan realized what she had picked up and shouted a warning to Jud. "Watch out. She has scissors."

Her arm sliced upward and Jud dodged just in time to take the blow on his bicep. He seized her hand and twisted. The scissors fell. Jud backhanded her and she crumpled to the floor.

In the excitement, Dan had been distracted from Victor who he thought was no longer a threat. But Victor saw his opening. He snared the scissors. Lashed out and sank them deeply into Paula's chest.

"No more insults. I win." A twisted smile lit his face.

Victor laughed aloud until his voice cracked and the tears came rushing down his cheeks. The laugh died and he wailed aloud. The realization of what he had done was too much for him. Krevins sobbed convulsively and tried to reach Paula.

"I just wanted you to love me."

He looked at Dan with his eyes vacant, his mind a vacuum.

"She didn't deserve me, not the way I worshipped her." He curled up in a tight ball and babbled nonsense, his mind gone.

Jud knelt to cradle Paula in his arms. "Hang on. We'll have help for you soon."

Someone shouted, "FBI," and the front door came crashing in.

Paula spoke in a halting voice. "We could have been so good together, Jud. You weren't like all the rest."

"Save your breath, Paula. Help is here." He brushed her lips with his.

"With you I could have been just Paula. I didn't need to dominate you. This time it could have been magic." Her words came to an abrupt end and she let out a low rattle. The light went out in those dazzling eyes.

Dan stood in a trance, unable to comprehend the sudden turn of events. He was rooted to the spot until a voice shouted urgently.

"Let's get out of here," an agent hurled at them. "Head for the patio. Get away from the fire. We'll sort everybody out later."

The attack team gathered up all four of the people in the room and ran to the patio as flames filled the hallway and licked at the doorway to the bedroom. Not until they had put distance between them and the fiery apartment did anyone breathe freely. Then Dan broke the silence.

"These two are murder suspects. We'll provide the evidence. She's beyond help and he's flipped out completely. My friend needs help for a stab wound."

* * *

The FBI agent took custody of Paula's body and the blabbering Victor Krevins. Dan begged off to rush back to the hospital and Ellen. Jud had a quick first aid job done on his arm. Dan and Jud were zipping along I-75 toward Tampa. Dan glanced over to see his friend lost in thought, staring out the window. Jud was brushing at the blotch of Paula's blood on his shirt as if hoping it and the scene it evoked would somehow go away.

"Gonna make it, Jud?"

"Yeah, I'll be okay. Just chewing over 'what ifs', pal. She was some woman."

Heavy silence for long minutes. Then, suddenly, Dan broke into uncontrolled laughter.

Jud asked him, "What the hell could possibly be funny about all this?"

"I was just thinking. There you sit with your arm slashed and your jaw scraped. I have this big bandage on my gourd, Drake's claw marks on me and I'm torn and grimy from my roll with Victor. We don't look like part of the winning team, do we?"

"Yeah, but we did it, Dan. Do you realize how thoroughly we kicked ass on this caper? We make a totally awesome team. I'd almost forgotten how well our minds mesh when we get down to serious business."

"Funny. I was thinking the same thing . . . guess that proves your point, huh?"

"Ellen won't believe it when I tell her what went down tonight. But I have her back and that's all that really matters." Dan cinched his seat belt and sank down into the seat to snooze.

"Wait. Don't conk out on me yet, Cooper. I have something to say to you."

"Shoot stick, but make it fast. Lala land beckons."

"I've been thinking," Jud said, taking a drag on his smoke. "There's a lot of scamming going on; computer crackers misusing their skills against unsuspecting victims. Now we know it can even be deadly as it was for your friends. Somebody's gotta go on the offensive against these bad dudes. We both have lots of time on our hands. Might as well be us." He paused.

Dan thought about it and asked, "You mean like hiring out as private eyes?"

"Something like that. I've been talking to our old partner, Pat O'Leary, about what we were into in Florida. Had a call from him just before I came back down. He's getting fidgety playing host at his Irish bar. Wants to be involved in some real action."

"You're serious, aren't you, Jud?"

"Serious and dead sober, pal. Pat says he may have a lead on a cracker crime up his way. Lady wants his help and it could involve a nasty murder. By my watch, it's now March 17th . . . St. Patrick's Day. What say we wake up the old Irishman and tell him it's a go? Even have a name—COB Investigations."

Dan wrestled with the possibilities and pinned a stare on the trees whizzing by his window. Finally, he turned to Jud with a broad smile.

"You want to make the call or should I?"